# Pathfinder

## THE GOD'S WIFE TRILOGY

## BOOK 2

### JW KINGSLEY

# Also by

In the Light of the Moon
Pathfinder
The God's Wife (coming early 2025)

Copyright © 2024 by JW Kingsley

All rights reserved.

No part of this publication may be reproduced, distributed, or transmitted in any form or by any means, including photocopying, recording, or other electronic or mechanical methods, without the prior written permission of the publisher, except as permitted by U.S. copyright law. For permission requests, contact Vellichor Ink.

The story, all names, characters, and incidents portrayed in this production are fictitious. No identification with actual persons (living or deceased), places, buildings, and products is intended or should be inferred. Where real-life historical persons appear, the situations, incidents, and dialogues concerning said persons are entirely fictitious and not intended to depict actual events.

Book Cover by JW Kingsley using Canva Pro

Interior art by JW Kingsley using Canvas Pro

Edited by Lindsey Clarke

First edition 2024

# Contents

| | | |
|---|---|---|
| Dedication | | IX |
| Previously On... | | X |
| Pronunciation and Character Guide | | XIII |
| 1. | Haunted | 1 |
| 2. | Ritual Death | 6 |
| 3. | Fight or Flight | 13 |
| 4. | Medicine and Memories | 20 |
| 5. | Before | 29 |
| 6. | A Cold Wind | 34 |
| 7. | After | 41 |
| 8. | Curiouser and Curiouser | 45 |
| 9. | Crystal Visions | 51 |
| 10. | Khonsu | 59 |
| 11. | Of Friendship and Fighting | 68 |
| 12. | Secrets Spilled | 74 |
| 13. | Anguish | 78 |

| 14. | Worry | 85 |
| 15. | Khonsu's Truth | 87 |
| 16. | Dashing Dreams | 94 |
| 17. | The Pain of Mated Souls | 97 |
| 18. | Breakthrough | 101 |
| 19. | Liminal Space | 109 |
| 20. | An Echo of Magic | 118 |
| 21. | The Ghosts That We Know | 124 |
| 22. | Cursed | 128 |
| 23. | Veiled Threats | 135 |
| 24. | Bird Set Free | 141 |
| 25. | The Egyptian Museum | 148 |
| 26. | Beloved | 153 |
| 27. | Failure | 159 |
| 28. | The Darkness | 165 |
| 29. | A Dark Path | 172 |
| 30. | Freedom in the Dark | 174 |
| 31. | Awry | 180 |
| 32. | The Shadow Man | 187 |
| 33. | The Truth | 192 |
| 34. | Unlikely Ally | 199 |
| 35. | The Reckoning | 201 |

| | | |
|---|---|---|
| 36. | Search and Find | 209 |
| 37. | Revelation | 217 |
| 38. | Minister of Secrets | 221 |
| 39. | Secrets No More | 228 |
| 40. | Dreams | 238 |
| 41. | Time | 241 |
| 42. | Plans | 244 |
| 43. | Gat a'la elgarh | 247 |
| 44. | With Sympathy | 252 |
| 45. | Infiltration | 255 |
| 46. | Gifts | 259 |
| 47. | Choices | 264 |
| 48. | Trial and Error | 269 |
| 49. | A Whispering of Shadows | 273 |
| 50. | Demands | 276 |
| 51. | Fever Dreams | 282 |
| 52. | A Healing | 286 |
| 53. | The Unthinkable | 291 |
| 54. | Another Kind of Betrayal | 298 |
| 55. | Pathfinder | 301 |
| 56. | All for Nothing | 304 |
| 57. | A Cold and Broken Hallelujah | 306 |

| | |
|---|---|
| 58. Consequences | 308 |
| Acknowledgements | 313 |
| About the author | 315 |

Stells, this one's for you.

An especially big THANK YOU for helping me figure out a big plot point when we were on a road trip to Wales. I didn't think you were even listening to me and Papa talk about the book, and when you piped up from the backseat amid Minecraft and snacks, you really saved the story! You are amazing—don't you forget it!

# Previously On...

I don't know about you, dear reader, but I read *a lot*. Sometimes I read series before they're finished, and no matter how excited I am for the next installment, I forget what happened and spend the first couple of chapters trying to remember key points. I can not tell you how many times I've longed for a recap like TV shows have. So, I decided to do one. I am, after all the author, agent, and *publisher*... I can do whatever I want! So, without further ado...

### *Previously on The God's Wife Trilogy...*

Julia Wheelright and her husband Andrew are on vacation in Egypt when she discovers that she has magical powers passed down from the ancient pharaoh, Hatshepsut. She is pulled into a secret world of magic and intrigue and becomes a member of a magical sisterhood, charged with protecting the pharaohs secrets and her grimoire (authors note: I *know* the word grimoire wasn't around in ancient Egyptian times, but its a word that fits what it is...a book filled with magic spells and information from the witch herself).

Julia stays behind in Egypt to learn about her newfound powers and it's there she learns that there's more to it than just lighting candles with a whisper or opening doors with a thought. There's an ancient brotherhood founded by Hatshepsut's stepson, Thutmose III and he and his followers wanted nothing more than to stamp out magic and witches, and erase them from history. His doctrine has also been passed down and the sisterhood is charged with protecting themselves from the dark clutches of the modern-day members of the brotherhood.

Julia's childhood trauma comes roaring to the surface when she recognizes some familiar faces on the sisterhood's watchlist. Warren and Gordon Mitchell—the pastor and his son from her childhood church (read: cult)—are more sinister than even she could have ever realized. The risk and terror from the Mitchell's was so great that Julia had changed her name and run from them all through her adulthood. Their sudden emergence from the shadows of her mind and memory shake her to her core.

Julia spends a year going back and forth between Bahrain, where she and Andrew live, and Luxor, Egypt, where she studies magic. Her powers don't come easily to her and she really struggles to find her place among the sisterhood. She and Andrew are preparing a move back to the US when she gets word her beloved grandmother has passed away. She leaves early and goes home to North Carolina—a place she's run from and not ever wanted to return to—to see to her grandmothers affairs. Her best friends, Edie and Dell, meet her there to help see her through her grief.

Julia ends up having to explain her magic to her friend Dell who witnesses a magical outburst courtesy of a panic attack. Dell is skeptical but understanding and Julia is terrified and realizes she still has a lot to learn.

Andrew is kidnapped on his way to Julia and kept hostage by Gordon Mitchell who found out his former flame was in town from a mutual friend. He comes calling and kidnaps Julia as well, taking her to his house of horrors. It's there that the magic Julia doesn't have control over explodes out of her and saves her and Andrew from certain death. They escape together and call on the sisterhood for help to clean up the mess.

Hanan, the leader of the sisterhood, Naomi, and Marwa come as soon as they can and when they return to Gordon Mitchell's home they encounter his father, Warren. Warren explains that Julia didn't actually kill Gordon (what she thought and feared), but he finished the job for her. He threatens Julia, and the sisterhood, and demands they leave and never return. In a bout of confidence, she fights back and stands up to Warren Mitchell before storming out and leaving North Carolina, and all the trauma she endured there, behind.

We start and end the book with scenes with our beloved pharaoh, Hatshepsut and in this story, we'll see a lot more of her!

# Pronunciation and Character Guide

**Hatshepsut** (Haht-SHEP-sut)—the fifth Pharaoh of the Eighteenth Dynasty of Egypt and the second documented female pharaoh. She ruled from 1479-1458 BCE. Upon the death of her husband and half-brother Thutmose II she stepped in as regent for her stepson, Thutmose III when he inherited the throne at age two. As the daughter of Thutmose I, she felt she had a divine right to rule and established herself as more than just a stand-in for Thutmose III. She wore a false beard and dressed as a male to gain more acceptance from anyone who would argue the need for a male ruler. Her reign lasted a little over twenty years and was prosperous and peaceful. She was one of the most prolific builders in Ancient Egypt and left her mark not only in the hearts of her people but in the landscape of Egypt.

Experts think she died of bone cancer from a carcinogenic skin lotion that she was probably using to soothe irritated and inflamed skin.

When she died Thutmose III took over as Pharaoh and towards the end of his reign he began to erase all evidence of her—statues were defaced and destroyed and her achievements were parceled out to other pharaohs. Even her burial was not what she planned—during Thutmose III's reign it is thought that she was moved from her father's tomb to another, unmarked tomb, with her nurse and separate from the rest of her burial things (including her canonic jars). Years of speculation and testing of teeth have led to believe that they've found her and she's currently in the Egyptian Museum in Cairo.

**Shesout** (sheh-soo)—nickname for Hatshepsut

**Julia** (jool-ee-ah)/**Jules** (joolz)—our female main character—she's 36/37 years old and carries the wounds of childhood trauma with her. She has had anxiety and depression her whole life and has found out that part of that anxiety has been her magic trying to manifest. Married to Andrew—they were friends in high school and fell in love and ran off together to keep her safe from the marriage that was arranged for her (see Gordon Mitchell).

**Andrew** (An-droo)—Julia's husband—around the same age as her, former Military and Government contractor, kind and gentle soul, and the love of her life. He's an avid reader, a musician and an all-around good guy.

**Hanan** (Han-ann)—The leader (*steward)* of the sisterhood. Her magic is pretty well-rounded and she's talented in many aspects of it. As the steward she knows the location of the scrolls of Hatshepsut and she takes charge of each ceremony and ritual, the deeper aspects of their magic attuned to her. She is typically very calm and cool-headed and a good leader. Well loved by everyone.

**Salma** (Sal-MA)—Hanan's second in command (*nebet).* Egyptian born and raised. Her mother (Marwa) was second in command to Hanan's mother before she died so Salma has always known the sisterhood and her place in it. High energy, outgoing, passionate. Married to Omar and mother to twin girls.

**Marwa** (Mar-wah)—Salma's mother and former second-in-command to the sisterhood. Her best friend was Hanan's mother, Aisha.

Magical strength is empathy and some healing—sends calming waves of magic outside of herself. Has become a mother figure to Julia.

**Hasina** (Ha-seen-ah)—The "brains" of the operation. Very intelligent and stoic. South African. Her magic revolves around plants and growing things. Married to Salma's brother Karim. No children.

**Reem** (R-ee-m)—British and Indian decent. Her magic manifests itself in her cooking. Very kitchen-witchy and loves to take care and feed everyone. Married to Simon and mother to two children.

**Marina** (Mah-ree-nah)—Italian. High Energy, scatterbrained, and artistic—her magic is channeled into her pottery. Imbues all her creations with magic. Also strong with meditation. Splits her time between Italy and Egypt—social media and website manager for a few different companies.

**Renee** (Rehn-ay)—Canadian—moved to Egypt with her husband whom she met in University when they were young. Widowed. Mother to a son who lives in Canada. Second oldest member. Her magic is healing energy. She is a massage therapist and has had a healing energy about her her entire life. She's a bit pushy and forced her magic onto Julia during her ritual. Because of this, Julia doesn't trust her completely.

**Naomi** (Nay-oh-mee)—The youngest member of the sisterhood. Egyptian and British. Comes form a wealthy family and is an advocate for the street kids of Egypt. Has a chip on her shoulder and she and Julia don't particularly get along. Abrasive personality but a fierce protector. Her magic is very defensive.

**Dell** (Deh-l)—One of Julia's best friends. Former Navy. Rescued Julia and Andrew after they escaped from Gordon Mitchell's house.

**Edie** (Ee-dee)—Julia's other best friend. Mother to four little girls (Elise, Enid, Emory, and Elliot) and married to Andrew's best friend, Eric. Doesn't know about the sisterhood or Julia's newfound magic.

**Lumee** (Loo-mee)—Julia and Andrew's cat. Adopted from Bahrain. Dilmun Cat—calico colored with yellow-green eyes (hence her name—Bahraini slang for lemons and limes) and *very* vocal.

**Omar** (Oh-Mar)—Professor. Salma's husband.

**Karim** (Kah-rim)—Doctor. Wife of Hasina, son to Marwa, and brother to Salma. Has grown up knowing about magic and the sisterhood.

**Simon** (Sy-mon)—Reem's husband. British. Works in banking.

**Gram** (Gr-am)—Julia's grandmother. Supportive and more of a mother to Julia than her own. Died towards the end of ITLOTM. Left Julia and Andrew with a ton of wealth after her death.

**Gordon Mitchell** (Gor-done Mm-itch-ell)—Died at the end of IT-LOTM after torturing Andrew and Julia. Pastor at a mega church in North Carolina and believed he would one day have the power to bring the dead back to life. Sadistic maniac who abused Julia during her teens.

**Warren Mitchell** (Waw-runn Mm-itch-ell)—Gordon's father and former pastor of the mega church, now a congressman. Also abused Julia as a teenager and allowed Gordon to run wild. Ended up killing his son to cover up the madness that had overtaken him. Also had Julia's parents killed for not agreeing to something when Julia was younger.

**Isis** (eye-sis)—Major Goddess in Ancient Egyptian mythology. Goddess of magic and wisdom, kingship and protection of the kingdom, mothering, and mourning. She was believed to have helped usher people into the afterlife.

**Khonsu** (Kahn-shoo)—Ancient Egyptian God of the Moon. His name means *traveller* and refers to the moon traveling across the sky. He is also known *Embracer*, *Pathfinder*, *Defender*, and *healer*, and was thought to watch over those who travel at night.

**Senenmut** (Sen-in-moot)— also rumored to be Hatshepsut's lover

**Thutmose (**THuwT-mows) **III**— Hatshepsut's Stepson—the first born son of Thutmose II. Next in line from the throne after his father, his stepmother stepped in as Regent when he was a young boy and reigned in his stead.

**Maatkare** (maht-car)— A name or title shared by many different women in Ancient Egypt. The name is roughly translated as **Maat (the goddess of truth) is the life force of Re (the sun god)**

The Golden Fields of **Aaru** (ah -roo)—The name for Heavenly Paradise in Ancient Egyptian Mythology (Also called The Golden Rushes or the Fields of Aaru)

**Heka** (heck-ah)—Ancient Egyptian word for magic

**Duat** (doo-aht)—Ancient Egyptian Underworld or Afterlife

**Neferure** (nef-er-ra)—Hatshepsut's daughter

**Habebty** (Hah-beeb-tee)— Arabic term of endearment meaning honey or sweetie

**Souk** (Sōok) —an Arabic market or bazaar

**Mashallah** (mah-shah-la)—an Arabic phrase that translates to "God has willed it"

**Bahrain** (Bah-RAYN)—Small island in the Middle East off the coast of Saudi Arabia

# 1

## *Haunted*

I had conjured the ghosts that were haunting me. They kept me awake, these specters that rose up out of my nightmares, moaning and rattling the chains that were tightening around me. No amount of magic that coursed through my veins could chase them away and let me find peace. Instead they hovered over my bed demanding attention, as if I'd called them forth from the ether and then ignored them. Phantom fingers wrapped around my throat, and I shivered and swatted at the empty air.

I gave up tossing and turning, not wanting to wake my husband, Andrew, with my demons. He wrestled with his own ghosts and was finally still in the quiet night. The injuries he'd sustained in the weeks before at the hands of a madman were grave, and when I wasn't reliving the trauma inflicted on me, I worried over his. I slipped on the faded peach cardigan that had been my Gram's. The loss of her was recent enough that her scent still lingered in the fibers. I wrapped myself in her arms and quietly went out into the garden.

The moon was barely a sliver, a *waning crescent*. I was becoming more accustomed to the moon's movements as I learned more about the magic that answered its call. Magic that had almost killed Gordon Mitchell and tortured his father, Warren. I shivered as I paced the garden, the night air chilly, or perhaps the chill was from the memories and ghosts that followed me from our room.

Luxor had been a sort of refuge for me in the last year. It had been a place of profound revelation, discoveries unmatched, and new friendships. Drew and I had come not knowing that our lives would forever be changed when we toured Hatshepsut's temple. There, I'd experienced a ritual that unlocked magic buried within. Magic I was still learning to control. Magic that had exploded out of me, unbidden, searching out the source of my fear and pain, trying to destroy that threat to keep Andrew and me safe. So much had happened in the last year. It was overwhelming if I thought about it too long.

I scrubbed my face with my hands, trying to force away memory and the guilt that weighed heavily on my soul. Rationally, I knew I had been in a kill-or-be-killed situation with Gordon. He'd had every intention of killing both Andrew and me, and there was no escaping that. I'd suffered at his hands as a teenager and knew the depth of his madness then. It had only deepened with time. No matter how unintentional, I had saved mine and Andrew's lives when the magic exploded out of me and attacked him. Until our run-in with Warren Mitchell the next night, I'd thought I'd taken his life. Finding out that Warren had finished him off did little to assuage the guilt and fear that was consuming me.

I pulled the cardigan tighter around me, trying to glean some comfort from the fabric that held the ghost of my grandmother's arms. I longed to talk to her. To get advice or cry on her shoulder and hear her soothing voice. Hers was the only ghost I would welcome in the garden and she was nowhere to be found. She and my Gramps were parents to me when my own betrayed me and put their faith in the cult they had been a part of above even my safety. I had been back at Gram's house after her sudden death, sorting through her entire life when Gordon had found me and, subsequently, Andrew. The shock of losing her might have waned, but the grief hadn't. I was struggling to exist in a world where she no longer d id.

"Jules?" I heard a quiet voice in the dark.

I turned and found my best friend, Delilah, who had come to Luxor with us in search of her own answers. She made her way over and put an arm around me, resting her head on my shoulder. I wasn't tall by any means, but Dell stood a few inches shorter than I did and always made me feel tall.

"Can't sleep?" I asked.

"Jet lag is a bitch," she said. She didn't ask after me, knowing the reason for my insomnia. Her presence was reassuring, solid, and comforting. We had known each other for almost fifteen years; she knew everything about me and loved me anyway. Besides Andrew, she and our friend Edie were my chosen family and were the sisters I had always wanted. Though, I knew I was also finding family within the sisterhood.

Delilah had been a wildcard I wasn't expecting. Hanan had come to me before we left Gram's house, the early morning light peeking through the trees distracting me from packing. I'd been staring dreamily into the dappled rays lighting up the bedroom, lost in a memory.

"You know she's one of us, right, Julia?"

I had looked up, eyes wide and mouth open. "Who? Delilah?" I asked.

She smiled and laughed softly. "Yes, Delilah," she answered.

"What? How?" I said, shocked.

"The same way it's inside any of us, I suppose," she smiled. No one knew why we were chosen by fate or Isis or Hatshepsut herself to carry on her legacy and magic. It just was. "She can always come with us if she wants to learn. Would you like to do the honors?"

I opened and closed my mouth, trying to wrap my mind around the fact that I would be able to merge both sides of my life. There had been no worry—I knew she'd want to come with us. She'd been drawn to the occult her entire life, to be able to practice *real* magic would bring her an immeasurable amount of joy.

I'd nodded, quietly gotten up, and found Dell packing her things in the guest room. I'd lingered outside the room, hovering at the threshold and turning inwards, reaching out to see if I could somehow tell that Dell had the same magic inside her. Focused as I was, a pulsing warmth radiated from her—something I'd never noticed before. I shored myself up, stepped into the room, and told my best friend that her life was about to change.

Her response had been one for the books. A loud squeal and hoot of laughter had brought Naomi running in. She looked us hugging and laughing, and then rolled her eyes when Dell told her she was coming with us.

"Took you long enough to realize," she'd snarked before walking back out to finish seeing to her own affairs.

We'd flown to Colorado then, and Dell had taken a day to wrap up her life for an extended leave of absence, grab her passport, and pack some clean clothes. I had no idea what excuse she'd used, but I was grateful for it

.

Nighttime garden wanderings had become a new ritual between us since we'd arrived in Luxor. Eventually she'd get over the jet lag, and I'd be left to wander alone; or as alone as I could get with my memories.

"You're going to have to sleep eventually, Jules," she said quietly.

I sighed. "Yeah? So are you. We've been here for almost two weeks now. Still fighting jet lag? And I sleep. Maybe not well, but I sleep," I trailed off.

"Yeah, but *you* look like hell. I'm at least sleeping at weird times. I love you, but you're making yourself sick with guilt, and he doesn't deserve your guilt or the sleepless nights, Jules. He really doesn't."

A tear slipped down my cheek, which frustrated me to no end. I didn't grieve for Gordon. The world was truly a safer place without him in it. I grieved for the loss of my innocence and for the choices I'd been forced to make. And for the fear that something else would happen and I'd lose control again. If I were being honest with myself, that kept me awake more than anything else did. The fear of losing control again stole my breath with a crushing weight on my chest that only seemed to grow heavier.

"I know, Dell. I know."

We stood together a few more minutes before she urged me to go back to bed. I left her sitting in the garden, lost in thought. I went back to Andrew, curled up against him, and willed myself to fall asleep.

## 2

## *Ritual Death*

"We have an idea," Hanan, my friend and leader of our group, said the next day at lunch. Concern was etched across her face, as plain as day.

The sisterhood, the group I had serendipitously become a part of the year before, had become our safe haven. It seemed that not only were they charged with the safekeeping of secrets of the long-dead Hatshepsut, but also the care and keeping of Andrew and me.

"For what?" I asked after finishing my bite of flatbread and hummus. I wasn't hungry and hadn't been since we arrived from the states, but I tried to go through the motions to keep everyone placated.

"Well, lots of things, but mostly to get you through this, Julia. You're disappearing into yourself, and none of us can stand to see it," Hanan said. Andrew and I were living in her guest house for the foreseeable future, so we saw her (and worried her) every day.

"Seriously, Jules, it's gotten bad," Dell added.

I nodded. I had no arguments for that. I was sinking into myself, a cloud of grief and depression choking in its intensity. I knew something had to be done but didn't know what.

"Renee and Hasina have tried to help Andrew, but he's not getting any better," Hanan started. "We are wondering if a focused, healing ritual at the next full moon would be enough to help."

"So, take him into the ritual room and focus all our energy on him?" I asked.

"That's what we're thinking. We aren't sure if it'll work, but it can't hurt to try." She looked sideways at Dell. "And, for you, we're wondering if maybe something a little more than just our energies is needed to heal you."

I looked at them, confused. "What do you mean?"

"Well, this is where it gets weird," Dell said.

I balked. Weird for Dell meant *really* weird. "So, you know how psilo-cybin is amazing for treating depression in micro-doses?" She paused, sussing me out and waiting, in vain, for me to catch up. "Mushrooms, Jules. Magic mushrooms." She sighed and shook her head.

"What?" I asked, trying to figure out what on earth she was talking about.

"So it's not all Santa lore and reindeers flying around." She waited a beat for me to get it but I didn't. She waved her hand. "Never mind. I'll tell you another day. Anyway, there are doctors that are really fighting and pushing for the regulation and legalization of psilocybin as med-ication. They were making noise about it just before I got out of the Navy—there were trials being done on service members for PTSD and the results were life-changing."

"Seriously?" I balked. "Mushrooms? Like, make-you-see-things-mushrooms?"

Dell rolled her eyes and kept going. "Yes. *Those* mushrooms. They've found that they kind of re-code the brain, in a way, to actually *heal* instead of just treating symptoms with medications and still dealing with the underlying trauma."

"Things like this have ritual histories, Julia," Hanan explained. "When I mentioned that I was thinking about something that would help you with your nightmares all those months ago, it was along these same lines."

I opened my mouth to argue.

"Look, before you say no," Dell jumped in. "Don't look at it any different than using cannabis. Or even the acacia in the full moon ritual. It's an all-natural substance that grows in the ground that might be able to help. It has to be worth a shot, yeah?"

I thought for a moment, quiet. It had taken a lot of encouragement for me to even *try* weed when we moved to California. Not only had my childhood been sheltered, but I'd been part of the D.A.R.E generation and deeply entrenched in a religious cult that vilified even the use of caffeine as a stimulant. Breaking old beliefs and biases hadn't been easy. Still, cannabis had really helped, and I was a big believer in healing by natural means whenever possible.

"I don't know. Let me think on it," I responded, finally.

"Can we tell you our thoughts on a plan?" Hanan asked.

I nodded.

"So, we would also utilize the full moon's energy for you. The day before we do the ritual for Andrew, the moon will be visible at ninety-nine percent. Obviously, it's not complete, but the strength will be there. We'll administer the psilocybin tincture in the ritual room—the safest and most warded place we have—and the two of us will be there with you. We'll ensure you're safe and comfortable the whole time."

I picked at the skin around my nails, leaning in to the prickle of pain to ground me. No matter my comfort with cannabis or even the acacia from the full moon rituals, magic mushrooms felt like a big thing to try. I hated the idea of losing control over myself and my thoughts.

"Okay. Safe and comfortable sound good," I said nervously. Taking the chance and performing the ritual to become part of the sisterhood had been a giant leap for me as it was. At best, the thought of another life-changing situation where I had to relinquish control and trust the process was nerve-wracking. At worst, I could lose myself entirely. But maybe I needed to. They were right, things were getting bad.

"Jules. They *are* safe," Dell said. "Truly. I'll send you some research on them if you want to read up before making the call, but for real, it's totally safe."

"These things, for longer than we realize, have been considered ritual death ceremonies where a part of you actually dies and is reborn into something new," Hanan explained. "The hope is that, with direct intentions set and the right mindset, the traumatized part of you dies and is reborn. The parts that are filled with fear, pain, self-doubt... we want you to purge yourself of those parts of you that are holding you back from being healed."

I nodded again and swallowed the lump in my throat that seemed like it was always at the ready lately. The tears in my eyes were hot and painful with their regularity. I felt like I should say more, but I was numb to the idea of ever feeling better—the little inkling of hope seemed to have fizzled out at some point in the last few days.

"Jules, I can't stand to see you like this anymore. I really can't," Dell said. "And I know Andrew can't either. None of us can. Maybe doing something like this will help. Maybe it won't. But you have to try something."

I nodded and then excused myself, needing some space.

I found Andrew in the garden, dozing in the warm afternoon sun, doing what he could to work on healing himself in the fresh air and sunshine. He still struggled to walk, his hands so injured he couldn't use crutches, and his feet a mess of wounds and broken toes and small bones. He hobbled from our bed to the toilet and all but crawled outside to get fresh air. It had been almost three weeks since he'd been tortured, but most of his injuries still looked fresh, save the sickly faded bruises on his face, all yellows and greens. He hadn't trimmed his facial hair since leaving DC, and his beard was longer than it had ever been before. Every look at him stirred a pang of guilt and anger at what had happened, but the worry over him was constant. I tucked myself into a chair across from him, sitting in the shade of the covered pergola.

"They tell you their plan yet?" he asked, eyes still closed.

"I didn't mean to wake you."

"You didn't. I'm just laying here, not really sleeping." His voice didn't hold any of the warmth it usually did. I knew he was in a great deal of pain despite everything that Renee and Hasina had been doing to help alleviate it.

"Okay. Well, that's good. And yes, they've told me the plan," I said softly. I was so nervous around him. There was a space between us that I didn't know how to close.

"Do you think you'll do it?"

I shrugged. I'd barely had time to think about it, let alone make a decision. "I mean, I don't know what else to do. I feel like there's this blanket of...guilt? Depression? Trauma? All of the above? I feel this weight on me. I can't get it lifted off on my own." I sighed, the sound heavy. I was exhausted with everything.

"My love," he said, sitting up and pushing his hair out of his face. "Why would you ever feel guilty for any of this? None of it is your fault. Come here." He opened his arms up to me and I scooted in close to him and let him wrap his arms around me. We'd had a version of this conversation a dozen times already, but I couldn't shake the guilt that sat heavy on my chest. Rationally I knew none of this was my fault. But grief was never rational.

"I know," I said, tears clogging up my throat. "I know, Drew. And I have no clue why I'm carrying this around like it's my fault. I just am."

He ran his hand up and down my arm, his touch gentle and careful. We were both so nervous around each other still—the pain and trauma holding us at arms length no matter how tightly pressed against him I was.

"You want me to try it first?" Drew asked after a few minutes. I shrugged.

"No. Not unless you want to, or they think it would help. I just don't know how I feel about it all."

"I get that," he said. "But if you think it would help to watch someone else go through it, I'll do it for you. And maybe it *would* help. What we went through was horrific." His voice dropped low, and I could hear him whispering around the emotion that was bubbling to the surface. "I'm barely hanging on too. Maybe we both need a reset, and this could be it."

I knew he was right, but the thought of a ritual *death* scared me, and I had no clue if it was the right thing to do or not.

"I know a few people who've tried them for PTSD, and it worked really well. My therapist and I talked about it for me, but there was nowhere that offered it as a treatment plan when we were in England, so it wasn't really an option then. You'll figure out what to do, J. Take whatever time you need—I've got you."

We sat in the garden for a long time, the birds and gentle wind the only noises filling the space. It was warm but not summer-hot yet, but I still felt a chill inside that no heat could thaw out. I knew I was withdrawing into myself and falling into a deeper and deeper depression. The heaviness was all too familiar. Though anxiety had been my constant companion, depression was like the random uninvited guest that cropped up every so often. It was far too easy to let it slip over me like a well-worn sweater. Not that I enjoyed the despair or the darkness, but it was almost easier to succumb and wrap myself in it than fight. I could find comfort in the numbness where facing the fear and the hurt carried unbelievable pain.

# 3

## *Fight or Flight*

The following two weeks passed unremarkably. Drew and I hovered nervously around each other, the space between us gaping wider and wider each day. He was managing his pain and moving around a bit more, though he still slept often and a lot, and his wounds were far from healing like they should. He was shrinking into himself, battling his own depression and demons. Deep down, I knew we should be turning to each other for comfort—it was what we always did, drawing in and battening down the hatches to work through something. But this time we couldn't seem to find each other. We were two ships passing in the night, and I worried about what that meant for us. I felt like he was keeping something from me—how much pain he was in, or something that had gone on in Gordon's basement that he just couldn't face yet. I wasn't sure, but it felt like there was an impassable chasm between us.

Dell was living her best life in Luxor. Finally tapped into true magic after a lifetime of studying the esoteric, she took to the group with a fervor I was jealous of. Dell fit in like she had been a part of it her entire life. She was never alone; someone from the sisterhood came to get her each day and helped her to unlock her potential.

Her ritual had taken place the day we arrived in Luxor. We'd flown in early that morning after a layover in London. Though we were all jet lagged and exhausted out of our minds, we got Andrew settled at Hanan's, our cat Lumee standing guard, and headed for the temple. Where my ritual had been a complete and utter surprise, Dell had the privilege of being fully prepared for hers. Our flight across the world had been peppered with questions.

"So, we go skinny-dipping?" She had asked, eliciting a laugh from Andrew and a mock look of horror from Marwa after we explained the American saying. Entering the pool unburdened by clothing not only allowed more access to the energy-laden water but was also seen as a rebirth. Going in and emerging as new was like a symbolic return to the womb. Which had been precisely what I'd equated it to.

The ritual that first night back in Luxor had been bittersweet. It was amazing to officially bring Dell into the fold and have her be a part of the sisterhood. Holding her hand and feeling the jolt of power course through us while we were connected hit on another level. I'd wept in relief that someone from my former life was now a part of my new life. I hadn't realized how much I needed that until we stood in the temple, bound together by magic and love.

Being surrounded by everyone was, in a way, bolstering. Still, it was also the beginning of my descent into a deep depression. Closing up Gram's house and leaving North Carolina in such a hurry had forced me to hold it together. Even with the stop in Colorado and the flight to Luxor... I'd been focused on Drew and the cat and getting away safely, not allowing myself to break down. But now that we were in Egypt and safe and distanced from everything that had happened, my control had slipped, and I no longer held anything together.

"Look, J, I will never force you to do something you don't want to do. You know that," Andrew said the day before my healing ritual was to take place. "But, I don't think this is a bad idea to at least give it a shot."

I looked up from my lap, my attention wholly focused on Lumee, who had taken to sunbathing in the garden before the hottest part of the day when she'd escape into Hanan's house and explore. I still hadn't made a final decision on whether or not I would go through with the ritual. I was at the point where I was sick and tired of everyone weighing in and wanted to be left alone to wallow.

"Drew, I love you, and I appreciate it, but I'm tired of everyone forcing their opinions down my throat," I said. My heart beat harder as adrenaline rushed through my veins as anger bubbled to the surface. "Between you and Dell and everyone else who saunters in here with their pity and commentary, I've had it."

"Whoa whoa whoa." Andrew held up his hands in surrender. "No one is pitying you, Jules. You saved my life down there—I don't *pity* you—I'm in awe of you. But we're all worried. Would you rather us ignore that your clothes are two sizes too big because you barely eat or that you could pack for a two-week trip in the bags under your eyes?"

I ground my teeth, anger fully present and accounted for now.

"Yeah. Everyone needs to back the fuck up. I almost killed a man, Andrew. And yeah, he was a sadistic asshole, but I could have taken his life. Not you. Not anyone else. Me. Not to mention losing Gram and you being tortured by said sadistic asshole. And *I* am the one who has to fucking deal with it, and it is okay if I am having a hard time processing it all." I upset the cat from my lap and stormed off to the guest house, slamming the door behind me with barely a thought.

Magic had been trickling out of me unbidden since I refused to use it consciously. I knew that I needed to get my shit together. Rationally, I knew everyone was worried and wanted the best for me. But it was either anger or apathy right now, and in this moment, it was anger coursing through my veins. I was spoiling for a fight. A small part of my brain told me to take deep breaths and calm down, but after storming around in the guest house for a few minutes and only getting hotter, I went in search of a punching bag.

I found Andrew where I'd left him, Lumee having taken up residence on his lap in my absence.

"You know what, Drew, fuck you," I said, words hot in my throat and pouring out of me like lava. "You want to talk about being worried? You won't talk to me, or even fucking look at me. You're not healing how you should be, and God knows you ought to be at least acknowledging the insane PTSD nightmares that have come back since the whole thing. How many years have I quietly laid there and let you have your nightmares? Huh? I didn't force you to do something that would change your brain chemistry to *fix* you, did I? No. I laid there and held you while you cried out in your sleep and woke up terrified."

The color drained from his face, and he looked like I'd slapped him.

"Well, they've started back up since all this. You want to let some piece of you die off in a ritual death? Or do you want to work through it on your own with some space?" I glared at him and thought for sure my eyes had to be aflame with how angry I was.

"Jules, no one is saying you need to lose a piece of yourself. We all just want you to be okay—okay as in *alive* again. *Present* again. Not lost in what happened and existing as a ghost of yourself. You deserve more than that. You deserve freedom and peace, and this is just offering you a chance at that. That's all. But if you don't want to do it, then don't."

I was fractious and in a fit of irrational anger, but depression *is* irrational, and I couldn't do anything to stop it from spewing out of me. No matter the tears that spilled down Drew's cheeks or the kind words I refused to hear. I kept going and lashed out at Andrew, the tiny voice inside me telling me to calm down drowned out in favor of pent-up fury. When I was finally done, I burst into tears and stormed out of the garden. I passed Hanan coming home from work, though she had the good sense to move out of my way as I shoved past her.

I walked with no real direction, just the furious pace of someone hurting and needing space.

Once I'd burned off some of the anger, I started to replay what happened in the garden. I knew my cheeks were already red with anger and exertion, but they flamed even more with shame.

Years before, something had happened on one of the deployments that haunted Andrew. He'd never talked about it. Whether it was classified or he couldn't stand to pick at the scab, he never went into detail. He'd had horrible nightmares and flashbacks for months.

The stigma around therapy ran deep in the military community, and the threat of losing his clearance was too great for him to feel comfortable seeking help for a long time. It took losing one of his friends to suicide for him to get up and fight. He got the help he needed and fought tooth and nail for his sailors to be free to get the same help without consequence. In time, the nightmares got better, but when he was stressed out or working so much that his sleep suffered, they always returned. Whatever had happened in the basement with Gordon had opened the floodgates of his carefully held control.

*Still*, I argued with myself, no one had suggested killing off a piece of himself. It just felt so extreme. Why couldn't they just leave me to wallow a bit longer? I'd eventually get out of it. Wouldn't I?

I fumed and walked until the sun started to set, and the rage simmered to manageable frustration. I pulled out my phone and opened the maps, unsure how far I'd walked or in what direction. I had missed calls and texts but ignored them, not ready to face anyone. I had somehow managed to walk a little over four miles away from Hanan's with no shoes. It wasn't until the maps pulled up my location that I felt the pain in the soles of my feet from my furious escapade.

I started back to the house, hobbling on cut-up feet, but the wind was out of my sails, and the last bit of anger fizzled out to nothing. I'd walked maybe half a mile when a car came up behind me, slowing down, and I felt a bolt of fear in my belly. I was in a foreign country with different customs and had no clue where I was. I held my shoulders back and head high, walking with purpose to hopefully stave off any unwanted attention.

"Jules, get in the car. You've been walking for almost two hours." I heard Dell say.

I sagged with relief and turned towards her. I hobbled over to her and climbed in, grateful I didn't have to finish my walk of shame.

Dell drove us back to Hanan's, but neither of us said anything until we parked. Looking at my lap, I spoke quietly to Dell once she shut the engine off.

"I'll do it."

Without looking at her, I left the car and went straight to the guest house. I climbed into bed and fell asleep, feet filthy and unwashed. Apologies needed to be made desperately, but my body shut down.

I blissfully sought out oblivion.

# 4

## *Medicine and Memories*

I don't know where Andrew slept the night of our fight. I woke up to a cold bed and knew he'd never been in it with me. The empty space where my husband should have been was filled with regret and shame. I had used him as a punching bag when I should have gone to him for comfort for the both of us, and I didn't know what it would take to make up for everything I'd said in my fit of anger. I was restless, but I dreaded getting up and facing the day. I rolled over, pulled the duvet over my head to block the light, and fell asleep.

When I woke again, the room was bright with the midday sun, and my bladder was full to bursting. After handling my morning business, I grabbed my phone to check my messages. It was well past noon. I groaned, incredulous that I'd slept that long. I had multiple missed calls and texts from Andrew the previous day that I had ignored. I put the phone back down, not ready to read through them all just yet. My mind was a mess.

I went to the kettle to make some tea to try and clear the last dregs of sleepiness from my mind and I saw a note on the counter from Andrew. I couldn't ignore him any longer.

*J, I love you so much and I never want you to feel like you're being forced into doing something you don't want to do. Whatever you decide, we'll get through this together.*

*You were right— I need to deal with my shit. I messaged the therapist back in the UK and I'm going to see if Jasmin can see me virtually. I just...I know I need to face everything that happened in that basement, but I'm struggling. You deserve to be free, but you also deserve a partner who is whole enough to support you however you need and that's just not me right now. I'm going to get some space and try to clear my head and give you some space without worrying about me. —A*

The paper grew heavy in my hands with the weight of his words. I reached for my phone again to respond to him. My fingers hovered over the screen while the kettle burbled and heated, but I had no clue what to say to him. I typed and retyped and by the time the water had boiled and settled back down again, I'd settled on *I'm doing it. I love you, and I am so, so sorry.* I hit send and waited for the three little dots to appear in response, but they never came.

I floated through the rest of the day in a haze. Andrew and I weren't perfect by any means, but this fight felt more significant than an angry one-off outburst. I felt untethered not having him near. When I'd finally surfaced from the guest house, having worked up the courage to face them, Dell told me that he was staying at Marwa's. She assured me it wasn't anger that had him leaving, but some misguided notion that I was better off without him near right now.

As the sun was setting, Hanan, Dell, and I met Renee and Marwa at the temple. I was a bundle of nerves, fraught with anxiety over every part of the day. Dell and I had talked, and I'd read the literature and watched videos online. Still, I was nervous that instead of the worst parts of me dying off and making way for healing connections in my brain, I would somehow get stuck in an endless loop of flashbacks with no escape.

When we walked down the passageway, my heart felt like it would beat right out of my chest. The air below ground was cool and was a shock from the warmth of the evening outside. I leaned against the cave walls, my skin needing a cold shock. Hanan unlocked the door, and I shivered; I wasn't sure if it was from nerves or the chill. The click and whirr of the opening of the locks were loud in our silence. I knew everyone else was anxious, even if they hadn't said as much. The tension was boiling off them in waves. We entered the preparation room and readied ourselves for the evening.

"I'm going to go get everything set up," Renee said, shifting her heavy backpack on her shoulders and heading into the ritual room. She lit the space as she crossed the threshold with only her words. As the resident healer, she was in for a busy couple of nights, but I knew I was in good hands. Renee had actually administered mushrooms before and had seen people safely through trips. That was the only thing giving me any confidence that it might not all go to pot. That and the fact that Marwa had agreed to be there and help keep me calm. No matter how I tried, I struggled to get past the point that Renee had used her magic on me without permission during one of the most defining moments of my life. No amount of time had yet to make it feel like she'd not taken my choice away that night in the temple. I didn't feel the same way about Marwa. She always asked permission.

"That will never get old," Dell said behind me.

"It really doesn't," I answered.

We worked quietly after that. There wasn't a terrible lot to prepare since I was the only one who would be partaking. Nonetheless, the other three wanted to be there to support me and needed their own things to get them through the night. We'd brought sleeping rolls and blankets, and I carried them into the ritual space, setting them up where Renee instructed me. She was setting out candles and herb bundles and burning incense, transforming the area into a warm and cozy place for us to spend the night. The room was warm from the water but not stifling, the cave walls keeping us underground enough to stave off the heat from the day. The moon cover had been moved, and a gentle current of warm air lazily drifted around the pool. I stood there for a few minutes, watching the dark water move gently, lapping at the edges of the pool, feeling calm for the first time in weeks.

"Okay, Jules, we're ready," Dell said a little while later, shaking me out of my trance. I turned back to them and the bedroll they'd prepped for me. Following the others' lead, I sat down and felt my hands go clammy.

"First, we're going to set the intention for the experience. That's the most important part of the whole process—the intent behind it. You have to come willingly and with a clear vision of what you hope to gain," Renee said.

Dell was next to me, and she reached over and grabbed my hand, squeezing it in support.

"Okay... I guess my intention for the experience is to find a way to let go of the past and the trauma," I said quietly.

Renee nodded at me. "Remember to be specific. The same way we set intentions for the New Moon, or you set them in your personal life, yes?" she said.

I considered this for a moment.

"Does anyone have any paper and a pen? I think it would help me to write it down."

"I brought some," Hanan said as she stood up and headed back to the preparation room. She returned with a small, spiral-bound notebook and a pen and handed them to me as she sat down again. I opened the book and spent a few minutes writing out my intention for the night, being specific but not too convoluted. I was doing this for one reason and one reason only, and I wanted that to be very clear.

*I am thankful that this medicine will help create pathways of healing in my brain, allowing me to let go of trauma, fear, and pain and find joy and purpose in my life separate from the things that happened to me. I am thankful that the traumatized part of me will die off and make way for my best and most whole self.*

I could have kept going. There were so many things I wanted to let go of and so many things I hoped for the future. But this was a start. Letting go of the trauma. Letting go of the burden that the pain and fear had forced me to carry.

"Okay, Julia. So we all have set intentions as well, intentions of support and healing, and we'll help you during this whole process. We will be directing calming energy and be here with you," Renee said.

She handed me my mug from Marina, and I sniffed cautiously. The warm liquid smelled earthy but not intense. Resolutely, I took a small sip. It was... odd. I could taste the herbs Renee had brewed with the shrooms, lemon balm, and lavender among them for their calming properties. Still, they weren't enough to mask the wild earthiness and funk that was distinctly the mushrooms. I took a breath, thought my intention in my mind, and knocked the rest of the cup back in a few gulps. I shuddered at the taste and handed the mug back to Renee. I laid on the sleeping pallet, making myself as comfortable as possible. Renee used pillows and blankets to bolster and support my body, making me more relaxed than

I'd been in a long time. After we were settled, Hanan led us all in a loving-kindness meditation—repeating the mantra: *May I be safe, May I be happy, May I be healthy, May I walk through this journey with ease.* It helped me focus on my intention and calm my nervous system.

A short time passed, and I started to feel an odd, floaty sensation slowly creep into my mind. My limbs began to feel heavy, and with a strange sense of detachment, I was grateful for the pillows and bolsters that supported my body.

"Julia, you've gone quiet. Are you starting to feel something?" Marwa asked quietly.

I nodded, not wanting to speak. My eyelids felt like they had small weights on them, and I don't know that I could have opened them if I'd wanted to. Slowly but surely, a deep sense of calm settled over me like a weighted blanket. Minutes or hours passed. I had no sense of time, only the steady beat of my heart in my ears and the peaceful sound of breathing around me. I was warm and cocooned in the ritual space and felt safe. Colors flashed in my mind, fading in and out like a kaleidoscope.

"Alright, Julia. We're going to start the hard work now," Renee said, her voice floating all around me in the room, disembodied. "Remember that we're here with you, and you're safe."

I nodded, focused on the colors in my mind. The calming smell of lavender filled my nose, wafting through me. Every few moments, something else intertwined with the herbs made its way through, disrupting the sensation of peace. I tried to focus on the odd hint of smell, and as soon as I turned my energy towards it, the stink of Gordon's cologne wiped out everything else. It was powerful and stung my nose. I fought back the urge to gag. My heart began to beat wildly in my chest as panic set in. My limbs were heavy, but instead of the pleasant calm they'd been suffused with initially, I felt trapped and thrashed wildly back and forth, trying to get them to move.

"Jules, stay calm. It's only a memory," Dell said.

Someone put their hand on my shoulder, and I screamed, a guttural sound that came from the depths of my body, and the hand jerked away.

"It's okay, Julia. You're safe here," Marwa said, her voice small and quiet. A slow calm radiated over me like a cool breeze. That same detached part of my mind realized she was helping, using her power to soothe me like we'd planned together.

The night carried on that way—a mix of terror and physical pain matched with soothing calm from Marwa and Renee's magic. Slowly, we worked through years of trauma together. I spoke freely, my tongue loosened, and the words poured out of me. A deep terror rolled through me as I recalled the things that had happened. Still, the longer I spoke, the more the memories almost loosed themselves from me, and it began to feel like I recalled someone else's memories. It was an odd sensation, this detachment from my pain. I was a ghost, hovering above the memories playing out in my mind as a spectator. I could see everything happening from all angles, from all points of view. And I became privy to knowledge that had been kept from my physical experience of the memories when they had originally happened.

I watched and felt slaps and punches, little moments of degradation, and significant moments of abuse all happen from above and within. The experiences and memories were tangible the longer I sat with them. I could smell the earth underneath me in the woods behind the Mitchell's house. The purr of an engine rumbled beneath me as we sped down the highway— screams from the driver's seat, an odd visceral experience through the mushrooms. The words popped out of Gordon's mouth like red bubbles of hot lava; my body felt the bursts of each one, melting holes in my skin. My body arched and shrank away in answer to his physical assaults. I felt the answering wall slam shut to keep him out and the roaring pain when he tore his way inside of me. I writhed in pain in the temple, Marwa and Renee sending waves of power over me, calming me as much as possible. At the same time, my body and mind expunged the trauma.

With each memory that rose to the surface, the feeling of mania grew from Gordon's perspective. When my mind started to play out everything that had happened two months before, it was pouring off him like a thick, oily fog. My mind slowed then and played out every horrifying moment with deeper clarity than the older memories. By this point, Renee had had me drink more tea, a small amount to keep me in and keep the purge—this reckoning—going.

I watched and recalled out loud the moments in Gram's house where Gordon had found me. I felt the splash of wine on my legs as I dropped the glass when I answered the door, the sharp, acidic scent mingling with his cologne. Felt the shard of glass embed itself into my foot, skin, fascia and muscle painfully slicing open. But the memory took a turn at that point, and I felt the splash on my legs that belonged to Gordon. I felt everything from inside of him. Elation, arousal, and a sick sense of retribution as I watched myself through his eyes. The excitement bubbled inside him as the color drained from my face in fear, the heat of my body pressed against him as he backed me against the wall at Grams. The memory continued like that, switching between us, my body going from hot to cold, fear and elation in a whirlwind that left me sweating and shaking.

By the time the memory played through to the end, I had a clear vision of Gordon's plans. They were worse than anything I could have imagined. I watched as *he* remembered the pain and abuse he'd inflicted on Andrew the night before. I saw the truth of what he'd done, saw the poison he'd swiped on his tools, and watched as he molested and defiled my husband's prone body while he was, blessedly, unconscious. I watched as Andrew lost himself bit by bit, breaking almost wholly. I watched Gordon's plans hover over his mind inside giant lightbulbs, the ugly pictures casting disturbing shadows in the room. He was, without a doubt, planning on killing the both of us, but not before keeping us alive for as long as he could. I watched scenes play out in real-time inside the weird light bulbs, his fantasies on an endless loop while the reality showed down below. It was odd and confusing, and I was lost to the temple room. No amount of anyone's energies or magic was strong enough to touch the horrors playing out in my mind.

My physical body tensed up when my power flared in the memory. Every muscle was screaming, my body burning like it was on fire. I arched up, my body physically lifting off the mat in a terrible climax of pain and fear that exploded inside me in a bright flash of white light, blinding me, memory, and soul.

And then, there was nothing.

# 5
## *Before*

My body had purged so much pain, anger, and fear that it shut down, and I slept on and off all day the next day. I had come to hours later as the sun was rising, delirious and fevered, and they half carried me out of the temple and to the car. I had no recollection of even making it back to Hanan's or being put to bed.

My fever broke around lunch, and I woke up sweaty and stinking. But I was lighter somehow. Like I had purged myself of at least a portion of the trauma that had been haunting me. Andrew was still at Marwa's. I knew he was hurting, but I wanted desperately to see him. To tell him what had happened and try to make things right. Marwa hadn't said much other than to assure me he was fine the night before.

"Just go over there," Dell said, late in the afternoon after I'd woken up and felt rested enough to leave the comfort of the bed. I had showered, washing my body of the residual sticky sweat and the dried fear sweat from the night before. That little act had revived me enough to feel human again.

"He wants space, Dell. I know I seriously fucked up this time," I said, nursing a cup of tea. My stomach was still uneasy, but the comfort of tea always soothed me.

"Jules, be serious," she said, rolling her eyes. "Yeah, you fucked up. Yeah, he needs space. But at a certain point, *someone* has to make the first move, and you're the one who caused the hurt, so it needs to be you. Go over there before tonight. I'm sure he's nervous, not knowing what to expect."

I sighed. I knew she was right, but I was struggling. I was embarrassed about how I'd treated him and was so anxious about making things right but not being able to.

Hanan and Dell dropped me off at Marwa's before heading to the temple early to get things ready. We'd left that morning without putting anything to rights, and I knew they wanted to get there and set things up for Andrew's ritual tonight. I had a wave of gratitude for these women, this family, who wanted to do everything in their power to take care of us and make us whole.

Resolutely, I stepped up to Marwa's front door, a heavy wooden thing with metal accents and a crescent moon carved into it. I raised my hand to knock, but the door opened before I made contact. Marwa, dressed in comfortable, flowy pants and a loose-fitting pale yellow shirt, looked at me with emotion clearly written on her face. Somehow, though she'd had just as long of a night as I had, she looked well-rested and put together.

"He's in the sitting room," she said, nodding in his direction. She touched my arm as I moved to go past her. "And *Habibti*, go easy on yourself. You're hurting, too," she said softly.

I found him propped up on the plush sofa, expecting me. His eyes were red-rimmed, and the bags underneath them were bruised purple like my own. All at once, there was a sweeping sense of guilt crashing with an overwhelming wave of love for him, and I hurried over, tears already flowing.

"I am so sorry"

"I feel like that's all we're doing lately, love. Just apologizing." He drew himself up, and I could see how pained he was even to be having this conversation.

"I know, Drew... How do we get back to us?" I asked. I reached for his face, but he stopped me and held my hand down. My heart lurched, and I pulled my hand back from him, stung. For Andrew to pull away from my touch meant more damage had been done than I'd even realized. His love language was touch, and he was always finding little moments to brush my hand or touch my hair, and he looked for those little touches from me all the time.

"I don't know," he said quietly. "It's not about our fight. It's nothing you've done, J. It's more... I don't know. I barely recognize us anymore, and that terrifies me. I feel like there's a lot to wade through." He looked down in his lap, refusing to meet my gaze.

I dropped to my knees by the sofa.

"I'm sorry, Drew. I really am," I started. "I... you don't know what it's been like for me. Between all of this, losing Gram, then everything in North Carolina, I... I don't recognize myself either," I said, finally voicing the fear I'd been sitting with for months.

We sat quietly then for a few moments. The silence that was usually so effortless was thick and awkward. I toyed absently with a loose string from the dark sofa, needing something to occupy my hand.

"Look, I know I'm still me. And hopefully, the whole thing last night will have helped me get rid of some of the weight that's been holding me down. But I can't do this without you, Drew. I can't. I need you. I need you to look at me again and to look at me without fear or pity... I need you to see me again."

"I want that, J, I really do. I... I need some time to reconcile everything."

The space inside of me where grief lay cracked wide open. My mouth went dry, and my palms sweaty. Marwa's cool living room suddenly became stifling. I sat back, away from the sofa.

"What do you mean you need time?" I asked around the lump in my throat.

"Just some space, babe. No big deal. I want to come back here for a few days after the ritual tonight and get some space. Heal on my own. Let you do the same." I opened my mouth to argue, but he kept on. "I'm not saying I want anything permanent. I... we both just need space."

I nodded, tears blurring my vision as I got up and hurried out of the room.

I found my way to the powder room and locked the door behind me, needing privacy more than Marwa's gentle touch. I wanted to sob and scream and freak out, but all I felt was a gaping sense of numbness. I had taken a big step in the right direction in the night; a part of me could fully let go of trauma, and I knew I was on my way to healing. But this... losing Drew for however long he needed was enough to feel the weight come crashing down again.

Andrew had always been the one who truly saw me. Even when we were younger, he saw me. He saw my truths, the ugly, the broken, and he loved me because of those things. He was the help I needed to be brave enough to stand on my own two feet. To lose that—even for a few days—felt like the rug had been pulled out from under me. He was holding something back from me. I knew that much, I just didn't know what it could possibly be.

"Julia, *Habibti*, we've got to leave to get to the temple," Marwa said through the door.

I wasn't sure how long I'd sat on the closed toilet seat, head in my hands, but I got up, splashed cold water on my face, and opened the door.

We drove in silence, the radio playing softly in the background. I leaned against the backseat window, doing everything in my power not to stare a hole in the back of Andrew's head. Even Salma, whom we'd picked up on the way, sitting next to me in the backseat, was uncharacteristically quiet, recognizing the sober atmosphere as soon as she climbed in Marwa's car.

# 6

## *A Cold Wind*

We were silent as we made our way to the temple. The air was still and stifling, more so than it had been the night before, but it could also have been the turmoil coursing through me that was stifling.

Andrew looked nervous. The light from Hanan and Dell's torches cast shadows on his face, highlighting his sickly pallor and the tiny beads of sweat that shone along his hairline. He hobbled along, hand along one wall of the underground passage to help give him leverage. This was the longest he'd walked in ages, and I knew he was in a lot of pain by the quick intake of breath every few steps. I didn't give him a choice but came up beside him and slipped his other arm around my shoulders, letting him give me some weight to carry. He paused, ready to pull away, but his nerves and discomfort won out over our fight, and he let me hold on. Tears pricked my eyes when we took the first steps together, giving me a little hope that we'd eventually be okay.

Andrew was quiet and reverent in the ritual space. He was a bit in shock that he was even there. Everyone had come together to decide that they felt comfortable enough with him being allowed in. It helped that everyone had seen him when we'd first arrived and had seen how bad his condition was. Either way, his awe was evident as he took in the space around him, his eyes lighting on the paintings that adorned the walls—the stories of Hatshepsut and the sisterhood that had been penned for hundreds of years.

The ritual room was warm, as always, and I had a momentary flash of the previous night and everything that had transpired. Dell and Hanan had cleared everything away and cleansed the space. I didn't feel any of my demons hovering around, for which I was blissfully grateful.

A large pallet was in the middle of the room, with candles and incense surrounding it. There was enough light to see clearly, but shadows danced along the walls, making the mood somber. That morning, the temple smelled like fear and sweat from a night of purging my trauma, but the white sage incense and myrrh had cleansed the space, so now it smelled clean and empty of my nightmares. There was an energy in the air that spoke to everyone's nerves. They'd watched with me as Andrew continued to deteriorate and withdraw into himself. I knew their fears, both spoken and silent, about what we would attempt tonight.

Andrew lay down on the pallet, and we formed a circle around him. Hanan turned away from the group, opened the moon door, and the beam of moonlight disappeared into the ritual pool. Andrew looked appropriately impressed with that little piece of magic, and I smiled in spite of myself. Hanan made her way back to the circle and began to speak, calling on the energy of the full moon to fill and guide us. All thoughts of watching Andrew's face vanished as my body connected with the innate power coursing through the room. I was still nervous and wary of my power, though the deep fear that curdled my belly had gone with ghosts we'd purged the night before. In spite of the fear, I closed my eyes and let the magic fill me up.

"Sisters, tonight we come together, drawing on the power of the moon, the power of the great Goddess of Magic herself, Isis, and our

Great Mother Hatshepsut. We call on them and ask that they bless our magics and give us the strength to help Andrew heal." Hanan lifted her hands and the hands of Salma and Marwa, who were on either side of her, and we all followed suit. The room was heavy with magic. The incense that was burning was strong, and the scent of it lodged thick in my throat. A breeze whipped down through the moon door and ruffled my hair, sending a chill down my spine.

We began to hum. A guttural yet melodious song and prayer lifted into the air and swirled around us.

The room grew warmer and warmer, and still, the frigid breeze wrapped itself around my body every few moments—a cold caress that startled me every time.

It was an odd enough sensation that it pulled me out of the trance-like state I should have quickly fallen into with our chanting. I opened my eyes and looked around, but no one else acted like anything was amiss. I closed my eyes, forcing myself to focus on the task at hand and then mentally chastising myself for losing focus in the first place. My hands were sweaty in Dell and Marwa's, and I fought back the urge to drop them and wipe them on my leggings. Sweat dripped down my back, and my body was covered in goosebumps. I squeezed my eyes shut tighter. The magic ebbed and flowed inside of me. It swelled like a wave, and before it could crest, it pulled back like the tide was sucking it away from me.

I was in and out of the trance. Magic pulled me but never entirely under. Distracted by the heat and the shocking cold of the breeze, I couldn't focus. Couldn't give myself over wholly to the magic.

Again and again, I tried. Energy shifted inside me, fighting to get out of the cracks within. And again and again, it settled, quiet in my veins.

Slowly, the chanting faded into humming and then back to silence, the cave walls reverberating our last sounds in a faint echo. I opened my eyes and looked down, expecting to see Andrew healed and whole again. Hoping to see his eyes full of life, and hope and promise... to see my husband again, the pain and fear stripped away.

Instead, his head drooped down at an odd angle, his mouth a little slack, and his skin the color of cream gone bad. I made a strangled noise in my throat and went to let go, but Marwa and Dell squeezed my hands in theirs, urging me to stay upright.

"Julia, you can't break the circle yet," Marwa said quickly, her voice strained.

I nodded, unable to speak, and tried to regain my composure. I looked over at Hanan; my eyes were wide and panicked.

"Stand strong and together, everyone. His body is trying to heal itself," she commanded. Her voice wavered, and she fought to hold control. Her face was unreadable, but the faces around the rest of the circle were a mix of concern and confusion. We had carefully planned. We had read and researched and were prepared for everything but this. He wasn't supposed to be unconscious before us.

The wind whipped around me again, starting at my feet and moving up, rustling my clothes and then lifting my sweaty curls off my shoulders, blowing them in my face. It whooshed past me and seemed to spirit itself up and through the moon door again, leaving the air around me still once more. It was too strong to ignore, and everyone around me saw it, though no one else seemed touched by the wind. I opened my mouth to speak but couldn't form the words, shock forcing me still.

"What the fuck was that?" asked Dell.

"I don't know," Hanan said, her stoic mask slipping slightly. "I need to close the circle first to keep us safe, and then, Julia, you can go to him."

A few more moments and words spoken that I couldn't hear over the roaring in my head, and Hanan slowly lowered her hands back down and released hands. Dell and Marwa loosened their grips, and I dropped to my knees, unable to hold myself up any longer, and crawled towards Andrew.

"Please, please, please," I chanted in prayer and demand.

His skin was cold and clammy, but his face was flushed, and he'd broken out in a sweat; his hair was wet with it, and his shirt was soaked. I swiped tiny wet curls away from his temple with my hand, feeling his fevered forehead under my own cold hands. The shock of his cold body and hot forehead were startling, and I looked around for Renee, who was next to me, checking his pulse. She looked at Hanan and said something to her, but I couldn't make it out through the pounding in my ears. Dell was at my back, her steady hand on my shoulder. There were murmurs around me, making it worse, like they were keeping a secret from me.

"He has a pulse, Julia, but it's weak," Renee said.

"What happened?" I asked. "This was supposed to help him, not make it worse!" I cried and dropped my head down to Andrew's chest. The rise and fall of his breaths were slow and shallow.

"I don't know," Hanan said quietly. "Nothing we did should have thrown him into unconsciousness. We had barely gotten started."

Everyone's eyes bore into me as I lay there on Andrew's chest, tears coursing down my cheeks.

"What if we form a circle again or even take turns directing our energies directly into him?" Renee asked.

I looked up and saw their concerned faces. Hanan's confident mask was gone and filled with confusion and fear.

"It is worth a shot, but we'll have to hurry. If he doesn't wake up, he will need medical care," she said.

"We have to try something," I said desperately. "Anything." Hanan nodded and took a breath, gathering herself.

We all took turns pouring magic into Andrew, hands placed on his forehead or chest or holding his hand, and then we tried together once more. Despite our efforts, he lay there, still and slowly breathing. Fear pooled in my belly like ice.

Minutes passed while everyone tried to formulate a plan for getting him out and where to go once we'd left the temple. Everyone had moved a little way from us, leaving me lying next to my husband, body pressed against his, willing him to wake up with everything in me. I channeled my energy, my magic, into him, and it grew weaker and weaker. I started to tremble, and Dell, who hadn't left my side, reached over and pulled my hand off his chest.

"Jules, you have to stop. You're draining yourself, and you're not going to be any good to him if you can't even stand up," she said.

I wrenched my hand back from her and gripped him tighter, heedless of her warning and frantic with needing to do something, anything.

It took Naomi to come over and bully me a bit, forcefully pulling me off Andrew to snap me out of draining myself dry. I wasn't sure how much time had passed, but I could barely hold my head up as she pulled me off and into her lap, wrapping her arms around me and whispering platitudes into my hair. I relaxed into her hold; all the fight drained out of me, and I looked around the room. Dell was next to Andrew, holding his hand, and Renee sat on his other side. Everyone else was grouped together near the doorway, save Hanan, whom I didn't see. I shuddered, my eyes closed, my eyelids heavy and burning with exhaustion. Naomi held me tight, rocking and humming under her breath, surprising me with how nurturing and comforting she was being in a way I hadn't seen before.

I heard deep voices by the doorway and opened my eyes. I struggled to sit up when I saw Hasina and Salma's husbands, Karim and Omar, at the door. Their eyes were wide as they took in the scene around them, and Hanan was talking in quick, clipped sentences in Arabic.

"We couldn't figure out a way to comfortably lift him and carry him out and through the passageway," Naomi said, supplying an answer to the questions getting ready to spew forth. "We're all exhausted from trying to heal him, so we couldn't even devise a magical way to get him out safely. This is absolutely our last resort."

I made to get up, my limbs weak and heavy, slowing my movements, and Naomi stopped me. "Wait, Julia. We're going with them, but let them do this and get him out. Then we'll go."

I relaxed against her, but only because the exhaustion was bone-deep, and my body gave me no choice. I watched the men calmly walk over to Andrew, Karim carrying a stretcher. I wondered how on earth he'd found one on short notice. They loaded him onto it; both men were gentle as they moved his limp body, Omar reaching down and placing his left hand on his chest. Then, each at one end, they lifted and carried him, following Hasina and Renee on the way out. As I watched, tears coursed down my cheeks, and the only thing I could think of was how distracted I'd been, and I wondered if, somehow, this was all my fault.

# 7

## *After*

"Andrew is in a coma," Karim said gently but matter-of-factly.

"But...I don't understand. How?"

"Honestly, I'm not entirely sure," he said, touching my arm lightly. "It really doesn't make any sense. His injuries are bad but not grave. Certainly not grave enough for a coma." Karim took his glasses off and pinched the bridge of his nose. He was usually confident and reassuring, a doctor who, I imagined, had the sort of bedside manner that could calm all nerves.

"Julia, I honestly don't know what happened or what *is* going to happen," Karim said. "I've never seen anything like it. He sort of defies all reason."

I could tell he was frustrated, not with Andrew or me, but with the helplessness of someone used to knowing what was wrong and how to fix it.

"What are we going to do?" I asked quietly. My eyes were sore and bloodshot from lack of sleep and constant crying. We'd driven straight to the private clinic that Karim ran with a few other doctors. They had put Andrew on an oxygen mask and hooked him up to every monitor the clinic had to offer. So far, every test they'd run had come back normal.

"Honestly, we have to treat him like a coma patient. He needs to be moved to a facility with round-the-clock care that can look after him and see to his needs. He's breathing independently, so he doesn't need more than a little oxygen, which is a good sign." He looked at me, concern written plainly across his face. "But, should that change, Julia, he needs to be in a place where they can step in quickly and keep him alive. I don't have that type of equipment here for the long term."

Dell, who hadn't left my side, squeezed my hand.

"Okay. So, do you have a place in mind? I don't even know how to go about finding a facility like that."

Karim had already asked around, and he and his partners had all come to the same general consensus: if we could afford it, there was a private clinic the very wealthy went to when they needed plastic surgery or drug rehab. They had everything from surgical suites to long-term care facilities. Not only were they the best in the country, but they were also discreet. They wouldn't ask questions about the multitude of apparent torture wounds peppering Andrew's body or his unexplained comatose state.

Favors were called in, and a lot of money was exchanged, but Andrew had a bed before the end of the day. I couldn't help but be thankful that I had my inheritance from Gram and didn't have to worry about getting him the care he needed. Though I'm sure they never dreamt we'd be using the money for something like this.

Instead of a stark white hospital room, we found ourselves in an incredibly state-of-the-art suite with every touch screen and luxurious comfort item someone in a magically induced coma could ever want or need. The walls were a soft dove gray with tasteful landscape prints of Egypt adorning them. The curtains were a subtle floral pattern with soft and inviting colors, making the room less hospital and more hotel suite. The bed was a queen-sized haven of comfort instead of a standard-issue hospital bed. Once we were settled, Andrew was hooked up to monitors and resting comfortably on a special pad that would keep his body from getting bed sores. Dell and Hanan stepped out. I crawled into bed and curled against his body.

His chest rose and fell steadily, the nasal cannula the only source of extra oxygen. He was attached to an IV and heart monitor, but otherwise, it looked like he was sleeping peacefully. I moved his arm, laid my head on his chest like I'd done a thousand times before, and let out a shuddering breath.

"Andrew, I am so sorry," I whispered. The words were thick in my throat, but I swallowed down the grief and kept going. "For everything. I'm so sorry. Please be okay... Please just wake up and be okay, and we'll figure everything out."

Tears poured down my cheeks, wetting the soft t-shirt they'd changed him into after we arrived. I lay there crying softly and whispering apologies until I fell asleep, utterly exhausted.

As I slept curled against Andrew, I dreamt vividly. I was back in Hatshepsut's temple but alone, swimming in the ritual pool in the light of the full moon. I was alive with power, the current under my skin electric. The water was warmer than I remembered—a hot bath that steamed all around me. The cold air bit at the skin that was out of the water. The heady fragrance of myrrh hung in the air as if it were bubbling up from the depths of the water. My skin was slick with oil, and there was a deep sense of relief and comfort as I floated in the water.

I heard a voice quietly speaking in a language I didn't understand, and I turned toward it. There was no one else there. I was alone. I realized at once that I was speaking, but the voice wasn't my own. As soon as the realization hit, the voice grew further away, and the temple faded to dark.

"Hey, come on, Jules, let's get you back home."

Dell was touching my arm and speaking quietly, waking me from sleep. I gave myself a moment to wake up, hugged Andrew, and kissed him before getting out of bed and heading for the door, leaning heavily against Dell.

I paused at the doorway and looked back, my heart heavy. I hoped I'd see Andrew's eyes looking back at me soon.

# 8

## *Curiouser and Curiouser*

D ays passed.
And then a week.
And then another.
And still, Andrew didn't wake.

My life became a balancing act of sleeping curled against Andrew in his bed and sleeping in my bed at Hanan's. I left only when the nurses shooed me out at the end of the day, urging me to take care of myself. I was barely functioning as anything other than what could only be described as a preemptive widow. I was wracked with guilt over everything that had happened over the last few months. Rationally, I knew no one was to blame but Gordon, but he was no longer here, and I was the only person to take the blame. I'd had to call Drew's parents and fabricate a lie that he'd been deployed for a contracting job, and they'd left suddenly. Luckily, his mom didn't bat an eyelash and drank down the lies that poured from my lips.

The only good thing to come out of the entire situation was that my nightmares were gone. For the first time in months, I slept peacefully. The dreams I found myself a part of were pleasant, albeit disorienting. I often dreamt of Hatshepsut, the moon, or the ritual space. While they were all dreams I happily delved into instead of the nightmares that plagued me, they were an odd assortment of things. When I woke from them, I woke with increasingly weird feelings that lingered through the day.

I was eating breakfast with Hanan one morning; Dell was off in Cairo with Naomi for a few days at my insistence so she could get a break from my constant grief. More than once, I recognized how much harder this would have been without my best friend here, and I gave thanks to Hatshepsut every chance I got for choosing Dell to be part of the sisterhood.

"I know it's a silly question to ask, but are you okay, Julia?" Hanan asked. "You seem more distracted than usual."

"Sorry, weird dreams lately, and last night's is kind of lingering," I said, waving my hand like it was no big deal.

"Have the nightmares returned?"

"No, no. Definitely not nightmares," I quickly reassured her. "More like an odd assortment of things. When I'm not dreaming about Andrew, I keep dreaming about Hatshepsut or the temple. Not bad at all. Weird, though." I took a sip of tea, finished my cup, and got up to put the kettle back on for another.

"Mm," she said over her own cup of tea. "Well, that's better than the nightmares, at least." I leaned against the counter and faced her while the kettle heated up.

"You want another cup?" I asked. She nodded, and I reached for the tea tin and grabbed two bags for our cups.

After a few moments, Hanan asked, "What is Hatshepsut doing when you dream of her?"

I shrugged and then turned to grab the kettle as it whistled, walking over to her and filling her mug.

"A few different things. I keep dreaming about her in the temple, but it doesn't look how it does now. The walls are blank, and it feels... unfinished, in a way. The pool is there, and I've seen her swim a few times. Sometimes, I *am* her, and I can feel the water on my skin and smell everything like it's me floating in the water. Other times, I sort of hover above everything and can see her."

"How do you know it's Hatshepsut?" Hanan asked.

"I—" I paused, thinking. "I don't know. I...it sort of *feels* like her. That sounds dumb."

"It doesn't. I'm wondering..." She trailed off, lost in thought.

I dunked my tea bag in the hot water, sousing it and watching the dark liquid swirl about.

"Does she ever speak?"

I looked up from my cup and nodded. "She does, but it's nothing I can understand. Sometimes, she sings, too. I don't know what she's saying, but I always wake up when she sings and feel the deepest sense of peace and calm. Almost like it was a lullaby."

"Have you always been a vivid dreamer?"

"Yes. Always. I had night terrors as a child, and then, you know about the nightmares I've dealt with. But when I don't have dreams that scare the shit out of me, I have really vivid ones—like, smells and feel, sounds and taste. It's all there."

"Last question—have you been meditating since we returned from the US?"

"No. Not besides the rituals altogether." I looked at her. "I know... I need to."

"You do, yes. But that's not why I was asking," she said. "I'm wondering if maybe you're having visions of Hatshepsut and not just regular dreams."

I stared at her, incredulous. "Visions? There's no way. It's just dreams. I don't even know if it's really her," I said, almost laughing at the absurdity.

"Maybe so, but I trust feelings, and I think you should look a little deeper. Maybe try some meditations with Marina—see if anything comes up." She shrugged, not forcing the issue, but I could tell her words had an undercurrent of seriousness.

Later in the day, as I lay curled against Andrew, I didn't let myself drift off to sleep like I had been. I lay there, awake, my mind rolling around the images and thoughts from my recent dreams. I wasn't having them every day, but they were becoming more frequent.

I tried to think about what exactly made me think I was dreaming of Hatshepsut. It wasn't as if she were wearing a name tag and shouting her name so I could know for sure. It was more of a feeling. The same feeling that wrapped around me in her temple—comfort, peace, and safety. No matter how I tried to talk myself out of it or deny anything, I knew, in my gut, it was Hatshepsut.

---

Alone in my bed that night, I propped myself up, got comfortable, and began to breathe deeply. I focused on my breath, counting my inhales and exhales and dropping into meditation.

My heart beat with anticipation, and I struggled to slow my breathing and focus. My mind kept flashing and buzzing, thoughts jumping in and interrupting my experiment, leaving me frustrated and annoyed.

I got up and sat on the floor, legs crossed, hands in my lap, spine straight to help focus. I sat until the muscles in the center of my back had passed the point of burning and felt numb and still, nothing beyond a few moments of breathless calm.

I gave up and crawled into bed, feeling silly that I'd even tried to... what? Summon up some magical vision of a long-dead woman? I shook my head and squeezed my eyes shut, irked at myself for even thinking what I was experiencing was more than dreams.

I tossed and turned all night, willing myself to fall asleep but not managing more than a light doze in and out all night. My mind wouldn't settle, and my body was restless. Finally, around five in the morning, I threw in the proverbial towel and got out of bed. I walked out to the garden and rolled out my yoga mat as quietly as possible, not wanting to disturb Hanan, whose bedroom window overlooked the garden.

I practiced there, in the early morning haze, in the place between night and day where the entire world seems still. The air was warm, the promise of a hot day hanging in the air, but a cool breeze blew through, leaving my skin pimpled with gooseflesh. I shuddered, mind calling back to the cool breeze in the temple that had distracted me. I went through sun salutations and long practiced movements, my mind quiet and body moving in time with my breath and muscle memory. Before long, my skin had a sheen of sweat, and my muscles were shaking, and still, I moved.

It had been weeks since I'd stepped foot on my mat. It was usually a place of peace for me. Where the stressors of life could be laid down and forgotten for the time I was on it, and, in my grief, I'd been unable to take the step to even get onto the mat. When the sun rose into the sky and warmed my skin, I finally stopped. I had been on the mat for hours by that point, soaked through, but I felt like I could finally breathe. Felt like I could make it through the day without the crushing weight of grief and guilt. I knew that when I stepped back off the mat and returned to the real world, I'd have to pick it back up again and deal with the ramifications of everything going on in my life. But, for that one beautiful moment, everything was... peace.

# 9

## *Crystal Visions*

I finished my practice and lay in *savasana*, palms facing up to the rising sun and eyes closed. Following the rise and fall of each breath, my body began to relax. Without even trying, I dropped down into a quiet space in my mind. I lay there breathing deeply like I was melting into the mat. The birds greeting the day were noisy but settled into background chatter and faded away.

As soon as the birdsong quieted in my mind, I heard singing. It was a quiet hum off in the distance. I had the oddest sensation like I was floating outside my body. As I floated through the darkness, eyes still closed, the singing grew clearer and louder. I blinked open my eyes and found myself in Hatshepsut's temple. It was dark, lit only by a single torch, and the ripple of shadows on the walls cast an eerie feeling throughout the space, though I wasn't afraid. I looked around, the singing ringing off the walls of the ritual room, wrapping me in its velvet sound. As my eyes adjusted to the lack of light, I noticed a figure in the water. She was standing in the middle of the pool, arms reaching up towards the sky, face tilted towards the moon door, but no light shone down on her as she sang, her voice clear and achingly beautiful.

*Isis—divine daughter of the Nile*
*Mighty Mother, most Holy Queen*

*in the dark of the moon*
*I beg you to be seen.*
*Isis, deliverer of fate,*
*I sing your praise.*
*If this be thy will,*
*Then show me the way.*
*I consecrate my body*
*Give thou my heart and soul*
*bathe me in healing*
*I will forever extol.*
*Oh, sweet Sovereign,*
*Grant me strength, and hope, and peace.*
*Protect my people.*
*From this suffering, I beg release.*
*Isis, my Goddess,*
*Most high and holy Queen,*
*On this, the darkness of nights,*
*Hear my plea.*

She stood supplicant to the sky, power thrumming through her like electricity. The cave was warm and smelled of ozone, and my power rippled inside me, wanting to answer her call. She wore a sheer white robe, similar to a kaftan, and it billowed around her in the water, giving off an ethereal glow. Her hair was unbound and dark as jet, hanging down to her waist in a thick curtain.

Slowly, she turned, singing softer now, more of a hum. Her eyes were closed, and tears tracked down her cheeks. Her face was soft and lightly lined with age, her skin giving off the gentle glow I had thought was coming from her gown. It was as if she had pulled the moon from the sky and nestled it inside her where it happily glowed from within her.

I stared curiously and unashamedly, grateful that her eyes were closed and that I could drink her all in. She had a commanding presence, even as humble and prayerful as she was. She was soft around the middle, a sign of her royal status and easy access to food, but she had a leanness that spoke to strength. Her gown was open, and an angry rash spread across her breasts and up her neck, scaly and red, standing out from her rich, umber skin.

I stood there; the floating sensation had ceased, and the ground was solid beneath me. The stone was cold against my bare feet. I watched Hatshepsut as she bathed herself in the water, repeating the prayer over and over again. Her voice was clear, deeper than I would have guessed, but with a lilting quality that gave her prayer musicality. She kept her eyes closed, administering her ablutions with tears and water from the pool. I could almost feel the burning itch of her skin and then the relief as the water sluiced over it. Her words became softer as the water calmed her inflamed skin and heart.

Eventually, the words tapered off into silence; the only sound in the temple was the water lapping against her as she stepped out of the pool. Water dripped down her body and pooled on the floor. Frozen in place, I watched as she stood, gown sheer and clinging to every inch of her body, nipples dark and prominent through the wet material. She opened her eyes as if sensing someone watching her and looked straight ahead. They were startlingly blue, bright, and glowing from within.

"Ah, you've finally come," she said softly.

I came to, sputtering and gasping for air.

"Oh my god," I said to the morning air. I fought to make sense of what had happened, unwilling to believe the obvious answer. I sat up, shaking my head and rubbing my face, trying to scrub away the incredulity. I had to find Hanan, damn the early morning.

To my immense relief, Hanan was awake and in her kitchen when I went to the door. I let myself in and went straight to her.

"It's visions! I just had a vision of her... of Hatshepsut. And she saw me, Hanan. She looked right at me and said *you've finally come*. Wha-how?" I sputtered, the words tripping over my tongue as I tried to get them out as quickly as possible.

Hanan stared at me, and I watched her face drain of color and her eyes glitter with excitement. She pulled the pan off the stove and set it aside, wiping her hands on the dishtowel slung over her shoulder before setting it down on the counter as she crossed the room to me.

"Let's sit down for a bit, and you can tell me everything." She tried her best to hide it, but she was practically vibrating with excitement. She led me to the living room, my favorite room in her house due to the floor-to-ceiling bookshelves packed with books. I settled down on the couch, my heart still pounding and my hands shaking.

Hanan, ever patient, let me sit and ramble for a few moments before finally getting it together long enough to recount what I'd seen in detail. With her gentle presence, I could focus and calm down, and eventually, my heart slowed, and my spirit settled.

"Well, I believe, if you were wondering what your *thing* was going to be, we've found it," Hanan said after I'd finished. "I think you've been having visions your whole life—dreams and night terrors, as you called them. I think they were more than just dreams. You are a powerful *seer*, Julia. And to be able to see our Queen... what a blessing." Hanan looked at me in awe, and I felt a little tug in my chest.

"What do you think it means that I'm seeing her?" I asked.

"Perhaps there is a message from her that we need to receive? Or maybe there's something you need to learn? I'm not sure." She trailed off, thinking, and we lapsed into silence.

"Oh!" I said suddenly, startling Hanan out of her thoughts.

"Yes?"

"I think my Gram came to me in a vision after she died. I had the most vivid dream about her before I left Bahrain. When I woke up, I could smell her perfume." A chill went down my back, and my arms broke out in goosebumps. Saying it aloud, I knew it was true. Gram had come to me with a message of love and comfort.

"That's amazing, Julia. What a beautiful thing for her to do."

My eyes stung with the burning tears, but I held them at bay. "She spoke to me and touched me. It was truly the turning point that got me out of bed and out of my grief."

"Do you remember what she said?" Hanan asked softly, her hand resting lightly on my arm in comfort.

I shook my head slightly and thought for a moment. I closed my eyes and turned inwards, loosening the walls I had put up to hold the grief of losing her at bay and let myself go back to Bahrain and that gaping maw of despair. I could see her soft form and loving energy filling my bedroom with warmth and feel her as she held me.

"She said something about not grieving her so hard, and I had a purpose that would become clear..." I trailed off. There was something else, just out of reach on the edge of memory. "There's something else, but I can't remember."

Hanan patted my arm, and I opened my eyes, firmly planting myself back into the present.

"Don't force it. Whatever message she had for you is there; it will surface when you need it most," she said. If there was one thing Hanan was besides assuring, it was confident. Being around her forced me to believe in myself a hell of a lot more than came naturally to me.

"Maybe I could talk to Hatshepsut, and she'd have a spell or something that could pull Drew out of his coma," I said, hopeful for the first time in weeks.

Hanan looked at me, mouth pursed, fine wrinkles forming around her mouth and forehead.

"I don't think that's a good idea, Julia," she said after taking a breath. "We cannot know if we'd cause more harm than good. And there are always sacrifices to be made with those sorts of things."

Annoyance rippled through me. "But what if we could save him?" I asked.

She had the decency to look down in her lap when she spoke, unwilling to meet my eyes when she continued. "What if this is what is meant to be happening?" Her voice was barely above a whisper. "We can't toy with fate any more than we already have. We aren't meant to disturb the balance in that way–"

"What?" I interrupted. "So you're telling me that if I found some way to save my husband from a ritual that *you* fucked up that sent him comatose, you wouldn't do it because it would *upset the balance?*" I bit out, hot anger flushing my skin. "We barely do anything besides parlor tricks as it is. We have real power we could be utilizing, and instead, we're lighting candles and sending out good intentions?"

"Julia, it's more complicated than that. It's–"

I shoved away from the counter and stormed off, not willing to hear her out, feeling betrayed. I slammed the front door behind me, already calling a cab from the app on my phone to take me to the hospital to escape next to Andrew and clear my head.

I spent the morning lying next to Andrew, recounting my newest revelation and anger at Hanan. I wished, more than anything, that he would wake up and help me navigate all of it.

"I hope you can hear me," I said, voice low so no one could overhear, though I'd written a sigil on his door for privacy. "All those wild and vivid dreams, my love? Apparently, they were visions, and I have this wild ability to see things." I absently rubbed his arm, his skin warm and soft under my hand, steadying me and burning away the anger from earlier in the morning.

"I'm dreaming of Hatshepsut. She is amazing. I can feel her power in the dream, and it is incredible. It made my own energy hum under my skin, wanting to answer her." I trailed off, thinking about the temple and what I'd felt. "I'm going to try and speak to her. To see if she has answers on how I can help you. I don't care what Hanan says. We got you into this mess, and I will find a way to get you out of it." I lay there, quiet, listening to his heartbeat in his chest, steady and rhythmic.

"I think I had a vision of Gram, too," I told him. "She came to me in Bahrain and pulled me out of that deep pit of grief. She had a message for me. She said I had a purpose that would be revealed soon and that I needed to lift the veil and see. Oh!" I stopped abruptly. "That was it. That's the part I couldn't remember earlier when I was telling Hanan. She told me to lift the veil. What could that have meant? That's weird, yeah?" I paused, thinking.

"Lift the veil..." I trailed off.

I lay there with Andrew for a while longer, going over every detail I could recall of my dream of Gram. It was easier to come forth then. Whether Andrew's quiet presence helped or knowing that it was more than a dream, I didn't know. But what she'd said and the message she'd passed on was clear. I knew that the veil she spoke of had to do with the visions and whatever that ability meant.

# 10

## *Khonsu*

*Andrew*

While Julia dreamt of Hatshepsut, Andrew had his own dreams.

As soon as the ritual started and Andrew closed his eyes, the heaviness of sleep dragged him under. He fought it hard, trying to stay conscious and take everything in. He knew he would never see the ritual room or the temple's inner sanctum. The pain in his body was throbbing and ever-present. Though he'd figured out a way to live life hand-in-hand with his injuries, they became more and more intense and impossible to ignore as he lay there.

The pain beat in time with his heart and to the rhythm of the chanting women. He heard Julia's voice ring out clearly above the others and heard the torment in her voice. He felt guilty that he'd caused her pain, and then her voice was lost to the crowd of the others. The throbbing went from bruise-like to white hot and searing as the chanting grew more insistent. In his mind, he hoped this was the 'worse before it gets better' stage of healing, and then all rational thought flew out the moon door above them. He lay there, body convulsing, pain writhing through him like angry snakes under his skin. And still, the women sang and chanted above him.

He began to panic, wondering if there was something they hadn't told him, if he was to be some horrible sacrifice to the gods or if they were somehow feeding off his pain. The fact that Jules would never intentionally hurt him was lost in his agony. The chanting and singing grew louder and louder, and his pain grew with it. Inside, his skin felt like fire, a fever burning through and lighting up his veins with its heat. But a cold wind seemed to wrap itself around Andrew from the outside. The once comforting glow of candles and moonlight grew dim behind his eyelids, darkening before vanishing altogether.

Andrew opened his eyes to darkness so thick he couldn't see or hear anything. It was wrapped around him like a cold shroud. The contrast between the fever burning within him and the frigid air around him was startling and terrifying. It was more than Andrew could take as he tried to grasp what was happening. He tried to move and get up from the pallet underneath him but was frozen, unable to move even his fingertips. The only thing he seemed to have control over were his eyes, and he blinked in the darkness, willing his eyes to adjust so he could find Julia in the dark.

Moments or hours passed, and he had no true notion of time, only that it felt like forever and a blink all at once. Finally, the pain overwhelmed him, and Andrew let go and slipped into unconsciousness.

The first thing he noticed as he woke was the absence of pain. His body had been wracked with an all-consuming pain he'd never known before, and now it felt like someone had flipped a switch. It was gone completely, and his body throbbed in relief. It was an odd sensation. He was still ensconced in darkness, but it wasn't thick and impenetrable like before. He could make out indistinct, bulky shapes around him.

"Do not be afraid, Andrew," a deep and unfamiliar voice whispered in the darkness, startling him and making his heart race. He couldn't tell where the voice was coming from. It seemed to be all around him.

"Who are you? Where is Julia?" Andrew tried to sit up, but his limbs felt like lead.

"Do not be afraid. No harm will come to you or your woman," the voice whispered again, its pitch so deep that it vibrated in Andrew's chest. "I am Khonsu, God of the Moon, and I need you."

Andrew relaxed, assuming he was in the middle of a fever dream.

"I can assure you this is no... fever dream, as you put it," the voice said. "You are dying, child, and I have come to offer you a bargain in exchange for your life."

A cool wind blew across Andrew's body, chilling him to the bone.

"Dying?" he asked, incredulous. He could feel his heart pounding in his chest and sweat beading on his upper lip despite the chill in the air. Whatever this was, it didn't feel like death.

"Yes. You are in stasis right now; my power is the only thing tethering you to the earth. But death comes for you."

Andrew heard the whisper of fabric against stone and quiet steps behind him. Fear shot through him, pounding through his veins with each heartbeat. Slowly, deliberately, the footsteps moved closer to him, and soon, he could feel someone standing next to him, though he still couldn't see through the darkness. He tried to find words but couldn't seem to form anything coherent. His mind was muddled, confused, and gripped by fear.

"Be calm, child. Do not be filled with fear. Death will come for us all, eventually," the voice said, looming above Andrew. "It is only your earthly body that fears death. Your soul has nothing to fear. Master the mind, and the body will forget the fear." He felt the presence shift beside him, and he struggled to move.

"I have a hold on your body, as I said, tethering you to my power to keep you alive. No amount of struggle or fight will break my hold. Be at peace." With the word peace, Andrew felt a hand touch the top of his head, and a calm poured over him like water. He stilled and ceased his struggle, giving in to the peace and feeling himself relax for the first time in months if not years.

"What will happen to my wife? To Julia?" Andrew asked, finding his voice.

"She already grieves for you, I'm afraid. It consumes her. She feels as if she has failed you... failed her sisters... failed herself." The voice paused for a moment. "She feels deeply, your wife. Deeply and absolutely. But she is powerful. I can feel her power from here, singing in her veins, waiting for her to take control." He trailed off, deep voice reverberating in the darkness.

"She hasn't failed anyone. She needs to know that," Andrew said, his own grief heavy in his chest.

"She can't know if death takes you. She will carry the burden of losing you for the rest of her life. But there is a way," Khonsu said.

Andrew could feel the man sitting beside him but still couldn't make him out.

"I will give you back your life, and you may carry on living."

"At what cost?" Andrew asked.

The man laughed a deep, booming sound that rang out and filled the darkness. "You are a clever one, aren't you?" he asked.

Andrew swallowed thickly, unsure what would happen. The shroud of peace slipped a bit, like the edge of a blanket falling away from his side.

"It *will* come at a price; you are right about that. But it is not too terrible, I think. I am thinking that you will accept the cost to be with your lovely wife."

"What is the price? And how do I know I can trust you and this isn't a trick?"

Another deep chuckle filled the room.

"You don't. You have to take it on faith." The words hung in the air.

"I only have faith in myself and Julia. I've lost any other faith I might have held once. I've seen what the faithful do."

A large hand touched his arm gently, suffusing him with peace once more. "I, too, have seen what the faithful do to each other. I watch from above and have seen wars and horrors you couldn't begin to imagine, all in the name of faith. What I am asking is faith in yourself and faith in love. As a god, I give you my word that no harm will come to you as long as the moon hangs in the sky."

"Why me? And why am I even dying? My injuries weren't that great."

"The injuries to your body weren't grave, no. But your soul was all but cleaved in two. Pain and suffering shredded pieces of it, peeling it back with each loss, each moment that was too much for words. You, too, have seen war and horrors, yes?" he asked.

Andrew nodded his head in the darkness, throat thick with emotion as horrors played out in his mind as if called forth by the man to his left.

"Trauma and pain leave marks, some deeper than others, and you carry heavy burdens of your own and those of others. Your soul couldn't hold any more weight, and the relief of the ritual the priestesses were performing and the grief of your heart weighed your soul down too much. It snapped, pulling itself out of your earthly body to protect itself from more harm." Another gentle touch of his hand on Andrew's arm and another wave of tranquility poured over him, and Andrew realized how weary he was.

"I have tried, in vain, to reach your wife. She is capable of power so great it would make you tremble before her. But the faithful of the other god hurt her so much she has closed herself off to receiving any gods' love. I have tried and failed to reach her many times. I hope I can reach her through you."

Andrew's mind whirred like a whirly-gig swept up in stormy winds. Somehow, everything that Khonsu was saying made sense. He *had* seen war and horrors that were unimaginable. He'd been faced with choices in his life that haunted him every day, things he couldn't escape and couldn't reconcile. He carried Jules' traumas, the things she'd told him, and the unspoken horrors he had known she'd endured. He knew she was closed off to anything related to God and religion. And then came his abduction by Gordon. The injuries inflicted upon him weren't terrible. Even when receiving the burns and cuts, they weren't the worst things he'd ever withstood.

It was only when Gordon had abused him over and over again, describing all the ways he'd done the same to Julia when they were younger, that something had broken inside of Andrew. Something had passed between him and Gordon in the hours he'd had him in his basement. The sadistic bastard had somehow taken his and Julia's love and commitment to each other and turned it into a vile and disgusting thing he was ashamed of. He could finally see the pain Gordon had inflicted upon her and how he'd pushed her to set those horrors aside at the beginning of their marriage and try to make new memories with *him*. He had known he was being selfish then, driven by hormones and lust so overwhelming he couldn't stand to think about what she'd gone through. He had been so consumed by her and so confident that he could burn away the memories of her past and replace them with himself. He knew that the weight of that realization had utterly broken him. And was, ultimately, the reason he had broken her heart and told her he wanted space. He hadn't wanted space from *her*... he had wanted to give her freedom from himself. From his desires and selfishness and the shame he felt curdling his belly and splitting him in two.

"It will do you no good to try and reconcile those battles now. They are over and done with. What I offer you is a chance to start anew. A choice. To lay down your sword and take up another. A new battle is brewing; you will be needed if they have any chance of winning."

"What do you mean?" Andrew asked.

"Ah, young one, would I show my whole hand before the deal is struck?" Khonsu answered with a chuckle. "No, I shall not. Know you are needed there, but the choice is your own."

"And if I say no, I'll just... die? And Julia will be left alone?"

"Yes."

"What happens if I say yes? Again, what is the cost? There is a price for everything."

"The cost is simple. Allow me to give you life; all I ask in return is one favor to be claimed at a time of my choosing. With my vow that no harm will come to yourself or anyone you love."

Andrew waited for a few moments, weighing his options and thinking through Khonsu's carefully spoken words.

"What sort of favor?" he asked finally.

"To be determined at a later date," Khonsu replied.

"I need some time to think."

"Ah, that is the other price, I'm afraid. There isn't any time. You must choose. Life or death." Khonsu's deep voice was soft next to Andrew.

In the space of a few months, everything he knew of the world had been upended. He'd seen his wife perform magic and been tortured by the monster of their past, and now he was face to face with an ancient god and a choice between literal life and death. As clearly as he was there with her, he could see Julia's face, grief-stricken and filled with pain and longing. At that moment, he knew he would take whatever deal to wipe away that pain.

"If I do this, if I make this choice, I'll return to the body that I have now, yes? With my memories intact? Nothing will change there, correct?" Thoughts of old fairy tales and bargains gone awry flitted through Andrew's mind.

"I assure you, there is no trickery here. I am the god of the moon, not the god of fools and tricksters. Your life, or your death, will be waiting for you when you make your choice," Khonsu said, irritation flickering through his voice.

Andrew took a deep breath and knew what he had to do. "Fine. I'll do it. Give me back my life, and I'll do your favor when you ask it of me."

"Hold out your hand, and we shall seal our bargain."

Andrew held his hand out and found it surprisingly steady. A cool hand found his, and they shook firmly, once, twice.

"It is done."

As the god spoke, tiny pinpricks of light appeared in front of Andrew, faintly glowing. With the final shake of their hands, the small dots of light grew larger and larger, a faint glow that ate away the darkness around him. He looked up and finally saw the face of the man who had been speaking. But calling him a man did him no justice. His skin was as dark as night, perfect and clear of blemishes or imperfections. His face was chiseled and looked like it was carved of the smoothest stone, yet it looked gentle and pliable as the softest skin. He was stunningly beautiful, so much so that he was almost unbelievable, yet he sat next to Andrew on the stone floor. He smiled, teeth bright white, and his whole face changed, lighting up with joy.

The most striking thing, however, was Khonsu's eyes. They were an intense study of light—the outer edges of them the brightest blue that melted away into iridescent gold, lighting his whole countenance with the glow of the moon. His face hovered right above Andrew's, so close they were almost touching, and yet, Andrew felt no discomfort, only p eace.

# 11

## *Of Friendship and Fighting*

Once I realized I had *the sight*, as everyone called it, the visions became easier. Or maybe they didn't *come* easier. Perhaps the realization that the dreams I'd been having were visions made it feel more accessible. No matter how it felt to have them, interpreting the visions wasn't effortless. Some were short bursts of light or feelings or even a quick moment with Hatshepsut that left me with more questions than clarity. Some were more fleeting dreams, the truth of which slipped through my fingers like sand. And others were clear as day and easy to recount.

Using magic less physically made me feel safer, and I grew more comfortable with myself and my powers. The hope that I'd be able to connect with Hatshepsut and figure out a way to save Andrew spurred me on. The first few weeks of intentionally meditating and navigating the visions filled my time. They lifted the burden of grief ever so slightly. I'd been begging and arguing with Hanan since Andrew fell into his coma, sure that there was more we could be doing. Now that I had something I could *actively* do, I had a renewed sense of purpose. But Hanan discouraged anything that might upset *the balance* and took it upon herself to remind me every time she had the opportunity at the cost of unfamiliar magic. She warned me against doing anything rash.

And so, I no longer talked to Hanan about my plan.

Anytime she had that look, or there was even a whisper of a lecture coming, I did my best to lie as convincingly as possible that I would leave it be and not try to find anything to save Drew. I knew that if the roles were reversed and she could have done something to save her mom when she was dying, she would have gone to the ends of the earth. I wasn't even trying to go to the ends of the earth. The answers I sought were hidden, protected by Hanan and her flawed sense of duty.

Everyone had a renewed excitement about them now that I'd found my niche. I think, more than anything, they were hoping that it would be a good distraction from my grief. And it was, if only for a few moments of each day. Marina and I came together often in those first few weeks; her meditation teachings were more profound than ever before and helped to hone my skill. Even Naomi was kinder and gentler with me, though I think Dell had a hand in tempering her more than anything.

It had all started in North Carolina when Naomi first arrived at Gram's, at the ready to rescue the damsel in distress. Dell had taken one look at her with piqued interest and, apparently, in our time here in Egypt, had fallen head over heels, much to my chagrin.

"For crying out loud, Dell. Seriously? Naomi?" I groaned at lunch a few days after my vision revelation when she finally decided to come clean about her crush on Naomi.

"What is wrong with her?" Dell grinned sheepishly, cheeks going pink.

"Only that she can be absolutely awful!" I said, rolling my eyes as I stabbed my fork into my lunch harder than was necessary. "Dell. Really. The only reason she and I are even halfway speaking now is because I finally got violent with my magic, and I had no choice but to call on her to come help with Hanan."

"Dude. You know that's not the reason," Dell answered quickly. "Jules, you've got her all wrong. She's not some evil bitch who wants you to be violent with your magic. She wanted you to know how to defend yourself in case it ever came down to having to do so. And she came to you because you're one of her sisters, and she takes the group very seriously."

I looked over the table at her, irritation written clearly across my face.

"That's fine. But she was a giant asshole about it. And she knows it, too." It was Dell's turn to roll her eyes at me.

"Just because she didn't fawn all over the new girl and kiss your ass doesn't make her awful. Sometimes, you *need* a firmer hand, Jules, and you know it. She knew it too and was trying to do her best by you. You didn't even give her a chance." Dell was hot now and on the defense of her new... friend, or whatever she was to her. But I was getting hot now, too, and my temper was about to boil over.

"Dell, I love you, but you weren't here," I said, trying to keep my cool. Dell and I were as close as sisters and could rile each other up like we were as well.

"You're right. I wasn't here. But I know you, and I'm getting to know her, and I know if you were being honest with yourself, you'd see that she didn't mean you any harm. She wanted to teach you so you could stop playing the victim and take control over your life."

"Oh. Seriously? Play the victim? Fuck that! Naomi was a cold and unwelcoming bitch whose idea of teaching was to berate me until I exploded at her."

Dell pinched between her brows and squeezed her eyes shut, breathing to calm herself.

"Jules. Two things. One, Naomi has pretty terrible social anxiety. She can handle herself around assholes and stick up for the kids she's fighting for in the city with no problem, but when it comes to intimate group settings with new people? She's a mess. She was so nervous about meeting you. The vibe the group had going on was comfortable for her. Adding a new person is never easy... you know that," she said pointedly. "And second of all, she knew you were holding back and scared of your shadow. She knew it would take a big moment to pull power out of you, and you *need* to be comfortable with what's inside you. So she did the best thing she could think of to shake it out of you. It worked, didn't it?"

I gritted my teeth in frustration. "Yeah. It worked great. And the next time something *shook* out my power, it almost killed a man. So, great teacher she is, Dell. Great person you're sleeping with, there." I bit out.

I regretted the words the moment they came out of my mouth and wished I could swallow them back down. Dell pushed her chair back from the table and glared down at me, eyes filled with fury.

"You can be such a bitch, Julia," she bit out, voice shaking with anger. "Regardless of your opinion of her, Naomi is supposed to be one of your sisters. And she came when you called. I don't know that I could say that you'd do the same for her."

She spun on her heel and stormed off, slamming the door behind her and leaving me in palpable silence. I stared down at my half-eaten salad and Dell's untouched plate. No longer hungry, I got up from the table, cleared the mess, and headed to my room, grateful that Hanan was working and we hadn't had an audience for our fight.

Dell and I avoided each other like the plague, which wasn't easy when we lived on the same property. When Naomi traveled back to Cairo and back to her work with street kids, Dell jumped at the chance to leave, and I had never been happier to see her go. Eventually, I knew we'd be okay, but we both needed some space to cool down.

She had been right, which is what rankled the most. I hated to admit it, but I *was* scared of my own shadow and absolutely needed a firmer hand in some instances—especially when it came to using my magic for the offense. No matter what I'd argued or how pissed I'd been, maybe Naomi was right not to coddle me and to be annoyed when that was what I wanted. I hated admitting I was wrong and had difficulty eating that particular crow. Especially since, unbeknownst to her, I'd taken matters into my own hands regarding finding answers for Andrew. No firm hand but my own was needed for that.

The bit that really stung was her pointing out that I played the victim. All I'd ever done was try and escape my past... to run from the things that had been done to me. And in all the running, I'd never really stopped and took my power back from my tormentors. Years of therapy and unending love and support from Andrew and my grandparents helped build my confidence in so many ways. Still, in others, I'd allowed myself to let everyone else make decisions for me. To continue to be someone who needed my hands held because I didn't believe I could do anything on my own. But surely that didn't mean I played the victim, did it?

Making a choice to join the sisterhood and to open myself up to extraordinary power was the first time I'd genuinely chosen something for myself. Running away with Andrew hadn't been a choice, not really. It was either that or Gordon would have eventually killed me. I knew that. Andrew and I were lucky that we had grown from desperate to escape to a deep connection that outweighed the past and tipped the scales into a balance between us. I knew I was standing on the edge of another precipice of choice and change. I was going to be the one to go further than anyone else to save the man I loved, no matter the cost.

# 12

## *Secrets Spilled*

After an hour of furious pacing, doing my best to wear a hole in the carpet, I gave up and grabbed my phone. I double-checked the time difference and hit call. Edie picked up on the first ring.

"Hey! I was just thinking about you!"

"Hey, Edie. How are you? How are the girls?" I asked, trying to calm my voice.

"They're good. The hellcats are wild, as usual. Elise entered a baking competition at school and has been practicing up a storm. Elliot is cutting teeth and screams if she's not attached to my boob. That about covers it. What's up with you?"

"Oh, you know, the usual. Was indoctrinated into an ancient, magical sisterhood in Egypt last year. My ex-boyfriend tried to kill Andrew and me, so I exploded magic at him and almost killed him. Andrew took a leave of absence and is now in a coma. Dell has magical powers, by the way, and is in this sisterhood, too. Oh, and we're fighting. She says I play the victim in my life and need to stop and take control. Oh. And she has a girlfriend now. I think that about covers it on my end."

There was silence on the other end of the line, and then the alert for the video option came through. I sighed and hit the button to accept it.

"Out of all of that, which parts are true?" Edie asked. I could see she was in the nursery, seated in the glider, baby Elliot happily nursing away.

I looked pointedly at her. "What if I told you all of it was true? Would you believe me?" I asked, daring her to question me. Apparently, I was all in.

"No. Not the magic stuff, obviously. And I would hope that if any of the other shit happened, you'd have called me long before now. Seriously. What's up?"

I took a breath and blew it out, exasperated. I was suddenly so, so tired.

"Look," I started. "You don't have to believe me. But, a really long story short, all that stuff is true. But I'm calling now because I need to know—do I play the victim in my life?"

"I'm going to need the long version before I answer that, Jules," Edie said, narrowing her gaze at me through the screen. She was no-nonsense and the least fantastical person I'd ever met. She was black and white without being a jerk about it and one of those people who needed concrete evidence to back up anything. I wasn't sure what had made me blurt everything out, but I was in over my head now and had no choice but to keep going.

I told her everything. Once I started talking, I couldn't stop. And to Edie's credit, she let me ramble and describe, in detail, the turns in which my life had taken over the last year with only the slightest noises of disbelief and doubt. I purged everything that had transpired and was thoroughly wrung out by the time I was finished.

"So, let me get this straight," she said. "All of this crazy shit has happened to you in the last *year,* and the thing you want to know from *me* is whether or not Dell is right?" I had no words to describe the look on her face.

I nodded, swallowing thickly.

"Jules. I love you. You're one of my best friends and the godmother to my kids, so like, I love you *a lot*. But you can't call me out of the blue, drop all this insane information on me, and then ask the most random question that puts me between you and another of my best friends. That's not fair at all. In fact, none of this shit is fair. Why wouldn't you tell me any of this when we were together?"

"Because it's *you*, Edie. You believe in science and reasoning and hard facts. How can I explain magic to someone who sees the world in black and white?"

"Is that really how you see me?" she asked softly. "Black and white?"

I shrugged my shoulders. "I mean, yeah? Aren't you?"

She stared straight at me, face pained, and then looked off-camera like she was gathering her thoughts.

"Not entirely, no," she said. Her voice pained, and I felt a stab of discomfort. There was no way that Dell and I both had been wrong about Edie all these years. She was the most straightforward, no-nonsense person I had ever met. We were quiet for a few moments, and then she spoke again.

"I don't know how I feel about all the magical stuff. That seems a little... far-fetched," she began. "I don't mean that in a closed-off-thinking sort of way," she added quickly, defending herself. "It's that part that is hard for me. But the rest of it? Jules, I saw your face when you told us about your past. I saw how terrified you still were of that maniac. Do I believe that he came and attacked you and Andrew? *Absolutely*. I'm just glad you got out alive, no matter *what* happened. Seriously." She paused.

"Yeah, that part is probably the least far-fetched of everything I've told you," I joked, trying to lighten the mood.

"Yeah, probably. But the rest of it? Andrew is in a coma? Why the hell wouldn't you call me? We love him too, you know? He and Eric are best friends. You don't think we'd want to know?"

"God, Edie, I'm so sorry. I know you would. It's a lot to explain, yeah?"

"Yeah, it is, but we've been friends for half our lives, and we don't lie to each other," She blew out a breath, and her bangs, in need of a trim, lifted off her forehead and out of her eyes. "Is he going to be okay?" Her voice was small and quiet, and that alone scared me. Edie was not one for small and quiet. Tears prickled in the corner of my eyes.

"I don't know." We tried to make small talk after that, but there was a gulf between us that couldn't be bridged yet. I hung up the call feeling simultaneously lighter from telling her the truth and weighed down by hurting her. Along with the heaviness of hurt, the weight of grief settled back on my shoulders, and I began to curl in on myself. Would I ever know the sweet relief of peace again?

# 13

## *Anguish*

I hoped that talking to Edie would shed some light on what Dell had accused me of, but it hadn't, and I was left trying to figure it out. After some soul-searching, I slowly warmed to the idea that maybe Dell wasn't entirely wrong. I sat with that for days, pulling further away and turning in on myself. And everyone seemed happy to leave me be. The excitement of my having visions seemed to have worn off, and once more, I found myself navigating life alone. I knew Dell was off with Naomi or learning magic from everyone else, and I rubbed at the pang of jealousy that it wasn't me standing in Reem's kitchen or gardening with Hasina. With her infectious joy and lack of recent trauma, Dell stepped in to fill the space I'd left behind. And really, I couldn't blame them. Who would want to be with me—all sorrow and grief—if they didn't have to?

The realization that I'd let myself become a victim to memory and to myself was startling. It filled me with an anger that simmered deep. I had held myself back from so much, and it was truly a wonder that Andrew and I had the relationship we did. Or even that I had the friendships I had with Edie and Dell, though those felt precarious at present.

When I realized that I needed to regain my own power, something unlocked inside of me. Whatever "veil" had still been settled on my shoulders finally lifted off, and I was free for the first time in my life. It was like waking up from a long sleep and not recognizing your surroundings; only my surroundings were myself, and the long sleep had been my life.

"I think it's time to let them go, *Habibti*," Marwa said one afternoon after I'd sought her out, tired of being alone to simmer.

"I know. But I don't know how."

She nodded and pulled out a white candle and a sheaf of paper from her drawer.

"I have an idea," she said. "Write them a letter. Confront them and say everything you wished you could have said before they died... the good and the bad... and the, how do you say?" She waved her hands around, trying to find the word she was looking for. "Oh. The ugly."

I laughed. Marwa loved English colloquialisms and wanted to use them as much as possible. Apparently, Arabic was filled with amazing ones that didn't always translate. Still, I was having her teach them to me in English as well, and we laughed over the similarities and differences between our languages. She was the steadiest person in my life, trying to make up for the loss of Gram, but I continued to push her away. And she continued to push back, enough to make sure I knew she was there to stay. It annoyed me, but I was also irrationally annoyed at my childish need for a motherly figure, so I swallowed the annoyance regularly.

"Okay. And then what?" I snapped as she slid paper and a pen towards me. I drank the last of my tea and set my cup to the side with more force than I'd meant. The anger that had been simmering was so easy to tip over to a boil. I was almost more consumed by it than worry or grief.

"Then we burn it," she said gently, ignoring my irritation. "And the smoke will take your messages into the universe and find them, wherever they are. And the matter will be settled." She spoke with such sincerity that I couldn't help but believe her. I shrugged. It couldn't hurt; at least it would get her off my back a bit.

I spent some time scribbling a letter to my mom and dad. I said everything I had always wished I could say. Hurtful, hateful, broken-hearted things that had my chest tight with longing and pain. And as I wrote, I poured every feeling I had towards them into the words. In the end, there were things unwritten in the margins that I would never be able to say or write that needed to be there. I didn't shed a tear for them—too many had come before that day, and I refused to give them any more. My hand ached from writing, and every muscle was tight with tension. But as I watched the letter burn, I knew I was finally letting them go, sending that hurt out into the ether, and that I would be okay. The weight of release was great, and I knew it was well past time to step into my power and take control of my life now my past no longer held sway over me.

"Okay. The thing is done. The universe will see to it now."

Something inside of me shifted at Marwa's words. I was no longer content to let someone else be in charge and guide my sense of purpose. I was through with that chapter of my life. Through with being a doormat. Through letting things *happen* to me. It was time to stand up and take charge.

Andrew falling into a coma was my undoing. But it would also prove to be my making. It was the catalyst I needed to shed the skin of my past and become who I was meant to be.

A few days later, it was the second full moon since Andrew's ritual... since the night he'd been taken from me. I had been so consumed with grief that no one had expected me to participate in the first one. And that, combined with the frustration with Hanan, meant I hadn't had time to worry over what another ritual would feel like, let alone plan for it.

I woke up late, sleep the only escape I had from myself. Dell and I weren't on speaking terms, and I hadn't heard anything else from Edie. While the letter to my parents and the burning of it had definitely lifted a weight off my chest, I was still heavy with grief and loneliness. The afternoon dragged on while I lay with Andrew in his bed. I had drawn the curtains against the bright sun as it made its way across the sky, ticking down the hours until the moon would take over.

My mood was stormy as I walked the passageway to the ritual room. I'd come alone, straight from Andrew, and my anger simmered into a righteous boil with each step I took. I paused at the door, lifting my hand and resting my palm against it. I closed my eyes and took a few deep breaths in and out, trying to ground myself. Trying to tamp down the anger. Little pulses of adrenaline swam through my blood, spiking my heart rate and making me feel out of control. I squeezed my eyes shut and willed my heart to calm down. Images of Andrew lying unconscious in the room beyond my palm flashed through my mind with each burst of adrenaline.

In... and out... I sucked in air with purpose and intent.

In...

Out...

And still, I raged.

My palm met empty air, and I opened my eyes to see Marwa standing in the doorway, eyes sad.

"We can hear you in here, *Habibti*. But more than that, we can feel you," she said softly, opening her arms up to me. I shook my head, eyes filling with tears, chest heaving with sobs. I could smell the ritual room now that the door was open—the moist heat of the water, the incense, and the candles burning. It took me back to that night at a visceral level. A wave of heat flushed down my spine, and my palms began to sweat.

"I can't do this," I forced out. The words were thick and heavy in the fragrant air. I stepped back from the door, stumbling a bit, unwilling to face the room or the women beyond looking past Marwa. "I'm... I'm sorry," I stammered before turning and returning the way I'd come.

The heat of memory and panic burst from every pore; I was dripping with sweat by the time I reached the entrance. My eyes were stinging with tears and sweat, and I tasted salt on my tongue. I could still feel my sisters' stares as I rushed away from them, itching between my shoulder blades, but I kept moving, hoping no one had followed.

I pulled out my phone and called for a cab, focusing all my energy on reigning in my emotions until I could return home to the freedom of a private breakdown. The cab driver took one look at me and didn't say a word. I barely made it through the gates before falling to my knees in the garden, great gulping sobs escaping my tight hold.

I collapsed to the ground. The mosaic stones beneath me were hard, but I was frozen in grief and fury. I let the discomfort spur me on. Facing the ritual room and the thought of going through the motions for another full moon ceremony had been more than I could bear. The guilt and shame of responsibility weren't the only things overwhelming me. The anger that the sisterhood, and that once safe and revelatory space, was the cause of my grief was more than I could take. The smells, the feeling of the air on my skin, and the faces of my sisters shook loose the last hold of sanity I'd held tight to.

I thought about Andrew, his body prone and quiet, and the grief swelled. Time, as it does, passed, and before I knew it, the moon hung bright and high above me. Alone in the garden, I held my own ceremony, calling on the moon and its magic.

I whispered my own words. Not Hanan's or Hatshepsut's.

There was no incense burning. No candles to light the way.

No ritual pool to bathe in. No womb-like return to the earth.

No sisters to hold my hands. No vibrant energy pulsing around us and building to a crescendo.

It was only me. Stripped down to my wounds.

Bared to the night.

Alone.

It was the alone that spurred me on. The fear. The hopelessness wrapped in a blanket of blind faith that something, *anything*, had to work.

I lifted my arms above my head, hands reaching for the celestial body that called to me.

I pulled and pulled and pulled. Siphoning everything I could in the selfish hope that it would help. That it would, somehow, hear me and take away the pain. Take away the anger. The anguish. Give me back my love. My self.

I imagined lassoing the moon à la *It's a Wonderful Life,* channeling my inner George Bailey. I held tight to that vision and pulled. The power swarmed like a thousand insects, buzzing all around me expectantly. A guttural, animal sound came from my throat, and I swallowed the buzzing energy. It filled me with electricity. And still, I pulled. And pulled. And pulled some more—mad with wanting.

My arms shook with exhaustion, and my skin was wringing wet when the sun began to peek over the horizon, painting the black sky with hints of color and light. I dragged myself to the guest house and into bed, asleep before I could even pass a thought for the clothes I'd left in the garden.

# 14

## *Worry*

*M*arwa

It was becoming more difficult to watch Julia pull away. With everything she had, Marwa tried to be a mother to her. But mothering her wasn't enough. Her heart broke when Julia closed the temple door in her face the night of the full moon ritual she missed. She knew Julia was hurting; they all did. But Marwa didn't understand, till that moment, the gravity of her pain. Marwa turned towards her sisters, searching for answers from them.

None of them had any.

"We must do something," Marwa said. Everyone's faces looked pained. They all worried about Julia, but she wondered if anyone else had felt how deep the wounds were. She had been an empath from birth. To Marwa, emotions were tactile things she'd learned to live with. Joy was effervescent and floated through the air like the bubbles she blew for her grandchildren. Excitement was a heady rush that tasted like champagne. Fear was sour and curled her shoulders forward as if protecting herself. Pain and suffering were heavy and weighed her down more than anything else. It had taken years of learning how to navigate her power to understand it fully. Even then, something could crop up that surprised her. Julia was one of those things.

From the outside, her needs seemed simple. Her parents had abandoned and abused her. She needed love and acceptance. All the things that should have been freely given to her when she was young. And so, Marwa tried. And continued to fail her.

"Yes, but what?" Marwa's own sweet Salma asked. "She keeps pushing us away."

"I tried to have her come with Delilah the other day to bake, and she refused. She barely leaves her room unless to go to Andrew," Reem said. Marwa nodded and looked at Hanan. If anyone had an idea of how bad things were with Julia, it was her.

"We all want to help her," she said, answering the older woman's look. "But she has to want our help, and right now, she doesn't."

"I don't think she knows how to ask," Marwa countered.

Everyone was quiet then. They made their way to the temple room to begin the full moon ritual, trying their best to ignore the empty space where Julia should have been, but it was impossible.

# 15

## Khonsu's Truth

*A*ndrew

Andrew's unconsciousness remained with Khonsu in his temple in a sort of stasis. Time had no real meaning on whatever plane they were on, and while his body slept, his soul wandered every corner of the temple at Karnak. Khonsu showed him details he'd missed when he and Julia had visited the year before. Though now it wasn't in ruins but intact and more amazing than Andrew could have imagined.

Thoughts of his wife were the only things that forced him to register the lack of time. But each time he brought up returning to his body to Khonsu, the god assured him that waiting was the best way forward. To allow his body to heal so that when he was reunited with it, he would be perfect and whole.

He caught glimpses of her in his dreams. He didn't sleep, per se, but went into almost a waking dream-like state. While there, he could see Jules. He watched her lying next to him, pouring her heart and magic out to his body, and he longed to be there. Longed to hold her and comfort her instead of lying there, the cause of the stress and tears.

When he wasn't in the dream-like trance, Khonsu was there. The god treated Andrew as a confidant and friend. They spoke of deep, meaningful things like world religions through the ages and trivial things like baseball. Khonsu was personable and likable. But still, Andrew kindled the small flame of distrust in his chest. He'd read too many fantasy novels and seen too many movies to trust this stranger implicitly. However, as time passed, it was getting harder not to let his guard down.

As Andrew relaxed around Khonsu and the pair got to know each other, Khonsu finally came clean about his intentions. And Andrew was left with more questions than answers.

"I am in love with Isis," the god had said late one night when the moon was high in the sky and only a few days from being full. With a jolt, Andrew realized that meant he'd been unconscious for almost a month unless he'd missed a full moon along the way.

"The goddess?"

"Yes. Who else?" Khonsu smiled, confused. He was matter-of-fact and so old and set in his ways and beliefs that there were sometimes moments of confusion as they sorted out the nuance of speech or common ideas or sayings that he didn't understand. The fact that anyone else could be named Isis, in Khonsu's mind, was a non-reality. There was only one. Andrew shrugged noncommittally.

"Alright. Have you told her?" he asked.

"No," the god said, hanging his head.

"But why not?" Andrew asked, the hopeless romantic in him stirring.

Khonsu waved a hand dismissively. "It is not so easy as telling a goddess you are in love with her. You must prove your devotion." He looked to the sky and the heavy orb that was his charge and essence. "I thought by giving her priestesses the power to draw from myself each month, she would take notice and fall in love with me. But alas, it has not happened as yet." He sighed, and Andrew realized that 'wistful' was not an emotion he'd ever associated with a god.

"Maybe she's noticed, but she doesn't know how to show her devotion to you?" Andrew said hopefully.

Khonsu made a sound of disagreement in the back of his throat. Andrew wasn't sure what he wanted from him. It wasn't like he had a direct connection with Isis and could play wingman for the god. He was a mortal and currently a mortal at the mercy of a lovesick god.

"I should think that she knows of my devotion. But Isis has many devotees and lovers. I should want to be her favored." Khonsu sighed again, face still turned toward the moon.

"The life of a god is long, but it is lonely without a mate. I spend my nights shining a light on wanderers and travelers, lighting the paths they seek, keeping them safe in the light and dark of the moon. But while the moon is high, I am the only one who wakes and walks this world. I am nameless and faceless to those who worship me and seek my light. I am tired, child, so tired of being alone." The last words were said softly, barely above a whisper, but Andrew heard the weariness in them and felt pity for the god.

"Is there anything I can do to help?"

"Perhaps," Khonsu said, slowly turning towards Andrew and looking at him, gaze seeking deeper than his eyes. "I hope that by restoring you to life, you can take a message back to the priestesses of Isis, and they can pass a message to my beloved."

"Do you mean the sisterhood?" Andrew asked.

"I do not know what this word is meaning. They are the priestesses of Isis, and they gather in the temple of the Queen Hatshepsut each cycle of the moon and draw strength and power from me."

Andrew nodded, letting his argument fall away, and a part of his brain wondered what Jules would think if he told her the gods thought them priestesses.

"Okay, what is the message then?" Andrew asked, hopeful that he would relay it and send him back to his wife and his life.

"I have seen many things. Things that have been and things to come. The moon sees these things and whispers them to me. The priestesses have no knowledge of what is to come, but they should ready themselves for war. *Ma'at* is in disarray, and they must do everything in their power to restore *ma'at*."

"What does that mean? *Ma'at*?" Andrew asked, fear for his wife curdling in his belly.

"Order. The world has been thrown into discord because of the misuse of *hekka*... of..." He waved a hand, searching for the familiar term Andrew would understand. "Magic."

"So the world is out of balance and needs to be put back to rights. Got it. But what does the magic have to do with it? Are the, uh, priestesses misusing it?"

"They haven't been in recent years, though there was a time. But now I can see the path that lies ahead. The world will become more unbalanced very soon." Khonsu said firmly. "The priestesses respect *hekka*, and they respect *ma'at*. However, your partner will soon begin to search out darker things. Magic to save you that will throw the balance off even more, tipping the scales into true chaos. Long ago, someone else did the same and used *hekka* for great and terrible things, and the cosmic order of the world must be restored. You will go and explain this to them before it's too late. The priestesses will go to Isis and tell her of the treachery that took place, and she will tell them how to put things to rights," Khonsu looked pleased with himself.

"Why can't you just talk to Isis?" Andrew asked.

"She will not come when I call her. And, I am a god. I should not expect that I have to go to her. She should come when I call."

Andrew internally rolled his eyes but said nothing.

"The chaos of the world is beginning to unravel. There are great plagues on humanity because of a deal that was struck thousands of years ago by one. Now that your wife seeks out powerful magic, things are coming that must be stopped, or the world will finally come to its end. And it is not time for that, as yet."

And so, Khonsu told Andrew everything, including what had long happened and what was to come. Some of it he knew, and some left him rocked to his core. Hours passed while Khonsu spoke, painting a picture of destruction and terror that left Andrew panting in fear. But he also spoke of hope. Of the sisterhood's true purpose, how he hoped to help them, and what Andrew would need to do. Andrew worried for Jules. He had felt her anguish from an entirely different plane of existence. Still, he couldn't believe that desperation would have sent her in search of the things she'd been warned against.

"Khonsu, I have to get back. I have to get to Julia and save her from doing something she'll regret," Andrew pleaded.

"Andrew, my child, you cannot save her," he said.

Andrew jumped to his feet, unable to sit still any longer while his wife was out there searching for what had sent the world toppling into imbalance.

"If I don't save her, who will?" he exclaimed. It was then that he noticed his lack of heartbeat. On earth, he knew his heart would be beating out of his chest in panic, but he felt nothing but a hollowness beneath his breastbone. It was more than a little unsettling.

"She must save herself."

Andrew shook his head at the god who remained reclined, arms behind his head, body stretched out before him like he didn't have a care in the world.

"Let me go to her, at least. I've been here long enough. Surely, my body is healed down there. Or, um, whatever direction *there* is."

Khonsu chuckled and rolled his eyes, a decidedly human gesture.

"You humans and your need to understand direction and the where and how of things. You're with your body. And not with your body. You exist, and you don't exist. It's not terribly hard to understand."

It was Andrew's turn to roll his eyes.

"Maybe not for a god, but my little human brain can't wrap itself around the whole here and not here, there and not there thing. Seriously, can you just... do whatever god woo-ey thing you need to do and put me back to rights so I can wake up and Jules will stop what she's doing before it's too late?"

Andrew knew that the desperation he felt to get back to wherever his body was didn't even touch the level of desperation his wife must have been feeling to start looking into darker magic. Meanwhile, Khonsu was belly laughing, the sound rich and vibrating off the walls, annoying Andrew.

"Your *little human brain* is capable of much more than you give it credit for, child," Khonsu said between laughter, clearly amused at the entire situation. "It is almost time," he finally said, sobering up.

"What do you mean, almost? Please, send me now," Andrew pleaded.

"I am Khonsu. The god of the moon. Protector of travelers. One of the gods of fertility. And, my friend... the Pathfinder. There is a path before you and the priestesses, and I am helping to keep you on the path. So when I say it is almost time, the way forward is clear, and it is almost time."

They didn't speak much after that. Both Andrew and Khonsu were contemplative and quiet, lost in thought. However long they'd been together, Andrew couldn't help but wonder if Khonsu had chosen the path that kept them together the longest to stave off his loneliness.

# 16

## Dashing Dreams

"I dreamt last night that we found a way to wake Andrew," I said to Hanan and Dell over breakfast. Dell and I still weren't on the best speaking terms, but we tried to be polite around everyone else. Hanan put down her coffee mug and looked at me.

"Julia, I know you're desperate for him to wake up, but I can't stress this enough: there's nothing else we can do. I cannot, and will not, use magic that way." She at least had the decency to look sad when she said it.

"Hanan, what if it isn't some crazy magic spell involving human sacrifice, and it's no more than a healing spell? Like what Renee does all the time? What if there's an answer in the scrolls?" I asked. The hope that was burning in my chest was sputtering with her dismissal.

"We've tried that sort of stuff, Jules. That's what the whole ritual was," Dell answered.

I glanced at her sideways, annoyed.

"Yeah, I know that. That's what got him into this mess. I'm trying to find a way to get him out of it. I don't know why everyone is content to sit around and let my husband waste away."

"Whoa, whoa, whoa, Julia," Dell interrupted my tirade. "No one is happy to sit around and watch him waste away. Take a breath and chill."

"Chill?" I asked furiously. "Chill? That's your answer. Take a breath and chill. Okay, cool, Dell. The next time your life partner is in a coma, and you're worried they'll never wake up again, I'll remind you just to chill, and we can see how much that helps you."

Hanan put her hand up and stopped us both. My chest was heaving, and my hands were shaking with anger.

"Everyone in this room needs to calm down," she said, steady. "Julia, no one is sitting around doing nothing. Renee and Hasina are deep-diving into every healing text we can get our hands on. There's nothing in the scrolls that would be safe enough to try. We're all visiting him and lending energy as often as we can. We all feel responsible, even though we had no way of knowing this would happen." She paused, gathering herself, and I sank back into my chair. The adrenaline in my veins was still making itself known, but I was exhausted.

"I wouldn't have even tried the ritual had I not had every confidence that it would work," she said. Her voice was barely above a whisper and choked with emotion.

My throat and eyes burned with tears. "But it didn't work. And now I might lose him, and no one will do anything about it." I got up from the table and walked away, tears making tracks down my cheeks.

Rationally, I knew that it was no one's fault. We all chose to do the ceremony. But I couldn't help but feel an untamable rage when I thought about Hanan's unwillingness to investigate something other than their traditional ways of magic. I knew there were answers in the scrolls. There was something more we could do, and I knew it. I just had to find it. Damn Hanan and damn anyone who stood in my way.

I woke up the following day angry at the world. Everything that could irritate me got under my skin and chafed. I left early to lay with Andrew in his hospital bed, hoping that being near him would help calm me down.

After an hour of tossing and turning next to him, I was sure I would disturb even the most profound coma, so I got up and paced the room. I traipsed back and forth, trying to find an outlet for the restlessness that was begging for a way out. My skin was tight with anger and frustration— like a panic attack, but instead of anxiety, it was rage boiling under the surface. I looked down at my clenched fists, surprised I couldn't see my blood boiling beneath my skin. I whirled around and looked at Andrew's peaceful face. It somehow made the rage worse.

"Wake up!" I shouted at him. "Wake the fuck up! You can't leave me here alone! I can't do this," I wailed, a sob catching in my throat. I kept on going, a string of incoherent sobbing and screaming, filled with all the anger and frustration that couldn't be contained any longer. On and on I went, tears streaming down my face, my eyes swelling with grief. But no matter how I raged at my husband, Andrew didn't even bat an eyelash. However, I did find out that the silencing sigil I placed on his door held up to the torrent of emotions I unleashed in the room.

When I had thoroughly cried myself dry and was no longer shaking with anger, I straightened up and smoothed my clothes down. I took in a deep, shuddering breath. With one last glance at Andrew, I opened the door and walked out, no longer desperate for release but still desperate for an answer.

# 17

# The Pain of Mated Souls

*A*ndrew

Andrew was pleasantly floating along on whatever plane he and Khonsu were in when he felt it. Or, rather, felt her. Shaken from a daydream of the mountains of North Carolina— the rich scent of crisp mountain air, loamy moss, and red clay dirt under his feet was swept away. He was jerked upright by a flood of emotions, jolted like being shocked back to life.

Violence.

Pain.

Rage.

Grief.

They were all-consuming and overwhelming. Peace and stasis were replaced with a clawing need to move, to breathe—for his heart to beat. He called out into the emptiness. No answer. Sharp bursts of pain shocked his system. Every place he had felt pain in his body was suddenly alive with nerve endings again in this place, and hot, stabbing knives shredded through his comfort. He didn't know if it was the sudden reintroduction to feeling, but the pain was worse than anything he'd known before. Andrew felt like he was being peeled apart, bit by bit.

"*Khonsu*!" He bellowed, breath gasping. He was doubled over in pain now, forehead on the ground in supplication. Andrew felt him before he heard him, the god's presence commanding the room. He heard words he couldn't make out on the periphery of his consciousness and then, blissfully, nothing. The pain stopped abruptly, lurching Andrew forward and tumbling to the side. He gasped, taking in great gulps of air, grateful again for the absence of pain.

"What...was...that?" he choked out between breaths. Andrew rolled over onto his back, rubbing the heels of his hands over his eyes, trying to shake off the last of the phantom pains.

"Your wife is in great pain," Khonsu said, voice rumbling. "She came to your body, hurting. Angry. Confused. She holds too much pain for one so young."

Andrew looked at the god who stood before him. He walked over to the chaise he'd been lounging on before and sat down, dropping his head into his hands.

"I have to go to her!" Andrew pleaded. "She has to know I'm going to be okay!" Worry and panic started bubbling up to the surface of his mind, raising his voice. Tears pricked his eyes, and it startled him that he could weep in this stasis. He opened his mouth to speak again, and tears choked off the words. Andrew wept unashamedly, the worry, fear, and pain pouring out of his eyes and down his cheeks. Khonsu stayed preternaturally still, watching. He scrubbed his hands over his face, wiping tears from his beard, and looked up at the god.

"It is not yet time to return," Khonsu spoke quietly and gently, mindful of the precipice Andrew stood before.

"But why?" Andrew pleaded more. "Why can't I go now? Heal me or do some sort of divine magic and let me get to her. I knew it was bad but couldn't have guessed it was *this* bad for her."

"The bond you share with her is not one I see often, Andrew. The two of you have spent lifetimes together. Your souls always find each other, and the bond gets stronger and stronger each lifetime."

Andrew shook his head. "I don't believe in soul mates, Khonsu. But I do believe that my wife needs me, and I need to be with her. If not now, when?"

Khonsu's eyes glowed softly in the fading light.

"Soon, child. Soon."

They sat together for a few minutes, then—with Andrew wracking his brain for any excuse to return to his body. Khonsu calmly and studiously ignored his frustrations. Eventually, he straightened up and quirked an eyebrow at Andrew as if to ask if he were okay. Andrew nodded. Khonsu walked away, leaving him to his thoughts, footsteps echoing in the temple.

The absence of pain was still there, throbbing after the torrent Jules' emotions had unleashed. He wished he could reach out and touch her... to let her know everything would be okay...eventually. He laid back on the chaise and closed his eyes, willing the dream of home to return...looking for peace and distraction. It was no use. His mind was stormy—thoughts and worries over Jules were no match for even the strongest will.

Soul mates. It sounded so cheesy. So silly. What he and Jules had wasn't written in the stars or preordained by some higher power. It was born out of hard work and dedication to one another. The choice they *both* made each and every day to show up for each other and their marriage. It was years of whispers in the darkest part of the night, entrusting each other with quiet truths and hard things. It was vows and promises. It was evolving together. And yet... there was something effortless between them, too. An undercurrent of something he'd never been able to define. Andrew shook his head and closed his eyes, not dreaming about the mountains he so missed, but he dreamt of his true home... of Jules.

# 18

## *Breakthrough*

After my meltdown in Andrew's hospital room, I began to sit in meditation almost constantly. I was convinced that the answer to waking him up lay somewhere with Hatshepsut and the scrolls, and I had to try hard enough to connect with her. I spent hours of my day seated, reclined, on and off cushions, using incense and every tool I knew to try and throw myself into a vision.

Try as I might, all I could glean was the occasional snippet of her life. While it was fascinating seeing glances of her in the ritual room or pacing her bedchamber, it wasn't what I needed or wanted. The frustration at not getting deep enough did precisely what one should have expected... held me back further. And still, I tried. Over and over. Every day. And finally, after weeks of failure, I had a breakthrough.

My hips and back were aching from sitting upright, trying my hardest to force a vision that wouldn't come. I turned the tap on the bath and waited as the hot water filled the deep tub. Within moments, the tiny bathroom was enveloped with steam. I poured bath oil and swirled it through the hot water, the heat stinging my hand. I turned the tap and added some cold water, not wanting to be boiled alive.

I tested the water again. It was hot but less than boiling, and I knew I needed the heat to soothe sore muscles. I stripped out of my leggings and T-shirt and sank into the water, groaning as the heat hit my skin.

I sank low into the tub, feeling my face flushing with water just a few degrees too hot. I rested my head against the tub and closed my eyes, skin throbbing. Slowly, I let myself melt into the water, tension leaking out of me and swirling around with the steam.

I took a deep, shuddering breath and let it out, thoroughly relaxing. For the first time in weeks, my mind went quiet. No longer was I trying too hard or making a failed attempt to find answers. I let the sensation of the water be my focus. Slowly, so slowly, the water settled from my entrance into the bath. As the water stilled, the last of my thoughts did as well. I gave myself entirely over to the sensation of peace.

And, of course, letting go was the key to unblocking my mind. It didn't take long; the steam was still rising around me, and I went under. I found Hatshepsut almost immediately. Or maybe she found me.

She was standing in a bedchamber, the bed draped in thin, barely-there netting and on a raised platform in the middle of the room. Lush fabrics in rich dyes were mussed and tossed about as if Hatshepsut had recently been lying in bed. She stood, her back to me, looking out her window, the moonlight being the only source of light in the room.

Something in her awareness shifted, and I watched her roll her shoulders back and pull herself up straighter.

"I wondered when she would send you," she said, still turned away. I looked around to see who had entered the room and found it empty. I leaned forward, trying to see if she was talking to someone on the balcony, when she slowly turned and looked at me head-on.

Her eyes weren't as bright as the first time I'd seen her in a vision, but the ethereal glow was still there. I turned and looked behind me, expecting to find a visitor, and there was no one.

"Do you have a message from Isis?" she asked, her voice deep and rich. Then, I realized she was looking directly at me and could see me. My heart should have been pounding out of my chest, but I felt nothing. No tell-tale beat of life, and I began to panic. I grabbed for my chest, hand fisting in fabric, as I stepped back. The wall behind me stopped me in my panicked tracks, and I gulped in deep breaths of warm air. My vision began to tunnel, edges going black and the room around me blurring. I heard Hatshepsut sigh, the exasperated sound loud above the panic in my ears. Somehow, her sigh anchored me to the spot, and the black edges around my sight receded.

"Oh. You're staying, then?" I heard her say. I squeezed my eyes shut, forcing calm into my system. I took deep breaths, steadied myself, and opened my eyes after a few moments. Hatshepsut was perched against her window, arms crossed against her chest, waiting patiently. I stood up, rolling my shoulders down my back, my body stiff with nerves.

"Can you see me?" I asked, voice quiet in the room. I felt small in her presence; she commanded the room, even as relaxed as she was. She quirked a dark eyebrow at me, a smile tugging at the corners of her lips.

"Of course, I can see you. You're standing in my bedchamber," she said dryly. She waved a hand, and candles sputtered to life all around the room; the shadows hiding me chased away instantly. "What do you fear, young one? Me?"

I shook my head gently.

"I fear a lot of things, my... queen." I wasn't sure what to call her. She nodded, and I took that as an invitation to go on. "I fear myself.

My power. What this means. And I fear for my husband's life. He is in danger." She moved from her perch and slowly made her way over to me. My back was still pressed against the wall, and I pushed harder against it. She stilled in front of me, a hairs breadth away. She smelled like the darkest part of an autumn night, the sticky resin of myrrh, and something sharp like ozone. I took a breath, drawing her into my lungs, her energy seeking out and filling the darkest corners of me. My magic rose in response, making me weak in the knees.

"I can feel your power from here, little one. It is fluttering underneath your skin like a bird that is trapped." She traced a finger down my cheek, along my neck, and between my breasts. She rested it where my heart should have been pounding. "What is that you fear of my gift?"

I swallowed, trying to find my voice. She leaned in closer, flattening her palm against my breasts, our lips almost touching, and she inhaled deeply, eyes fluttering closed as she seemed to take me in the way I had done her. She stood there, unmoving, for a long time. I was frozen in place, wrapped in her power. She opened her eyes, the gold flecks glowing in the candlelight, and I spoke, voice barely above a whisper.

"I fear too much power. Corruption. Loss of control. Hurting someone..." I trailed off, not wanting to give a voice to the deepest part of my fear... enjoying the power and the loss of control. But I knew that, somehow, she knew. She stayed close, our breath mingling, hers sweet and rich on my tongue.

"You will only corrupt the gift if you don't use it how it wants to be used. Yours is a heart that is true. It would not have been given to you if you would misuse it." She pulled away then, leaving a tangible absence in her place. I ached for her to come back. For her breath on my lips and her hands on my skin. "Do you come bearing a message from Isis?" she asked again, her back to me as she strode to the window.

I peeled myself off the wall and tentatively stepped towards her.

"From Isis?" I asked, confused.

She turned and nodded, eyebrow quirked again. "I have no message from anyone. I... I came to find answers. From you." She clicked her tongue and shook her head, looking down at her feet. She looked... lost. And as quickly as the mask of formidable presence slipped, she pulled it back on again and looked directly at me.

"I don't know who you are or how you have found me, but Isis has promised me a message from a priestess, and I await it. Many nights I have paced this room, waiting. And a handful of nights, I have seen a flicker, a spectral shadow, come to deliver me from this waiting. And yet, nothing." The mask slipped again, and I saw her pained face, tired and frustrated in the shadowed light.

"I don't know anyone named Isis. Our Steward's name is Hanan, and she didn't want me looking for you."

Hatshepsut's head snapped up, and her eyes blazed.

"Your *steward*?" she said. "Steward of what? And Isis is no human for you to *know*. She is a goddess. *My* goddess. The one who gifted me with power. The one whose power also sings in your veins."

I stilled, confused, and it must have been written as plain as day across my face.

"Come!" she commanded. And I did. She placed her hands gently on the sides of my face, fingertips on my temples, cheeks cradled in her palms. She closed her eyes and took a deep, practiced breath. The space between her breaths was long and measured. I closed my eyes, and moments and memories flashed across my eyelids. Internally, I itched to move, to get out of her grasp. Externally, I was frozen by her hands and her magic, anchoring me to the spot. I existed between spaces. Hovering betwixt her inhales and exhales, lost to magic outside my control.

Time passed, and Hatshepsut's hold on me relaxed. My body twinged with tension from standing still for so long, and I shifted my weight as unobtrusively as possible. She still held my face in her hands, but she'd yet to open her eyes. Her breaths were even, with less time between them, and slowly, I watched her come back into her body. She opened her eyes, and the flecks of gold were bright and glowing, like amber liquid held to the light for clarity.

"I have seen a lot of things in my time. Felt pain and the sting of betrayal. I have been lost. Broken. But also whole. And powerful." She swallowed, and I watched her throat work and felt a lump forming in my own. "My dear, sweet one. You feel so many things and feel them so deeply that they are written in your bones and stitched onto your soul. Your power is tainted by your fear. It is a dark veil that covers you from the top of your head to the soles of your feet, and you must find a way to lift it off or be smothered under its weight." A single tear traced down her cheek, and I watched it, entranced by the trail it left on her skin. The gravity of a Queen's tear, shed for my pain, was not lost on me. She pulled me to her, cradling me in her arms, and I wept. My heart may not have had a beat in this liminal space, but my tears flowed freely, and I soaked the gown she wore.

When I was thoroughly wrung out and emptied of tears, the weight of grief lightened ever so slightly. I pulled away and looked at Hatshepsut. Her face had softened; the regality was still there, but gone was the mask of the Pharaoh, the role she played. In its stead was a face of empathy and compassion. It was the face of someone who saw me—the dark and the light and didn't shy away from either.

"I have seen you. Your life and your journey. The ritual that brought you to me. And I see, too, that the Priestesses of Isis have lost their way." Her voice was gentle, the forced depth replaced by what I assumed was her natural pitch. It was soft and more feminine than she wanted to portray to her kingdom.

"I don't know what you mean by *the Priestesses of Isis*. Is that what you call us? The sisterhood?" I asked.

She led me to her bed, and we sat next to each other, legs touching. Her heat warmed me, and she held my hand in her lap.

"I see that time has not been kind to our purpose," she said. "So many things lost. Lost to time. To fear. To a madman," she spoke dreamily, eyes cast down to her lap, her mind whirring, I was sure. "It is what I feared most."

She began to speak earnestly then, telling me the truths lost or watered down throughout time. The purpose of the Priestesses of Isis, or the sisterhood as we were called in my time. She was calm, though worried, as she spoke of balance. The dual natures of good and evil. How Isis had come to her, first in visions and then in person, and they'd struck a deal of sorts. Isis had entrusted Hatshepsut with almost god-like power, gifting her with a small piece of herself for control. At that point, she formally named herself *the Good Goddess Maatkare,* shedding her title of *The God's Wife.*

Her magic took on a different role at that point as well, and she began to be able to do things she'd only heard whispers of. Walking through the dreams of others, concealing herself in plain sight, and seeing the truth of someone by touching them. I shivered at the thought of more power.

And then I shivered again. And again. Until my teeth were chattering, and the cold was deep inside of me. Hatshepsut had stopped speaking and was looking at me, confused. The air in the room hadn't changed. She wasn't cold. But I was shaking, and my fingertips were mottled with purple. She wrapped her arms around me, running her hands up and down my goose-pimpled arms. And still, I shivered. The room around me also began to shiver, blurring again at the edges of my vision, Hatshepsut's voice tunneling like she was far away.

With a gasp, I returned to myself in the bathtub, water frigid and corporeal body violently shaking with cold.

# 19

## *Liminal Space*

In terms of loneliness, I discovered that the cure for mine was getting lost in visions. The space between reality and the plane upon which I resided with Hatshepsut was the space where nothing hurt. The grief and worry were gone when Hatshepsut and I were together. It was as if my mind could place them in a box and leave it there while I sat with my Queen. It was always there, waiting for me once I returned to my body. But I was at peace when I was in a vision.

The bathtub experience was my first real brush with choosing to stay in a vision and have some control over it. As time went on, it became more accessible and easier to navigate and sort of *drop in* wherever I wanted. However, the bathtub also taught me how the outside world affecting my physical body could impact my soul, mind, or whatever was off traveling with Hatshepsut. And that was how I came to view it... traveling.

When I wasn't with Hatshepsut, I longed to be with her. I made excuses with everyone and locked myself away in Hanan's guest house, curtains drawn, body tucked up in bed to ensure I was comfortable and not in a bathtub with rapidly cooling water. I didn't even light candles or incense and didn't drink or eat beforehand, not wanting to be pulled out of a vision to deal with bodily demands.

"You grow stronger each day, Julia," Hatshepsut said one day when I came to her in the ritual room. I practically preened over her approval. She was alone as she'd been each time I came to her. I thought it odd, but I also felt lucky not to drop in on some crucial meeting with her advisors or anyone else to whom we'd have to explain my presence.

"It gets easier each time," I said. "I know exactly where I'm going, who I'm looking for now, and what you sort of *feel* like. I think that helps focus my mind and my power." I had stopped exploring much else since making such strong connections with her. Nothing else seemed to matter. It was easy with her. Both in terms of finding her and existing with her. She'd begun to tutor me in magic, and I was growing stronger and more confident in my abilities.

"Do you relay our meetings to the other priestesses?" she asked. We were soaking in the ritual pool, the water hot and soothing even in my vision state. I tilted my head back against the lip of the pool and closed my eyes, trying to find the right words.

"I haven't, no," I started. "They don't understand. They're playing at magic and have forgotten so much and don't want to do anything to change up how they're living life. And... I don't feel like sharing you with them. Is that wrong of me, your grace?"

Hatshepsut laughed, throaty and rich.

"My darling, you must call me Shesout. Enough with these formal titles. I am Hatshepsut, Pharaoh out there, but when together, we are Julia and Shesout. Friends." My skin blushed with joy and pride.

"*Shesout,*" I tried out, the name foreign in my mouth. "I like that." She smiled at me, and I warmed from the inside out. I had pulled further and further away from the sisterhood. The grief carved a vast gap between us, but I'd allowed it to continue to gape and grow, and I felt like the only person in the world who saw me was across from me now. And she was a long-dead queen that no one else could communicate with but me.

"The priestesses have grown complacent in their beliefs and rituals, but you have not, beloved friend. You sought me out. Found me across time and space in your search for answers. They will have to face the truth soon, and you will be the one to bring it to them."

I let her words sink into the water around us and into my skin. I didn't feel like some harbinger of truth. I felt like a woman desperate enough for answers to do the unimaginable. It ended up with me here, in this bizarre reality that no one knew existed.

We soaked in the ritual pool for a long while, the comfortable silence of friends who don't need to fill a void with empty words. I let her presence wash over me. Besides her kind words of friendship, her presence was soothing. Our magic called to one another, and I was comforted and seen when we were together. Her praise and assurance that I was on the path to truth burned like a flame inside my chest. I felt a dark nudge of pride that *I* was right. Everyone else was wrong... a validation Shesout fanned each time we came together. Before long, whenever I was with the sisterhood, little bubbles of anger popped around me like champagne bubbles-tiny and furious on my tongue.

"Come, let us practice together. I will teach you to see someone's truth in their mind."

We left the ritual pool, wrapping ourselves in soft cotton towels, and made our way to thick cushions on the floor.

"Senenmut wanted to bring more formal things to this place, but I don't want to be a pharaoh here. I didn't want pretension or extravagance. I have enough of that in the palace. I only want to be a priestess on equal footing with the others here in this place of magic. He argued, but I insisted." She smiled, the corners of her eyes crinkling. "He's the only one who will argue with me."

"He sounds like he deeply respects you," I offered, trying not to pry but wanting to know more.

"He does. He is also deeply devoted to me and has been for a long time." She had a dreamy look, and I knew the devotion went both ways. "I don't know what I would do without him."

My stomach lurched, and the grief waiting on the other side of time and space found its way to me. "I know that feeling," I said softly. "It has been impossibly hard without Andrew."

"Well, if I am to help you find a way to help him, we have to get to work," she said, though her face was soft with empathy. "Come, sit close to me, and we'll begin."

Until then, we had mostly talked and performed elemental and healing spells together, though those were more potent and efficient in this place. She also tested my abilities and gave me histories and things to prepare me for whatever I needed to help Drew. I'd tried and had little success with the new healing spells she'd shown me, and I hoped that whatever we would do next would be one of the keys to unlocking answers.

"You have to perform this with pure intentions," she said once I scooted closer. We were facing each other, legs crossed, knees barely touching. "You have to make physical contact. I find it easier to use my hands, my fingers focusing my magic where I want it to go. Like this," she said. She placed her fingers gently on the sides of my face, thumbs bracing my chin, fingers on my temples and the sides of my head. "Close your eyes. Breathe. And think about what you want to know the truth about."

I breathed gently, feeling her fingers on my skin as I watched her. She concentrated, furrowing her thick brows ever so slightly, a crease forming between them. Her magic sought me out, the slightest tingling pressure on my skin, and I closed my eyes. A few short moments passed, and she sighed, a sad song that seemed to escape from her lips without realizing it. I opened my eyes and saw a tear tracing down her cheek.

"What is it, Shesout?" I whispered.

"So much love. So much joy. And now, so much pain," she answered back with a yearning in her voice. "I sought out your truth with your lover, Andrew. I wanted to see if he is worth saving." She opened her eyes and looked at me, sadness and love spilling over her cheeks. "Hathor has blessed you, Julia. Truly and deeply blessed you both. I am sorry I ever questioned it."

My sadness and love spilled down my face. Tenderly, she brushed the tears away, bringing her wet fingertips to her heart in a gesture so heartfelt it brought more tears to my eyes. I wiped her cheeks and did the same with my wet fingertips. It felt reverent. Holy. We sat together for a few breaths, hands over our hearts, cheeks shining, silent and contemplative.

"Okay. So, tell me how you did that," I finally said, words soft and quiet in the candlelit room.

Shesout sat up a bit straighter and swiped the backs of her hands over her face.

"You have to focus your power on whatever you're seeking. Really focus on it. The same as when you travel to visit me, I imagine." I nodded. "And you shouldn't look for anything unrelated to what you're searching for. It isn't pure or kind to delve further into the mind than what is necessary." She narrowed her eyes. "And you might find hidden things you don't want to see along the way."

With that ominous warning, she pulled my hands to her face and placed my fingers along her skull as she'd held mine. Her skin was warm from the pool and slightly damp from her tears. I held her gently as she'd held me.

"What should I search for?" I asked. Our eyes met, and the bright amber pools of hers shone.

"I have seen your love with Andrew. Seek out my truth with my Senenmut." I took a deep breath, the fragrant oils she used filling my nose. I focused on Hatshepsut and the dreamy look of love she'd worn earlier. I didn't have a face for Senenmut, but I hoped her love would be strong enough. "Gently press your fingers on my temples and along my jawline." She pressed her hands along my fingers, showing me where to apply pressure.

"Now, think of a word, something strong and resonant when you think of searching and finding an answer... a truth... opening a locked door...lighting a flame in the darkness..." she trailed off, giving me the space to ruminate.

I pictured a locked door. Strong and thick wood bolted shut with a huge metal bolt that came down across the center, keeping me out. I imagined touching the door and the bolt lifting with ease... only it didn't. It stayed locked. I tensed up and focused harder.

"No, no. You're using too much pressure. You must finesse it. There's a nuance to the searching. You must be gentle with the mind you're seeking, or its own defenses will keep you out."

I forced myself to relax, breathing deeply.

The locked door was too heavy. Too much. I imagined lighting a candle in the darkness. I felt the effortlessness of the lighting. The whisper of a thought that would bring forth the light. Pinpricks of light shone behind my eyes, growing larger until an image formed. Hatshepsut, in her formal attire, a false beard and crown, turned towards a man. He wasn't tall, maybe an inch taller than Hatshepsut, with broad shoulders and a commanding presence. Senenmut came to her, steps confident and stride certain. Slowly and tenderly, he removed her crown, the heavy double crown of a united Upper and Lower Egypt. He turned and placed it on a low table in her bed chamber. He reached into a bowl and pulled out a cloth, ringing excess water into the bowl. He turned back towards her and reached for her false beard, gently wiping the fabric along the edges, loosening whatever fixative she'd used to hold it in place. It came loose, and he washed her face, peppering her with kisses between ablutions.

He turned and placed the cloth back in the bowl and the beard next to the crown and turned back to his lover, for she was no longer his pharaoh. He reached up and unbound her hair, running his fingers along her scalp, massaging the hair loose and gifting her with the comfort of solid fingers. I heard a sigh escape her lips. He laughed a throaty, smoky chuckle and kissed her on the mouth, hands still buried in her hair. She wrapped her arms around him, holding tight, keeping him in place. I wanted to turn away from such a private moment but was transfixed. She pulled away after a few moments, breathless, and he began to undo her robe. They fell to the floor layer after layer, and she stood bare to him. His hands were gentle on her body, not needy or wanting, but comforting and filled with love. He knelt before her, hands roaming, still kneading and caring for her. His devotion was apparent, as was hers, as she looked down at him.

"You are the only one who can truly see me. Who I truly am. Not who they want me to be or who I pretend to be. But me. You see me,

Senenmut." He looked up at her, his face shining with admiration, his strong jawline and prominent cheekbones made more so by the smile that lit up his face. He rose to meet her, and they came together again, mouths and bodies pressed tightly together, and I forced myself to turn away and let go of what I was seeing.

"And did you see my own truth, *Merit*?" Shesout asked, her face flushing the way I knew my own was.

I looked up at her, confused. "*Merit*?" I asked.

She smiled. "It means beloved. And you are a beloved friend to me, Julia."

I swallowed a lump in my throat and nodded, my hands dropping to my lap.

"So, did you see my own truth?"

"I did. It was... beautiful." I was warm in the room, but what I'd witnessed made me hot all over. A throbbing between my legs sent waves of embarrassment down my spine and longing through my heart.

"Yes. He is a beautiful soul. A beautiful man. And we, too, have been blessed by Hathor." She was wistful, the dreamy look across her face once more.

You told him he was the only one who truly saw you," I said. "I feel that way about Andrew as well. I have to play a role with everyone else, but he sees who I truly am." I trailed off, and Hatshepsut held my face in her hands and looked me in the eyes.

"We will find a way to bring him back," she said, voice unwavering. "On my honor, we will."

I didn't stay long after that. There wasn't much more to say, and I could sense that all the talk of Senenmut had lit a fire of desire in her that she wanted nothing more than to see to. We parted with plans and promises, and I left her to return to my own time, desires, and longing.

# 20

## *An Echo of Magic*

Weeks passed, and before I knew it, I was facing down another full moon ceremony. Hanan had told me I didn't have to come or participate and could take as much time as needed. But I knew I eventually had to face it head-on. It helped that Hatshepsut and I often met in the ritual room and bathed in the pool after practicing magic together. That space held new memories from Andrew's failed ritual. Even if they were memories from that liminal space or inside my mind—wherever they existed—I held tight to them.

Even still, entering the space with the group felt heavy. A weight settled in my chest as I shrugged off my clothes and donned my robe. I moved like I was wading through water, memories thick in the air around me.

Hanan chanted.

My palms were sweating. They were clammy in the hands of Marwa and Dell, who were silently at my side after hearing how I'd reacted the month before, though we still hadn't made up. They lent their support. But it only added weight to my chest.

Images fluttered through the smoke on the periphery of my vision, distracting me. Taunting me.

I imagined cool breezes winding around my ankles, though the air was still and warm with the early summer heat.

Hanan continued to chant. Called down power. And still, my mind betrayed me. Wandered. Disconnected. The thread that had once connected me so deeply to her was growing thinner and thinner as I pulled away.

Thoughts and visions of Hatshepsut and Andrew flitted through my mind, twining together to create a perfect distraction of the two people I longed to be with most. Hanan's call was not strong enough to keep me focused. The herby smoke wasn't enough to keep my mind empty.

Finally, I let go of the hope that I would have a good experience and let my mind take over. It was kind enough to zero in on Hatshepsut and give me a reprieve from grief. I'd practiced enough magic with her to know what it felt like when our power intertwined, and I craved it. The pulsing energy that threaded through my palms was barely registering as a current compared to what it was like when I was with her.

Hatshepsut was raw, unbridled power. It encouraged my own and made me wild with energy and magic but held in a way that gave me control. Her strength was visceral. Strong. It set me alight. The magic that wound its way around me and through my sisters felt like play. It whispered cool breath over the light that burned with Hatshepsut and made my power flicker in and out.

Hanan chanted. My sisters answered. I stayed silent... folding in on myself. Their voices echoed off the temple walls and bounced off my skin. Time, words, and weak magic passed back and forth around me. I stood, unmoving, hands clammy, body keyed up but pulsing magic untapped.

Finally, we moved to the pool. I went through the motions, anointing my body with oil and melting into the hot, fragrant water. The moonbeams pulsed in the night air. And still, I longed for Hatshepsut. Longed for her magic. Longed to feel *something* like what I felt with her.

I plunged beneath the water, holding my breath until my lungs burned. Spots danced behind my eyelids, forcing me to seek out air. I rested my head against the lip of the pool and closed my eyes. Almost instantly, I was thrown into a vision. It was as if Hatshepsut was waiting for me in the pool across time and space.

"You feel different, *Merit*," she said when I opened my eyes and found myself in the ritual pool beside her. She was alone, soaking in the water, the moon door above us thrown open, the night sky bright with stars.

"Shesout, I was desperate to find you. It is a full moon in my time," I sighed. "And I'm in the middle of the ritual, and it feels like nothing compared to how I feel when we work our magic together. It is a shadow... an echo of magic." I tilted my face to the sky and closed my eyes, restless energy finally settling down.

"I worry for the other priestesses," she said quietly. "They have forgotten the old ways, and there will come a time when they are called upon to stand for themselves and your world, and I fear they will fail. You *must* find a way to open their eyes, *Merit*. You must."

The urgency in her words settled deep in my bones. After spending time with her and knowing what the magic should feel like, I knew that what we were practicing was nothing that would save us if it ever came down to it. But I also knew that Hanan wouldn't take anything I said seriously right now. I had been so adamant about practicing more potent magic to heal Andrew that I knew she'd think I was still only concerned about that.

"For now, let us draw down the power you need." She tilted her face to the sky and began to hum, a guttural sound that sang to my core. I mirrored her and met her chant, my bones vibrating with the sound of magic in my throat.

The water churned... bubbled... spit. The beams of moonlight grew brighter and brighter, a dizzying display of raw power. My eyes squeezed shut against the light. Ozone, thick and heady, filled the space around us. The smell of energy and power grew more potent with the light.

She pulled me to her, oil and water-slick skin hot against mine. She pressed flush against me, breasts and stomach flattened against my back, one arm wrapped around my waist, holding me in place, the other arm raised in invocation. I pressed a hand to my chest, pressing hard against my breast bone, integrating myself into my body in the moment... an old coping mechanism from therapy and a technique I'd learned to use to ground myself in my magic. My body was sandwiched between my hand and Hatshepsut, magic flowing through and around us. Wind whipped our hair away from our faces. I was startled for a moment—the memory of another cool breeze grappling to the surface. Hatshepsut held me tighter, feeling my attention slip. The memory lashed away with her fierceness.

Her hand fell away, wrapping across my chest, holding tight.

A lover's embrace.

The humming became a song we sang together.

A prayer to Isis.

An entreaty to the moon.

A love song to magic.

To each other. To our sisters.

My body arched against Hatshepsut's, magic filling my body to the brim. I was electric. Every inch of me alight with power. Limbs trembling with the ecstasy of it. I turned towards her; bodies pressed tightly together in the still bubbling water. I tipped my head back, lips parting slightly as Hatshepsut quirked her head at me, bending down and gently-

"Julia! Julia! Are you okay?" Rough hands shook my body, snapping me out of my vision. My heart was racing, the throbbing loud in my ears.

"What?" I growled, angry that they'd woken me. I panted, my body still keyed up with magic and the abrupt ending to a vision.

"I'm sorry, *Habibti*. You were moaning and sounded like you were in pain," Marwa answered softly, her arm resting gently on my shoulder.

"I'm fine," I said, pushing away from the pool wall, making for the edge to climb out.

"Were you having a vision?" Hanan asked.

I shrugged my shoulders, trying to act nonchalant.

"What was it? Did you see her? Hatshepsut?" She was so eager, so earnest in her curiosity.

I shrugged again, not wanting to share Hatshepsut with her. Not wanting to answer her questions. Wanting to protect my time with my queen.

"I'm not sure what to make out of it," I said, still breathless. "It's a lot to sort through and figure out." I avoided Hanan's gaze and felt the stares of everyone else bore into me. Their surprise was as apparent as their frustration. I hadn't shared much with them, and no one knew how deeply connected I was to Hatshepsut. I had toyed with telling them, especially Marwa, but couldn't bring myself to. There was too much hurt I had let fester. Too much pain. My time with Hatshepsut was the one thing that was truly mine and mine alone. She was the only one who seemed willing to help me find something to help Andrew. And so, I stayed quiet, ignoring the curious stares and the pointed questions from Han an.

We closed out the night and made our way back home, and I crawled into bed, magic stronger than I'd ever felt before, but my heart and mind unsettled.

I slept the dreamless sleep of the exhausted.

# 21

## The Ghosts That We Know

*Marwa*

"We need to do something about Julia," Marwa said. Hanan sat across from her, nursing a cup of coffee. She'd called her and Salma, who was, as always, right next to her, to come over. Something was deeply wrong with Julia, and they needed to do something before it was too late.

"Maybe so, but every interaction she and I have had lately has been an argument, or we barely speak at all. She is angry and wants to blame all of us for what happened that night. I won't have it. I understand, I do. But it is no one's fault, Marwa."

"You mistake where she lays the blame, my dear," Marwa argued softly. "She is angry with herself, and that is the worst kind of angry to be."

"Mama, I think you're blinded by your love for her," Salma said. She crossed and uncrossed her arms, the defiance she'd been born with constantly warring to come to the forefront, no matter the interaction.

"*Habibti,* I do love her, but I am not blind. She is hurting. She has pulled away, and we've all allowed it to happen in the hope that time and a little space would help her to heal. But it hasn't. Enough time has passed. We must do something or risk losing her forever."

"I get that, Mama, I do," Salma argued. "But she's been absolutely horrible to Hanan about the scrolls and—" Hanan reached out and laid a hand on Salma's arm.

"I can fight my own battles, Sal," she interrupted. "She doesn't know enough about the scrolls to know what she's asking."

"So, maybe it's time to tell her."

"Mama, you can't be serious," Salma said, sitting up in her seat, ready for a fight.

"I am."

"Marwa, you know I love and respect you, but—"

"Before you tell me that I wouldn't understand, need I remind you that only a few years ago, it was your mother and me who sat side-by-side deciding the fate of this group?" She narrowed her gaze at both of the younger women. "I may be an old woman now, but I remember. I know the risks. And she deserves to know the truth. She must understand you're not withholding the power to wake Andrew just to spite her."

Salma opened her mouth to argue more, and Marwa gave her the look that had quieted her down when she was young. It didn't always work back then, but there was enough time and respect between them that it worked now. Hanan stared at the cup of coffee in her lap. Marwa gave a tiny shake of her head to Salma, and they both sat quietly, letting Hanan think.

Finally, she looked up and bit her lip, fighting back tears.

"I don't want to relive it all."

"I know, *Habibti*." Marwa nodded. "I know. But sometimes our greatest pain can be our greatest strength when we need it to be." She knew this to be true because losing Hanan's mom, Aisha, was the greatest pain of Marwa's life. Aisha had been her steward, her lifelong confidante, her best friend.

The girls—for they would always be girls to Marwa, no matter their age—sat quietly for a few minutes. She knew Hanan was replaying everything that needed to be said to Julia in her mind. Salma waited to see what Hanan needed. Marwa was always struck by how similar they looked to Aisha and herself when they were together like this.

Aisha and Marwa had grown up together— like the girls who sat before Marwa now—raised as sisters but more than that. Aisha and Marwa had been inseparable and knew each other on such a deep level that she knew there was no way they could have been anything other than soul mates. Just as Marwa knew, Salma and Hanan were soul mates. It had taken time, but Marwa had learned to turn the pain of losing a part of her soul into something she knew Aisha would be proud of. She guided Salma, Hanan, and the rest of the women with as much empathy and love as possible. Marwa wanted them to know love and support with no conditions. No... she searched her brain for the American saying... ropes attached?

"I know you'll do the right thing, *Habibti*," Marwa said.

Hanan looked up at her, eyes filled with tears that she fought to keep from falling. She looked so young for someone who carried the weight of the world on her shoulders.

"Maybe we tell everyone?" Salma asked. "I mean, they all need to know. Naomi has asked about learning from the scrolls before, too. Well, all of them, really, have asked. Naomi and Julia have been the only ones not okay with being told no." Salma was right. They had all been curious, and how could they not be? Hanan pinched the space between her eyebrows and searched for an argument.

"Hanan, she's right. They've all wondered," Marwa said. "And it is a testament to their trust in you that they've let it go and not pushed back with their curiosity. It's time. They're your sisters. They'll understand and support you." Hanan finally let go of her face and nodded at both the women before excusing herself and walking out into the garden. Salma made to go after her, and Marwa reached out a hand to stop her daughter.

"Let her go, *Habibti*," she said. "She needs some space."

The girls didn't stay much longer, and Marwa was left alone with her thoughts and her best friend's ghost.

"I'm trying to do my best by her, Aisha. How I wish you were still here," she said to the empty room, wishing it wasn't so empty for the millionth time.

## 22

## *Cursed*

Days passed after the ritual, and I did my best to avoid Hanan and her questions. I rose before she did and went to Andrew's room to hide out, or I made it look like I was gone or still asleep till after she'd left for work. I knew, eventually, I'd have to answer her, but I didn't want to. The full moon ceremony had left me confused. What I'd felt with Shesout had been incredible, but it was also laced with some uncomfortable truths I needed to search for and about myself.

I was pulling further and further away from everyone. I knew I would one day have to reconcile that, but I couldn't get past the hurt. Projecting the responsibility I'd felt in Andrew's demise made it easier for me to at least halfway function. The rational side of my brain wanted to call me out on my own bullshit, but I had long since quieted rationality in favor of emotions.

A part of me felt a little like my hope was slipping. Andrew had been unconscious for two months, and it was starting to feel like he'd never wake again. It was harder to hold on to hope when the one person who always helped rally me in my darkest moments was lost to me. The longer his eyes stayed closed, the more not only my hope slipped away but little pieces of myself also. A shift was happening, a rearrangement of the fragments of my very soul. I wondered if, and when, Andrew ever woke up, would he even be able to recognize the person I was becoming?

Would I?

Eventually, I couldn't avoid Hanan any longer. Though I'd gotten up early to head to the clinic to see Andrew, she beat me to the garden and was waiting on me, steaming cup of tea in hand.

"Before you run away, come and sit by me this morning," Hanan said.

Her voice was soft and her tone light, but I couldn't help but feel like I was in trouble for something. I walked over and sat across from her. She nodded towards the cup on the table, and I gratefully picked up the warm cup of tea and took a fortifying sip.

"I wasn't going to run away," I said.

"You and I both know that's not true," Hanan said, smiling. "And that's fine, I understand. We don't see eye to eye on everything, but I think it's time I explained why to you."

She leaned forward and set her cup down on the table between us.

"A long time ago, before my mother was born, there was a member of the sisterhood who wanted to do more with our magic. She wondered the same questions you and Naomi have wondered. *Why don't we use the scrolls? Why don't we use stronger magic and do greater things?* At first, it was harmless. She was young and curious. And then she mastered her powers and grew hungry for more."

I shifted uncomfortably in my seat.

"Somewhere along the way, she found the scrolls. No one is clear on how, exactly, she did it. My grandmother was Steward then and pregnant with my mom when she discovered the scrolls were missing."

"Wait, this woman found them and stole them without them knowing?"

Hanan nodded. "Yes. We don't often go to the scrolls. They're protected, more so now than they were back then, obviously. It had been a few months since my grandmother had strengthened the wards. When the woman disappeared, she went to check them and found them gone. Ilse had spent months and months asking for the scrolls, and then suddenly, she stopped. She missed a full moon ceremony. And then everyone started realizing they hadn't seen her in a few days or weeks. I still don't know how they didn't realize what was going on..." she trailed off. I didn't say anything and let her sit with the weight of leadership and the past.

"How did they find her?" I asked.

"She actually came to them," Hanan said. "She had been trying to find a spell to bring back the dead and needed something from the ritual room. She snuck in one night, but it was close to the full moon, and my grandmother was there, bathing in the ritual pool, trying to find some peace so she could try and piece together where this woman, Ilse, could be. Imagine their surprise when she walked into the room. My grandmother was convinced that Hatshepsut herself sent her directly there in that moment. She saw it as divine intervention and an answered prayer."

"What happened then? Surely she tried to run?" I asked, fully invested in the story.

"She needed something, so she couldn't very well run, could she?" Hanan shrugged. "Ilse actually took the opportunity to plead with my grandmother one last time. She told her of the impossible things she'd learned and the power they could all have at their fingertips if they'd only look." I opened my mouth to say something, but Hanan raised her hand to stop me.

"But she had gone mad from the magic. My grandmother could see it in her eyes and feel it in the chaotic energy rolling off her like an oily fog. What happened next is not very clear—my grandmother would never talk about it in depth. It terrified her. They argued and fought, and in the midst of their fighting, Ilse pulled out a notebook she'd written some spells on and fought dirty. I don't know what happened in the temple. No one does but my grandmother and the night sky now. But dark magic was wielded, curses were hurled in all directions, and, in the scuffle, some spell backfired and hit Ilse in the chest, killing her instantly. Light from all the magic that was being used exploded like fireworks in the room and rained down on my grandmother. Every spot on her body that the light hit left burn marks and burrowed under the skin." I sucked in a breath.

"But what did they do with Ilse?" I asked.

"They said she died of natural causes, had a funeral, and she became the example for why we don't go looking through the scrolls," Hanan answered. "What else could they do? There was no way to go to the police or tell anyone the truth of what happened. So, they did what they had to do and covered it up."

"God, that's just...crazy,"

"It was. Afterward, they waited for a long time. Watching and waiting for something horrible to happen. But nothing did. My grandmother was terrified to give birth to my mom, convinced that the baby was going to die from the trauma she'd endured, from some sort of curse. But she was healthy. My mom thrived. I don't think she had more than a sniffle her whole childhood. And still, my grandmother worried herself sick. It took years for her to let go of the worry that something catastrophic would happen. Eventually, by the time my mother was a young adult, everyone had taken a deep breath and thought they were in the clear." Hanan looked dreamy, her eyes unfocused, her thoughts in the past. I had a feeling in the pit of my stomach that this wasn't going to end well.

"When my mom first got sick, no one thought anything. We waited for her diagnosis. They ran test after test and couldn't find anything."

"What do you mean they couldn't find anything?"

"She was incredibly ill, and every test came back normal. Every scan, blood test, everything was within normal limits."

I paled. "The curse."

Hanan nodded, tears in her eyes. "The curse finally came to fruition," she confirmed. "My grandmother was beside herself. She knew that this was her comeuppance for what she saw as her greatest failing. We left Egypt for a short time and flew to London and then France, trying to find answers. No one could find anything. And no doctor could find any medication or treatment that would alleviate her symptoms or her pain."

Hanan explained that the sisterhood tried everything. They made medicines, performed rituals and spells, and even went to the scrolls to find answers, but her mom refused to let them try anything from them.

"She was worried that something else would happen and someone else would suffer later for her relief. It was horrible."

Hanan no longer looked like a leader shouldering the responsibility of the sisterhood. She looked like a grieving daughter.

"I was convinced that the scrolls had the answer we needed to bring her back from the brink. You have to understand she was in excruciating pain every single day. She wasn't eating or sleeping. It had been years since she'd first gotten sick. She was a shell of the woman she once was."

I stopped myself from narrowing my gaze at her. It wasn't the time to remind her that I did understand very well.

"It got to the point where she no longer wanted to be alive. She had done some research into euthanization and was making plans when, blessedly, her body gave out, and she didn't have to make that call," Hanan's voice caught on a sob. She mumbled an apology and dabbed at the tears on her face.

"I'm so sorry, Hanan, I really am," I said. And I was. My heart ached for her. To watch someone you love waste away and want to end their life was a nightmare. I wanted to reach out to her, but the distance between us had grown too big to close with a touch. I squeezed the mug Hanan had given me when I sat down, the heat from the tea stinging.

"It's been many years now, but it feels like it only just happened," she cleared her throat, trying to clear the emotion to tell the rest of the story. Her grandmother had left then. She'd left Hanan and the sisterhood a note that explained she couldn't face them or her failures anymore and fled.

"She eventually came back, though?" I asked. I remembered Hanan mentioning that she and Salma's grandmother were living together and were both widowed.

"Eventually, yes. But she was gone for years. I think that's why my dad left in the beginning. To try to find her and bring her back. And then he realized it was less painful out of Luxor, and he didn't come back."

My heart dropped into my stomach as I really saw the hurt she must have gone through. To lose not only her mother but her grandmother and then her dad, I couldn't imagine how awful that felt. It made sense that she blamed the scrolls and the power they held.

"My grandmother was convinced that if she left us, she'd take any of the curse's lingering magic with her and protect the rest of us. Personally, I think the curse took what it wanted, and it wouldn't have been an issue, but there was no arguing with her. When Salma's grandfather died and left her grandmother alone, she finally returned, and they both live together." Hanan paused, and her eyes dropped to her lap. "She refuses to speak on the past and what happened. She does her best to live an uncomplicated life but will have nothing to do with magic or the sisterhood. That part of her is broken beyond repair."

Her words hung in the air, heavy with unsaid things, and I got the feeling that she was keeping something from me. What, I had no clue. I'd met both her and Salma's grandmother's at breakfast the morning after the big send-off ritual we'd had for me earlier in the year. Hanan's grandmother had been warm and friendly, but now that I thought on it, she hadn't participated in the ritual itself or spoke of magic at all.

There wasn't much left to say after that. I couldn't make any promises to Hanan about the scrolls. I still felt like there was more we could do in a safer way than what Ilse had tried to do. I wasn't looking for power for power's sake. Therein lay the difference.

# 23

## *Veiled Threats*

Despite hearing the reason for not utilizing the scrolls, I couldn't overcome the frustration of not looking through them. I understood Hanan's fear, but there was more we could do, and she was letting a cautionary tale stop me from finding answers. It felt like Hanan hoped her explanation would erase all the tension between us, and we could return to normal and move on.

But months of Andrew being unconscious with no sign of waking wasn't something I could just move on from. I wanted my old life back. I hated this new normal. Hated the routine of clinic visits and tears. During the first few weeks of Andrew's coma, it felt like nothing would ever feel normal again. It was like a huge hole had been carved out of me, and I simply existed in a place of trauma response and fatigue. I wasn't done searching for ways to reverse the damage we'd done and get back to how life was before.

A few weeks after Hanan explained why we didn't use the scrolls, I was leaving the clinic, my nerves frayed and tender. Andrew, though he still looked peaceful, the devastating changes of being in a coma for months were taking their toll. He was almost unrecognizable, and my heart ached. My phone buzzed in my pocket and I answered without even looking at the screen.

"Ah, Missus Wheelright, finally!" The syrupy southern voice sang out into the phone—Luke Willis from the lawyer's office handling Gram's estate.

"Um, yes?" I said, confused, wondering how he'd gotten my number.

"I have been trying to get ahold of you for a few weeks now. It seems like the number you left with us is no longer active. I contacted Miz Coker, but she didn't know how to reach you and was just that worried about you, you know. You really ought to give her a call so she doesn't worry herself to death, poor thing."

I shuddered. His voice immediately threw me back to that terrible week. The fog of cleaning out the house that held my happiest childhood memories and the memories of my grandparents' happy life. And then the horrors that unfolded a few short days later.

"I'm sorry about that," I stammered, hating how nervous I sounded. "I've moved in the last few months—"

"Yes, I am aware," he interrupted. "After searching your file, I finally found a separate contact for an Edie Stewart. When I got ahold of her, she gave me your new number, and lo and behold, here you are."

I sighed, annoyed with Edie, but I understood he probably weaseled it out of her.

"What can I help you with, Mr. Willis?" I wanted nothing more than to hurl the phone across the street and never deal with him again.

"Well, your grandmother's estate is finally coming out of probate, and everything is settled and finished here. All the documents have been signed, and you are the legal owner of the house on Pollardswood Drive."

I exhaled a sigh of relief.

"That's great news. Thank you." I hadn't even thought about probate or estates or wills in months. Finally, selling the house and washing my hands of North Carolina sounded heavenly.

"Yes, I thought you'd be happy to hear it," he said. "Now, have you had a chance to talk to your husband and see what he wants to do with the house? It's in a great neighborhood, you know. Great place to bring your kids and raise 'em right."

I rolled my eyes and let out an annoyed breath.

"As the house is in my name and not my husband's, I have decided to sell." I wasn't giving him an ounce more detail than he needed to know. Hopefully, this would be the last time I had to deal with him.

"Well, now, that's a real shame. A real shame." I could almost see his disapproving head shake.

"It'll just have to be a shame. I'm not coming back there. Thanks so much for your time, Mr. Willis. Is there anything I need to do, or can you email all the information to me?"

"Now that we've spoken, I can send everything over via email. The documents are password protected, so my secretary will send over a second email with the password and directions on how to access them."

"Great. If that's all, thanks so much."

"Well, there is one last thing, Miz Wheelright."

I closed my eyes and leaned my head back in annoyance. "Yes?"

"I have a message here from Gordon Mitchell's father, Warren. You'll have heard by now that poor Pastor Mitchell went to be with the lord suddenly last year. Such a wretched thing. I'm sure you were just so upset about your old flame passin' on."

My blood ran cold, and adrenaline shot down my spine. I made a noncommittal noise in my throat, and he continued.

"Well, seems like Mister Warren wanted to make sure you knew that his son had passed on. And, since you all were like family, he wanted to help in any way with sorting out your grandmother's estate."

I swallowed down bile.

"He said to be sure and let you know that he hurried the process along. He made a few phone calls and made sure the judge got to it right away." I heard papers rustle on his end. "I've got a message he sent over the other day. Let's see... ah, here it is.

*Dearest Jolene, I know this message is finding you far, far away from the great state of North Carolina. I wanted to extend my deepest condolences for our mutual loss. Gordon was such a special boy; you'll remember him vividly, I'm sure. You meant a great deal to him and to me. I wanted to be sure to reach out and remind you of our history together and how important those ties are. Regards—Warren Mitchell, Senator of North Carolina.*

What a great family the Mitchells are..."

The blood was pounding in my ears, and a roaring, panicked noise played over the continued ramblings of the Mitchells' greatness from Luke Willis. I couldn't take any more, couldn't hold the phone to my ear any longer.

"I'm sorry, I've really got to go. Thanks so much for your call." I hung up without waiting for a response. I gripped the phone tight, my knuckles white with tension as I stared at the phone and sucked in stuttering breaths. I don't know why I ever thought I'd escape the Mitchells. Their reach was vast, and Warren Mitchell was not content to sit back and let anything go.

I made it back to Hanan's on autopilot. When the taxi driver pulled up to her house, I had no memory of how we even got there. I didn't even thank him as I got out. I went to the gate, steps shaky and nerves frayed.

It was sobering to think that Warren Mitchell's veiled threats could rattle me this much, even after all this time and all this distance.

I found Dell in the kitchen, making lunch. She was humming softly under her breath, swaying to a song playing from her phone.

"Hey, Dell," I said.

She turned around, her smile faltering when she saw my face. "Oh... what happened? Is it Drew?"

I shook my head. "No, no, sorry. He's fine... well, the same. It's something different." I took a breath, still not calmed down from the encounter with the estate lawyer.

"I heard from Luke Willis, the lawyer in North Carolina in charge of Gram's estate."

"That little weasel is such an asshole," she said, rolling her eyes.

"Yeah, he is. He definitely asked if my husband had decided to sell the house yet."

She rolled her eyes again and groaned out loud.

"But that's not what's wrong. Apparently, Warren Mitchell tracked him down and left me a note."

Dell's face drained of color, and her mouth fell open in a surprised *o*.

"Yeah. He didn't come right out and say anything, but the threat was there. He reminded me of our long history together, which was... dripping with veiled threats. I don't know. I hoped he'd forget about me and leave it be."

"I know I had only one very brief meeting with him, but he didn't strike me as the type to let things go so easily."

I nodded.

"Yeah, I know. I hoped that I could be well and truly done with them. My whole life has been running from my past and what those men did to me. I just feel like I'll never be free of them."

Dell took in a deep breath. "Well, I hate to sound so blasé about it, but you're at least free of one of them. And Warren Mitchell won't live forever. Besides, you don't want to return to North Carolina, do you? It's not home, right?"

"It's never really been home. Not since everything happened. And it certainly won't be now that Gram is gone. There's nothing for me there."

Dell finished making lunch and left me to my thoughts, looking over her shoulder a few times to check on me. I was lost in thought, images from my traumatic teenage years playing out on a loop punctuated with the nightmare that had been the catalyst for our move to Egypt and, ultimately, Drew's coma.

Dell and I ate lunch with the quiet silence of longtime friends. While things weren't completely better between us, the anger had fizzled out. I hadn't quite figured out what I would do about Warren Mitchell. Dell was right. I had no desire to move back to North Carolina, so sticking to his demand to stay away wouldn't be difficult. But, him tracking me down and leaving a message with the lawyer was a lot to process and, if I was being honest with myself, terrified me.

# 24

## *Bird Set Free*

The worry over Warren Mitchell kept my mind occupied. I struggled to sleep and focus on meditation. Before I knew it, it had been over a week since I'd seen Hatshepsut. It took a lot of focus—like I had to warm up a muscle that hadn't been used in a while. I had flashes of moonlight and visions of a spectral figure I couldn't quite make out, but Hatshepsut, my friend Shesout, was nowhere to be found.

It took some time, but I found her. She was alone in her bed chamber, and her back was turned away from the door. She didn't turn to face me when she spoke.

"It's been too long, *Merit*," she said, her voice icy and strained.

I sighed. Of course, she'd be upset with me for avoiding her.

"I'm sorry, Shesout," I started. "There's been a lot going on. It's only been a few days." I tried to think of an excuse but came up empty. As tempting as it was to make something up, she'd see a lie if she touched my cheek and searched it out. I walked towards her, tentative at first.

"It's been longer than a few days for me," she said. "Time must work differently between us. It feels as though it's been weeks. I have been lonely here without you. And worried."

I hung my head; her back was still to me, but shame flared and warmed my cheeks like I was standing in front of a roaring fire.

"I'm so sorry, Shesout. Truly. It's only been a few days for me. I just needed some space. My mind is so busy. I feel…" I trailed off, not knowing how to quantify my feelings. I'd spent the last few days digging deep and trying to figure out what was going on with myself. My mind was muddled, and my heart heavy. I didn't know what to say or how act around anyone, least of all myself.

"I understand. There are many times that I have needed to pull away and take some time to be with myself. I wish I had known. Or that we knew how time worked between us."

Hatshepsut was sad. I could see it in her eyes and the way she held herself. I knew she was upset with me, too. It seemed the theme of my life right now—displeasing everyone around me.

"I really am sorry," I said. "I wish I knew what to say to make things better." We sat in silence. It wasn't the comfortable silence we often shared but the stilted silence of two upset people who didn't know a way forward yet. I closed my eyes and rolled my head side to side, trying vainly to work out the kinks in my neck.

The minutes ticked by, and Hatshepsut seemed to decide to forgive my absence.

"I have been thinking," she finally said, gathering herself up. "Do the priestesses use my amulet to gather power between the moons?"

"What amulet?" I asked.

Hatshepsut shook her head, pinching the bridge of her nose and squeezing her eyes shut.

"I truly don't know when so much was lost." Her exasperation was a tangible thing across the room. I crossed over to her and stood closer. I didn't know what to say or how to apologize for something I had no control or knowledge about.

"When Isis and I made our agreement, she gifted me with an amulet that would harness the power of the moon. Should I need it, I would be able to call on an immense amount of magic in a time of need. With Thutmose's threats, she felt we needed something to protect people from him should he get his hands on the scrolls again." She pulled on the chain around her neck and held a small stone in the palm of her hand. "It doesn't look like much," she said. "We wanted it to be unassuming. But it is very powerful. It holds the moon's power at the very fullest of its strength."

She lifted it over her head and handed it to me. The chain was light as a feather, but the amulet was heavy, only about the size of a man's thumb, and warm from her skin. Roughly set in gold, the shimmering moonstone glowed with power in my hands, the pearlescent colors shimmering in my palm. I ran my thumb over it and felt it ripple with energy, the power lighting up and making my fingers tingle with wanting. I could feel the power in my hand and felt the pull to draw it into myself to feel the freedom in its strength.

"You can feel it, can't you?" Hatshepsut asked, breaking me out of my trance. I swallowed and nodded. "I can see it calling to you. The power. The strength. You want nothing more than to drain the amulet and draw it into yourself." Her words were a whisper, but they shouted and throbbed in my ears. The pendant pulsed in my hands, the beat matching the pace of my heart.

"Take it," she said, her eyes glowing in the light of the moonstone. "Pull it in... draw it into yourself and feel it feed your magic." Her words were magnetic, pulling me closer to her with wanting.

"How?" My voice scratched. The desire to harness the power vibrating in my hands filled me to bursting with its own kind of energy. Hatshepsut gently took the amulet from me, and the moment she touched it, I felt its absence. She slipped the chain over my head and placed the amulet between my breasts. Her fingertips grazed my skin and held there for a moment, electric against me, and then the pull of the moonstone dragged my attention back.

"Close your eyes and focus on the vibration. Once your heart beats in time with the moonstone, you can pull it inside of you. Similar to how you pull the power from the moon when it's full. Use your incantation...the words you call on." She spoke slowly, letting her words hang in the air and resonate deep within me. "Let the magic fill you up—let it race through your veins and give you power like you've not felt before."

Another breath and another long pause, urging me on.

"Don't let go, let it consume you."

Her face was inches from mine. Her breath on my cheek was sweet from the dates she loved so much. I closed my eyes. My heart pounded in my chest, hard against my ribs. I took a breath, long and slow. My heart continued to beat wildly in anticipation. I longed for the power of the moonstone. Hope tingled inside of me for the first time in months. Hope that this was the answer to healing Andrew. More power. More magic.

Hatshepsut placed her hands on either side of my face, cradling my cheeks. "Be calm, *Merit*. Your heartbeat needs to match the moonstones. Yours is wild and racing right now. Breathe slowly...with purpose."

We breathed together, a meditation of inhales and exhales. Every sense was on fire—Hatshepsut's fingertips were electric on my skin. I was hot all over, salty sweat beading on my lip and dripping slowly down my spine.

My heart began to slow. The throbbing vibration of the moonstone kept pulsing, beating against my chest like a drum. Every time I zeroed in on the sensation, my heartbeat would pick up out of rhythm, sending ripples of frustration down my spine. I focused my energy on my breath, breathing deeply and intentionally.

Every few breaths, my heart beat in time with the moonstone for a moment until they finally synced. A gentle knowing settled on my shoulders, and I began to chant.

Instead of feeling like I was asking the moon to lend me her energy, my focus was turned inward. Standing in the quiet room with Hatshepsut, with no moon to be seen, no other hands to hold, no taking turns or sharing the power, felt like liberation. I was a bird set free. I drank down power from the moonstone like a traveler lost in the desert who'd come across an oasis.

My skin tingled and burned as I was filled with raw power. My back arched, and I gasped, light leaving the moonstone and pouring down my throat. Hatshepsut held tight, helping to anchor me to the moment and keep me steady... heart beating with the moonstone's energy, holding tight to the connection. Magic raced through my veins—strengthening my hold and power. Flashes of light and warmth flooded me. After a few moments, the bright light from the stone faded, darkening to a black as dark as a moonless night.

I was dripping with sweat; it stung my eyes and was salty on my lips as it dripped down my face. I was lightheaded, dizzy with magic, hysterical with a giddiness that couldn't be contained. My skin was tight, and every nerve ending was lit up like a Christmas tree. Hatshepsut still held my face in her hands. Both of us were breathing heavily, eyes locked on each other. The resinous scent of myrrh was overpowered by her own sweat and heat, a primal smell that matched my own. Restless energy bubbled through me, chaotic from the moonstone.

I was drunk with power. From the moonstone. From her. My queen. From myself. It was like nothing I'd ever felt before. Power sang in my veins and hummed all around us.

"This is incredible," I finally said.

Hatshepsut laughed. The sound of her mirth filled the space, echoing off the walls.

"It is, isn't it?" She stepped away from me, but the magic I'd drawn from the moonstone was palpable between us. "The moonstone holds a power greater than anything I've felt before, save Isis' own power."

"What is she like?" I asked. Hatshepsut mentioned Isis before but hadn't spoken about the goddess other than to talk about her magic.

"Incredible," she whispered. Her face softened and looked dreamy as I watched her think about Isis. "She is incredible. Remember, I have spent my whole life worshipping the gods and goddesses. Before we can even speak, we're told stories of the gods who rule over our lives and afterlives. So, when she came to me—in a similar way that you come to me—I was speechless. I truly thought the god of dreaming was blessing me with such a gift." She paused, thinking back, I was sure, on their first meeting.

"It was like that when I first met you," I said, smiling. "Like I was dreaming." Hatshepsut smiled back at me and continued.

"Ah, *Merit*, there's no way I am comparable to our goddess. No matter how important I am to you." I shook my head and took her hand.

"You are a dream, Shesout. Isis may have gifted you with magic, but it is *your* call I answered—you that I sought out through time and space. You, Shesout, are incredible."

She smiled a coy smile that spoke to her humility and continued. She told me about Isis and how she came to her and taught her magic—how they formed the original sisterhood, Priestesses to Isis.

"Stay with me a while, *Merit*," Shesout said quietly after she'd finished her tale. "I'm not ready to be alone yet."

# 25

## The Egyptian Museum

My pull to stay with Hatshepsut was strong enough for me to remain even when we slept. I didn't sleep deep enough to dream but dozed in and out, our bodies nestled against each other. She stirred, and when she opened her eyes, they glowed in the darkness with the power of the moon. I wondered if my own were shining back at her.

"You need to find my amulet in your own time to utilize it there and gather power to hold when you need it. I think having that strength will be what you need to help wake Andrew," she whispered in the dark. "I don't think it is buried with me. I will have left directions with my priestesses to keep it close so they can use it if the need arises."

"I'll ask Hanan if they've ever heard of it. Maybe it's hidden away with the scrolls, and they think it's a special trinket and don't realize its power."

Hatshepsut sighed, the sound heavy with frustration. I knew it was hard for her to have so much power in her own time and be so helpless in mine. And for everything to have changed and things to have been lost to time. We talked of time then. Of the impossibility of it all—how it felt like it slipped through our fingers, but such a vast gap separated us. We'd given up trying to grasp the concept of thousands of years. We both agreed that time existed differently for us in this space, and we were content to leave it alone and not try too hard to understand it. It was easier that way. But she struggled. I know I did. I wished I could pull her through the liminal space with me and drag her back to my own time to help. There was so much power in my abilities. Still, they were limiting and small when faced with longing and inability.

Most of the time, I forgot I was living in Egypt. My day-to-day routine consisted of visiting Andrew, badgering his doctors about his progress and treatments, and seeking out Hatshepsut to practice magic. I had all but forgotten that first fateful trip filled with museums, tombs, artifacts, and mummies—an insatiable curiosity that brought us to Egypt in the first place. But learning about the moonstone amulet Hatshepsut used, I was on a mission to find it.

I'd asked Hanan and Marwa if they knew about any unique jewelry Hatshepsut might have worn, but neither one had.

"I'm sure there were special things she wore for ceremonies, *Habibti,* but nothing of import to us. Why?" Marwa had asked one morning in Andrew's room. It was the only place anyone could be sure to find me. I could tell by how she looked at me, sadness watering her dark eyes and concern knitting her brows together. She was deeply concerned about me. I tried to make an effort to reassure her.

"Oh, no specific reason," I answered, plastering my best fake smile on my face. "I just wondered." Marwa smiled, her eyes crinkling and watering a bit more.

"I'm happy to hear an interest starting back up in our Queen, *Habibti.* You've been growing so distant from all of us and from your magic for so long." She patted and rubbed my forearm comfortingly. It made my skin crawl with annoyance where it had once brought comfort, but I swallowed it to keep the peace and attention away from what I was genuinely searching for.

"Mm, I've never lost interest in her," I said quietly. "I wish I could do something to help Andrew. I hate seeing him like this."

Marwa nodded and muttered empty, placating words.

We talked of inconsequential things then—both of us trying to grasp onto some normalcy while Andrew's vitality continued to leech out of him in front of our eyes. I wondered, absently, when I'd grown to dislike even Marwa's attention. Still, I knew it boiled down to no one being willing or powerful enough to help me find a way to heal Andrew. Only Hatshepsut could do that.

And so, I'd taken it upon myself to play tourist for a few days and pore over the Egyptian Museum in search of the moonstone. I hated to leave Andrew in Luxor, even for a few days. I called every morning and evening to check on him, and I knew, deep down, that nothing would change until I could find answers and help him myself.

Despite leaving Andrew behind, I found the physical space from everyone else was therapeutic. There was no one to answer to or make small talk with if I ran into them. I could lock myself away in my hotel room after a day of traipsing around the museum and cry, wail, or space out entirely, and no one knew any different. It was liberating when it should have been lonely. I continued to spiral into the darkness of my mind, reveling in isolation. I was blinded by my grief and drive toward answers to recognize the dangerous game I was playing with my mental health.

By the end of the third day, I was restless and frustrated. My eyes were blurry from museum lighting and searching out row after row of ancient jewels worn by the nobility who had once ruled over Egypt. I'd been dazzled by sparkling gold and deep blue lapis lazuli, entranced by endlessly dark obsidian and overwhelmed with precious metals and jewels, but no moonstone among them.

I avoided the mummy room, skirting around it, unable to see Hat-shepsut laid out for the world to see. The first time we visited, I'd been fascinated and a bit repulsed by the idea of someone's dead body being on display, no matter how intriguing their preservation processes were. But now, intimately knowing one of those mummies... those *people*, it felt so dehumanizing and disrespectful. I also knew there was no way I could stomach seeing my beautiful friend stripped of her shining life force and magic. It was hard enough to see Andrew in the state he was in, and he was not a mummified husk of his former self. I knew I had seen her before; I remembered making a note of her, but I made a futile attempt to block the memory.

Frustrated and annoyed, I made one last loop through the museum's ground floor and, as luck would have it, I ended up blocked in by a tour group, the guide chattering on about the history of the museum itself in thickly accented English.

"What you see here is not only what we have at the museum. There is so much more. So many more jewels and riches," she said. Her voice was flat and unenthusiastic, and I wondered how she was engaging her group, but one look at their glazed eyes and bored faces told me she wasn't.

"Yeah, I guess the British Museum in London houses the rest, eh?" Someone snarked. She crossed her hands under her chest, rapping her long nails along one arm in annoyance. The Brits' theft of precious artifacts and their claim on Egyptian history was a sore spot for many Egyptians.

"Actually, no," she said. "While they have *some* things on display, we have much more. There are at least two or three more museums worth of things beneath us. Stored away, not to be seen right now."

I froze in place, my heart in my throat.

"We have many historians working on curating the best museum experience, and they do restorations on our beautiful artifacts, so you only see the best."

I was convinced they could hear my heart pounding in my chest. Surely, if the moonstone wasn't on display and the sisterhood didn't have it, it had to be below, tucked away in storage somewhere. I mumbled *excuse me* and *pardon me* under my breath and waded around the tour group, hope kindling in my chest for the first time in days.

# 26

## *Beloved*

"I need to know how to get into a closed, locked space. Unseen. Unheard." I was practically vibrating with excitement when I found Hatshepsut as the words spilled out without pretext.

"Hello to you, *Merit*. It is nice to see you, as well," she answered drolly. As we'd grown closer, I'd discovered a quick wit and a sarcastic streak from the Queen. The more time passed, the more her mask slipped, and I was let in to see her true self.

"Ha— sorry. Hello, my beautiful and amazing Queen and wonderful friend, Shesout." I laughed. "So… is there a magical way to get into a space that's locked and secured from the public? Unseen and unheard? Or is that a pipe dream?"

She rolled her eyes at me and laughed again.

"I do not know this dream of a pipe. But the magic is possible, yes. And you are strong enough to perform it, I think."

It was my turn to laugh again. "Sorry. Pipe dream. It means…" I trailed off, trying to think of how to explain what exactly the euphemism meant. I blanked. "I don't know how to describe it. It's like a hope or an impossible plan?"

"But what does that have to do with pipes?" she asked.

I made a face and shrugged my shoulders, hands open in the *I don't know* gesture.

"Honestly, I have no clue. I'm sure there's some explanation, but I don't know what it is off the top of my head."

Hatshepsut made another face. "The top of your head? Your hair? The curls?"

I laughed, a deep belly laugh then, and found I couldn't stop. Hatshepsut joined in, and we ended up laughing until tears rolled down both of our cheeks.

"It's another euphemism... a common saying from my time to emphasize a point or paint a picture with words. I don't think I realized how many I use in my normal speech till we started meeting."

We settled down then and moved on to the magic and my reason for needing it.

I explained to Shesout about the amulet and not being able to find it. She was distressed at the thought that the sisterhood wasn't using it as it was meant to be. Again, I wished to pull her through time with me and have her sort everything out. Maybe we should be searching for a spell for *that* particular magic. The responsibility of all the information lost to time weighed heavily on my shoulders. I kept putting it off, the weight of Andrew's health having more gravity at the moment. I knew everything would come crashing down when I finally found the magic he needed. I wouldn't have a choice but to pull Hanan in and explain everything so we could do what we could to compensate for all the loss and time.

"So you think in this... museum, my amulet is stored away in a box somewhere?" she asked once I'd finished.

I nodded and shrugged my shoulders at the same time. It felt a little incredulous now that I was saying it out loud... I was hanging all my hopes on the basement of a massive museum without knowing for sure what was down there. I had a moment's panic, envisioning a network of tunnels, mazes, and loads of different spaces in absolute chaos that I'd have to sort through on my own. I shook my head to clear that nightmare and focused on learning what I needed to do to at least discover the truth of what lay beneath.

"I have no way of knowing for sure. I know they have so many artifacts and things they don't have on display. They're constantly lending things to other museums across the globe, spreading the word and stories of your people. Even in my time, we are fascinated by you all. By the amazing things you were doing and learning with less technology than we have in my present." I knew things would get murky with her if I kept on with everything. We'd spent many long hours discussing my time and the marvels I lived with daily. It was enough to boggle her mind and, if I'm honest, mine too when I broke things down into their barest form. Imagining how quickly humanity evolved and developed in the last two thousand years was wild.

"I don't understand why you are fascinated. It is nothing more than life for us. Normal. It seems impossible that my sandals should be on display for everyone to see. They're dusty and plain— made to protect my feet. You wear sandals as well, and they look similar to mine."

This was a version of the same conversation we regularly had. Talking to Hatshepsut about her life and how it was lived day to day was as fascinating as any movie I'd ever watched or book I'd read. But to her, it was mundane. Ordinary. As mundane and routine as my own life was to me. It made me wonder who would be poring over my diaries or taking pictures of my faded favorite jeans or our favorite band t-shirt behind museum glass hundreds of years from now. I shuddered to think our bodies or cremated remains might be laid out to witness and remark on. I hadn't had the heart to tell Hatshepsut that their mummies had been unearthed and pulled from their resting places to be studied and documented. It seemed more than cruel.

"I know. It's hard to explain and hard to understand, I know. It's... you and your people were so advanced for the time." I waved a hand dismissively, knowing we'd get caught in a loop if we kept going. "Anyway, there's supposed to be loads of stuff below the public part of the museum. I don't know how to get down there without attracting attention."

She nodded. "Yes, you need to go in without being seen or heard. It is challenging magic, but not impossible." She paused, thinking. "I think it would be similar to what you're doing to come to me. Mastering your mind and manipulating something, in this instance, time, to your will."

"Yes, but I'd need to get in with my physical body. When I come to you, it's in my mind. My unconscious being or soul or whatever is the thing that comes to you. My actual body is in my time in a sort of...stasis? I guess. I don't know. I can't think too hard about it, or I'll lose my hold." I could already see the edges of her room, sort of shimmering under my scrutiny. I closed my eyes and took a deep breath, focusing back on Hatshepsut, her time, her sitting room where I'd found her. I steadied enough to open my eyes again and look at her.

"Ah. I see what you mean," she said. "Then, we'll have to look at it differently. Give me a moment."

She paced the room as she thought, muttering under her breath every now and then. It wasn't a massive room, but large enough that she got quite a few steps in. There were cushions strewn about the floor, low settees, and wooden benches along some of the walls. Paintings and papyrus decorated the walls, and scrolls half unfurled and partially read on a low table in front of her seat. It was a room where she received only her closest friends and family members. It felt comfortably lived in. It was attached to her bedchamber, and I found her here often.

"You've told me that you have some way of silencing a room, yes?" she finally asked.

"Yes. I paint a sigil on the door and imbue it with magic when I say a few words to shield and silence."

She nodded at me then.

"I think you have to do the same thing on your person. Paint the... sigil on your body—something for silence and something to conceal. Do you know one to hide or make invisible?" she asked, hopeful. Her face had a dreamy yet excited look to it. Sigils were obviously a different way of performing magic than she used, and she was eager to learn more. We'd sort of touched on them, and I'd painted the sigil for soundproofing her room on more than one occasion so we wouldn't be disturbed, and she watched with interest every time.

"I don't know them now, but I'll learn. You really think that will work?"

"I don't know, but it is the only thing I can think of. There are ways to manipulate shadows and become part of the darkness, but it is complicated and needs more than your will and innate magic to work. When you become a part of the darkness, you have to accept part of it inside you; once it resides there, you can't be rid of it. It is a great sacrifice and not without consequence, beloved." I paled and visibly shuddered.

"I don't know if I'm that desperate just yet," I said. The thought of inviting *more* darkness inside of me was terrifying. I knew I'd do it if I had to. I'd do anything to save Andrew and live with the consequences later. We could handle anything together.

"We can discuss the darkness if your sigils don't work." Hatshepsut looked at me; her face mirrored Marwa's concern from earlier and it stopped me in my tracks. My grief and desperation were leaking out of me like a fog, unfurling onto everyone I came in contact with. I wanted to find the amulet and draw in enough power to do whatever it took to end this feeling. I knew I would happily invite the shadows in if I could wipe the pity off everyone's faces when they talked to me.

# 27

## *Failure*

I'd come back down to Luxor after three days at the museum, unwilling to leave Andrew alone any longer. While I was with him, I pored over old texts and searched Google till I was blue in the face, and my eyes watered from staring at sigil after sigil. I finally found what I thought might work and the words to enable the magic. I'd found the Latin words that I would attempt to use... *caecus* meant blind, obscure, and unseen. *Obtego* meant to cover and conceal. *Confuto* was to halt or silence. *Selenium* was silence, quiet, and stillness. I'd also come across the words *dormeo* and *sopor*, which meant to fall asleep and deep sleep, respectively. I held them in my back pocket in case I encountered any security at the museum.

My best plan was to go at night when I'd have the longest uninterrupted time to search. I knew that I needed to test my sigils first. I painted them on using an eye pencil on the backs of my hands and my cheeks—of the mind that they probably needed to be visible. I walked out into the garden where Hanan was working.

At first, she said nothing, and my belly warmed with excitement that it had worked. Then she looked up from her computer, her hands stilling from whatever she was working on, and smiled at me.

"Hi, Julia. Everything alright?"

My stomach dropped. It hadn't worked. "Yeah. Everything's good. Going for a walk," I mumbled.

"What's that on your cheeks?" she asked. "New makeup style you're trying out?"

I forced out a laugh and touched my hand to my cheek.

"Oh. It's..." I wracked my brain for an excuse. "I was FaceTiming my friend Edie and her kids, and we were being silly." I mentally thanked Edie for having children and coming to mind so quickly. "I'm glad you caught it before I walked out of here!" I turned on my heel and returned to the guest house, trying hard not to slam the door shut in frustration.

I stared at myself in the bathroom mirror. The sigils weren't large but outlined in dark, waterproof eyeliner, curves and lines standing out against my pale skin.

"What the fuck?" I said to the girl in the mirror. I barely recognized her. My skin was pale from spending too much time inside in meditation. My hair was stringy, and I had dark circles under my eyes; the purple skin was the only color that popped out at me. Even my eyes, once bright and exciting, seemed dull and wan. I ran my fingers through my greasy curls, pulling at the roots in frustration, little zaps of pain forcing me to focus.

"I don't know what I did wrong," I said, studying the sigils in the mirror. I picked up the paper I'd finalized them on and looked back and forth between my face and the original sigils. A near-perfect match. I inched closer to the mirror, leaning over the sink. Water I'd spilled on the counter earlier dampened my shirt and sent a chill down my spine when the cold water seeped through to my skin.

I'd practiced multiple times, steadying my hand each time to ensure it was sure and confident. I couldn't see any discrepancy. I blew out a frustrated breath and pulled away, scrubbing my hands over my face and rubbing my eyes. I was tired. Irked. I braced my hands on the counter, hunched over and angry. I squeezed my eyes shut, the blood throbbing in my ears. The last little bit of hope I held onto was slipping further and further away. I knew that I would have to choose to go to Hatshepsut and do the one thing she'd cautioned against.

I didn't see how accepting any more darkness into myself would change anything other than giving me the freedom I needed to find the power to save Andrew. Grief was eating me alive, and I would do anything to stop it in its tracks. Whatever dark magic Hatshepsut offered couldn't possibly be any worse than what I was experiencing right now. I looked up into the reflection in the mirror. Tears I hadn't realized I was crying were streaming down my face, running across the sigils, the waterproof pencil holding as promised. And then it hit me.

"Oh my god." I squeezed my eyes shut as a wave of relief washed over me. "I'm such an idiot." I picked up the sheet of paper, held it next to my cheek, and looked into the mirror again... I'd mirrored the image on my cheek to follow the pattern. "Mother fucker," I muttered under my breath, both in relief and annoyance. It was little mistakes that were holding me back. Little fuck ups were keeping Andrew from me. I reached for the bottle of makeup remover and a washcloth and scrubbed my face and hands clean of the makeup. My skin was red and stinging when I was done, the pain unnecessary but a tiny punishment I afforded my frustration.

"Okay. Let's try this again, correctly this time," I said as I picked up the paper and headed out to the bedroom to rewrite the sigils in the opposite way so I could copy them to my skin more easily. I forced myself to take a few breaths to settle myself down. I was no good to anyone if I let my anger get the best of me. I practiced the sigil backward for a few minutes before returning to the bathroom and doing it all over again. This time, I was sure they'd work.

I walked out into the garden, but Hanan was nowhere to be found. I sighed and walked out of the gate, hoping to find someone out for a walk I could test my magic on.

I walked for a few minutes and only had two cars drive past me, neither of which responded to my waves, but that could be magic or the nature of the drivers. I had to find a way to actually figure out if it was working or not.

I walked to the bakery on the corner that was getting ready to close for the night. I had frequented them enough that the owner, Farida, knew me by name.

She was clearing a table, her hair on top of her head in a messy bun, bright fabric holding it off her face, and tied in her signature knot. My heart pounded, and I clenched my teeth. This *had* to work. I had to be unseen.

"Ah—Juleea, my friend," she said in her thick Arabic accent. "You no been to see me in long time. You want some *kunafeh*? I have a small piece left for you," she said, and my face flushed with anger. I spun on my heel and ran back home, ignoring her shouts of concern behind me.

I was well and truly livid when I finally got back home. I fumbled with the key to the gate, dropping the keys to the ground, spurning on my anger. I let myself in and headed straight for the guest house, slamming the door behind me as I hurried to the bathroom to pore over my face and any mistakes I might have made. When I saw nothing, I crumpled up the paper, threw it across the room, and then swept my hand across the bathroom counter, swiping everything off and onto the floor. A cacophony of things falling and shattering filled the space, along with my heavy breathing. It did nothing to make me feel better.

I stormed back into the bedroom and thought about swiping everything off the kitchen counters and onto the floor, but I refrained. I did the only thing I knew to do in that moment—I threw myself onto the bed, closed my eyes, and forced my racing heart to calm and meditate to get to Hatshepsut.

It took me a long time to find her, and I knew it was because I was so angry. I couldn't steer, or whatever it was I was doing when I was feeling an overwhelming emotion. When I found her, she was bathing in the ritual pool. I fell to my knees when I landed in the room, crying out with the pain of failure.

"*Merit,* what has happened? Is it Andrew? Has he made his journey to *Duat*?" She rushed out of the water and came to me. She was dripping wet and soaked my clothes as she wrapped herself around me. I sobbed in her arms, full, body-wracking sobs that left me exhausted and the anger drained.

"I failed, Shesout," I said, deflated. "I tried the sigils and the magic, and it didn't work."

I sank against her further, all the fight gone out of me. She kissed the top of my head and held me, rocking me like a mother would a hurt child. She murmured words into my hair; some things I understood, and others I didn't. But I lay there, letting her console me, for a long time.

Finally, my heart slowed, and the pain ebbed enough for me to speak.

"I don't care what the consequences are, Shesout. I must get into the museum unseen. What do I have to do?"

She sighed against me, and I knew she would argue but eventually relent. She had to. I wouldn't give her a choice.

"My dear, it is not something to do lightly. This is not magic like we have been learning. This is something darker and with repercussions. Magic that demands payment."

I sat up and pulled away from her arms.

"I will pay whatever the magic asks of me," I said, voice steady. My clothes were cold and stuck to my body with the water from Hatshepsut's skin. But, there was no chill at my words, only the fevered assurance from a woman making her actual descent into madness. The last tether I held on my sanity snapped when I failed. The moment Farida had been able to see me, I felt it go. And I felt myself leaning into the madness, sure it would be the thing to keep me going. The thing that would drive me toward answers... to whatever it took to get what I wanted.

# 28

## The Darkness

Hatshepsut wouldn't let me make any rash decisions. Even after I'd calmed down and long after our fingers and toes had shriveled in the ritual pool. She was adamant. I left her with the promise to think about what she was asking and return after at least three days.

I struggled to go about my life for those three days. I finally packed my bags and headed to Cairo again. I figured I'd at least be close to the museum and ready to go when Hatshepsut taught me what I needed to know. Because I had known the moment the sigils failed that I would do whatever it took to find answers. There was no thinking about consequences or worrying over what might happen. There wasn't a shred of doubt in my mind.

I thought about returning to her and lying about the time it had been since it worked so differently between us, but I couldn't bring myself to deceive her. It was one line I was unwilling to cross.

On the third day, I settled myself into the cushy hotel bed, the air conditioning whirring loud enough in the background to drown out the busy streets of the city below me. I breathed deeply, the myrrh oil I'd anointed myself with beforehand filling my nose and helping to center me. I thought about Hatshepsut, focusing on her face. On how it felt to be together. To wield magic together. Moments passed, and the now familiar tug on my mind, the belly-dropping and breath-stealing pull through time and space, sent me traveling. When I opened my eyes, I found her waiting for me. A sadness crossed her face when our eyes met.

"Oh *Merit*. I had hoped you wouldn't come back with such determination. It flows off you in waves so strong I could sense your decision before you fully formed in front of me."

I ignored her sadness. The weary worry of someone who cared for me but couldn't see that this was exactly what I needed. That I was out of options.

"Do not be sad, Shesout," I said defiantly. "I will be fine. I need this. And I am strong enough to handle it." Her eyes fluttered closed, and she took a breath before standing up to meet me. She put one hand on her heart and one on my arm.

"Once you choose this, there is no turning back," she said. "You have to accept... to invite a piece of the darkness inside you... to become the darkness. To truly become unseen, you must become the shadows and move about within them." I nodded, more sure of myself than I should have been.

"It cannot be worse than the darkness already inside me." My voice was steady, as was my heart, and both should have been erratic and panicked at the thought of what I was about to do. Hatshepsut leaned forward and gently pressed her lips to mine before pulling away and looking at me, unshed tears in her eyes shining in the candlelight.

"The darkness can always get worse, Julia."

I started a bit when she used my name. She'd been using her pet name for me for months now, and I'd come to view myself as *Merit* when I was in this place... almost like it was a different identity from Julia or Jules.

She turned away from me, and I could practically see a weight settle on her shoulders.

"If you can't be dissuaded, then we'll begin. It isn't terribly complicated, but it does require focus, intent, an invitation, and a bit of your blood."

I chewed on my lip and nodded, more to myself than her since her back was facing me.

"I'm ready," I whispered. More than nerves, a deep sense of guilt settled into the pit of my stomach that my choice was weighing so heavily on her. But I knew I couldn't help it. It was my choice, in the end, for better or worse, and I was making it.

She simply nodded and walked to the shelves recessed in the temple walls, where I'd come to her. She turned back towards me, a bundle in her hands. Approaching the center of the room, she took a seat, motioning me to join her. I walked over and sat, crossing my legs beneath me, straightening my spine.

The bundle was a short, fat candle wrapped in herbs, which she placed unlit in front of me. Before we began, she guided me through what to do, going over everything in great detail and then scooting a bit away from me and leaving me to it.

I took a deep breath, readying myself, and began.

I lit the candle, and the flame sputtered to life as I waved my hand across it. A quick flush of heat and light danced across my face, bringing with it the smell of beeswax, sage, and something else I couldn't quite put my finger on, something dark and syrupy.

I took another breath and rolled the words I was to say in my mind before opening my mouth to speak the incantation.

"To the shadows I seek

I ask the darkness
to give a piece of itself to me.
To allow me to walk about unseen.
To become one with the shade...
to cloak me in obscurity.
In return, I invite a small piece
to reside inside of me.
To nestle in and amongst myself.
Finding a home in this vessel I offer up."

I let the words ring out in the quiet space, the room's silence throbbing in my ears. An absence of sound so deafening I was sure the darkness had stolen my hearing.

The air was still. So still. Not even the candle flames flickered. The presence of something greater than Hatshepsut and I loomed in the room. Greater than magic. And darker as well.

Then fear began to thread through me, niggling at first but growing stronger. Before I could lose the gumption to finish the spell, I leaned closer to the flame. I pricked my finger with Hatshepsut's small ceremonial knife beside me. I had no idea if I would bleed here in this liminal space or what I would do if it didn't. After a moment, blood welled up, dark in the candlelight. I raised my hand over the flame, its heat wavering underneath me. With a squeeze of my hand, I snuffed out the flame with a drop of blood.

The room went dark, all the candles snuffing out at once. Not even the whites of Hatshepsut's eyes shone in the darkness. It was velvety and thick, permeating everything.

With a whisper, Hatshepsut lit the candles that lined the walls, and the glow of the flames slowly came to life. I looked at her, and she looked at me. I searched inward, feeling out any differences. I found none.

"Now, you must master the shadows to use them." Her voice was hoarse like she'd sat in silence for a long time, and I wondered how long it had taken me to perform the spell. And whether it had even worked. I stood up, joints stiff from sitting for a long time in the same position, and I knew then we'd been there longer than the moments it had felt like.

I walked over to the wall and stood directly underneath a glowing candle. I reached up and waved my hand over it, the heat of the flame stinging my palm as I whispered, "*Deflammo.*" With the extinguishing of light, something unfurled inside me, like the smoke slithering through my fingertips. I didn't fight it. It felt familiar. Comfortable. It felt like my grief was made tangible. I held it close against my chest, protecting it like something fragile. I heard Hatshepsut suck in a breath behind me.

"I have never seen someone master the darkness so quickly."

The words were reverent. I felt warm all over. Her praise was always a balm to my soul. I pressed my hand back into my chest, grounding myself and reassuring the darkness that we were safe together. To hold it and allow space for it felt like the most organic thing in the moment. I sighed as it settled into me. It felt like I was wearing a warm cloak fitted around my soul. I walked towards Hatshepsut and stood a breath away from her when I released my hold on the shadows.

Her gasp made me laugh out loud, the sound ringing off the temple walls and back at me.

"So, it worked then?" I asked, still laughing.

"Yes. I would say that it worked very well," she said darkly. She sounded more worried than anything, but I dismissed her apprehension and danced around the room, flickering in and out of the shadows at will. It was the first time magic felt genuinely effortless, and I reveled in it.

"How does it feel to become the darkness?" Hatshepsut asked, voice threaded with melancholy.

I smiled despite it. "Like I'm being wrapped in a warm cloak on a cool autumn day. It smells crisp, like the clean scent of the sky when it's beginning to turn from autumn to winter… and it's as effortless as breathing."

"I know what it feels like for myself, and it's nothing so much as all of that. It feels heavy, like a burden I cannot put down. And it smells of brimstone." The melancholy wasn't only threaded through her voice now but dripping with it. I looked at her, and shock must have registered on my face. "You don't think I have wanted to move about unseen? Unheard? To judge who truly stood on my side? To be Pharaoh is to rule knowing there is a knife to your back at all times. After Thutmose's betrayal, I did what I had to do to assure our purpose would continue and with whom I could truly entrust my secrets."

I thought for a moment about how different our experiences with the shadows were. I couldn't imagine it feeling like a burden. I was free in the darkness. I felt the pull from my physical body and looked at Hatshepsut.

"I must go. I can feel my body stirring, pulling me back." She looked at me, the sorrow and gloom a physical thing winding around us.

"Be careful and do not let the darkness have free rein, Julia…it will take more than you are truly willing to give up…" she tapered off, eyes filling, hand to her chest. It felt like there was more between us than time and space, but I didn't have time to deal with it. The tug of my body yanked me forward, the pit of my stomach dropping at the lurch, and I found myself waking up in a body that was damp and shivering on the hotel bed. I'd been gone so long I'd wet myself.

I should have been ashamed, but all I could think was that I'd pee all over myself again if it meant feeling this free and this hopeful. The darkness stirred, stretching inside my body like waking from a long sleep. It felt like a comfort...like a friend, like something I'd been waiting on my whole life. I smiled.

I looked down at my hand and saw my fingertip was crusted with blood. I smiled again and knew that it must have truly worked. I got myself up and washed off, showering and dressing quickly, and then took myself out into the hotel, practicing my new abilities and mastering the shadows.

This time, I was wildly successful.

# 29

## A Dark Path

*Andrew*

"I must tell you of your wife," Khonsu said one morning. He had been coming to see Andrew almost every day. He found the human entertaining and a balm for the loneliness that plagued him.

"What's happened?"

"She is trying to find a way to heal you, as you know, and she is desperate in her search," Khonsu spoke carefully, choosing his words intentionally. "She has made a choice that sits her firmly on a dark path." The god's voice was deep and rumbling in Andrew's chest. He squeezed his eyes shut, wondering what decision she could have made that led her down a path so dark the god of the moon sounded worried.

"Is she going to be okay?" Andrew asked. The god looked at him, his shining eyes soft with concern.

"I cannot answer that just yet," he said. "I only know the path she has chosen. There are different branches that path can take. Different roads she can travel. It all comes down to more choices. And before you ask, no, there is nothing I can do to change the course of her decisions."

Andrew, who had been standing up, walked over to a lounge and sat down heavily. He hung his head in his hands and worried over his wife.

"I don't understand," he said. "I know she's upset, but what could have driven her to set out on a darker path? What choice did she make?"

"She has performed a spell to become the darkness," Khonsu answered.

"To become the darkness?"

"It is an old spell that was used long ago to disappear. To be able to move about in the shadows, unseen. But to do so, she had to accept a piece of the darkness inside her." Andrew looked up at the god, startled.

"She has a piece of darkness inside of her? What does that mean?"

"It can mean many things," Khonsu said. "It will depend upon how she embraces the darkness."

Andrew's stomach dropped. There was a darkness in his wife—she had been so scared of it after what happened with Gordon Mitchell. For her to have invited something darker inside of her, he knew she was desperate.

"I have to get back to her," Andrew pleaded. He could taste the fear on his tongue—static and bitter. "It has to be time for me to go."

Khonsu shook his head.

"It is close, child, but not time yet." They sat quietly then, Andrew's mind racing and Khonsu pensive beside him, lending his calm demeanor. But nothing could temper Andrew's worry for Julia and what holding a piece of darkness inside of her was doing to the love of his life.

# 30

## *Freedom in the Dark*

I scoped out the Egyptian museum again; this time, excitement danced through my steps instead of frustration leading the way. I made notes of the closed-off doorways and which ones were locked, making notes on my phone as discreetly as possible, though no one was paying a lone tourist any attention.

The Egyptian sun warmed me through as I lounged outside the massive museum building, plotting and thinking. I got online, searching again, in vain, for blueprints of the underbelly of the museum. It seemed like no one else found any interest in the storage archives. My plan was to hide behind the museum, at the employee entrance, and sneak in with someone unnoticed. The last thing I wanted was a wayward door caught on the security camera footage opening and closing of its own volition. Not to mention, I hadn't the foggiest idea how to even go about picking a lock.

Ideas of what to do about security cameras were still few and far between, and while I didn't really want to, I was going to wing it and hope for the best. I was too desperate to get moving and get ahold of the amulet to spend more time planning. It was rash, and I knew it, but I was done waiting around.

That night, I dressed in black leggings, a tight-fitting shirt, and a dark cardigan wrapped around me. My hair was pulled back in a tight knot at the base of my skull, curls tamed and hidden by a dark scarf tucked under and knotted at my neck. I felt like a thief, which I was getting ready to become. Shame swirled about in my belly, but I swallowed it down, shoving it away, telling myself that the true owner of the amulet wanted me to have it. Had encouraged this. Taught me how to get it. The curators of the museum had no claim—at least not one stronger than my own.

With that thought, I shored myself up and took a breath, inviting the darkness to surface. It was fluid and organic and felt like it had always been a part of me. I wondered if the darkness inside of me... the fear and anxiety, the depression, the trauma... if all of it had been waiting for the freedom to take the reins all this time. If shoving it down and ignoring it for my entire life had somehow compacted it into this sentient thing waiting for me to feed it more power. If that's why becoming the darkness was so effortless. The shadows wrapped around me, cloaking me in darkness and confidence. I skirted around the museum building, the pink limestone cool against me, though it had been warming in the hot Egyptian sun all day.

I found the doors and picked a spot close enough to be able to move quickly but far enough away to remain unseen and unnoticed. I was confident that the magic would hold... the darkness was happy to be given some freedom. I knew it wouldn't let me down.

I leaned against the building, shifting my weight and trying to make my hammering heart slow down, sure that any passerby would hear it beating away. It wasn't long before a couple of security guards came out for a smoke break. They held the door open with a brick. They walked a few feet, one propping himself up against the building nonchalantly, foot and back bracing him, with an unlit cigarette dangling from his lips. The other man dug around in his pockets and produced a lighter, touching the flame to his cigarette before handing it to his comrade. They spoke quietly in Arabic, the back and forth a friendly banter. I inched closer to the door, pausing next to the cracked opening. The cold air from the air conditioner poured out of the entrance, dissipating into the warm evening, but it wasn't wide enough for me to squeeze through.

They smoked two cigarettes each before putting their butts in an old planter whose plant was long gone, cigarette butts and trash taking its place. My heart throbbed in my throat, sweat beading at my temples and down my spine when the two men reached the door. They paused, and I was sure I was going to be caught, but they stood, the taller of the two's hand on the door handle when the shorter man said something, and he waited for a few beats longer, listening. The scent of cigarettes and body odor was overwhelming, and I tried taking small sips of air through my mouth to keep from sniffing too deeply. Tasting the fetid air hanging around them wasn't any better.

Finally, by the grace of some god or goddess somewhere, tall and rangy cracked the door open more. He held it with his hip, letting out more cold air as they stood talking another minute more. Without hesitation, I made my move and slipped in right under their noses and into the dimly lit entrance of the underbelly of the Egyptian Museum.

My heart was still hammering away in my chest, and I could taste the beaded sweat on my upper lip. But I had made it inside. Now, I had to find the archives and storage, and then I would be golden.

I knew it wouldn't be long before the guards outside came in behind me, so I made a swift decision. I turned to the right, pressed myself into the shadows against the wall, and took stock of my surroundings.

It was funny how different this part of the museum was from what the public was privy to. The walls were unadorned, no *canopic* jars or mummies on display. It felt industrial and cold. Nothing like the otherworldly upstairs with its riches and history on display.

As luck would have it, there were signs on the walls ahead, similar to what was above me; the rooms below were organized into security, a break room, offices, paper archives, and then separate sections for each dynastic time period. I headed towards Hatshepsut's Eighteenth Dynasty section, skirting along the walls, sticking to the shadows, and praying to Hatshepsut and anyone who would listen to keep me hidden. The darkness was comforting. The shadows were a cloak—its weight wrapped around me from head to toe. I could hear the whirr of the air conditioners and the static hum of the dim lights that lit the corridor I was in, but other than that, the archives were silent as a tomb.

I followed the signs and took a few more turns before finding myself in the Eighteenth Dynasty. I stepped into the room and found it lit only by emergency lighting along the floors. But along with the power of melting into the shadows, accepting the darkness into myself also meant that I could see in the dark. It wasn't like seeing things bright as day, but a soft glow emanated from the shadows to my eyes, allowing me to see as if I had a wide-beamed, low-lit flashlight.

As far back as I could see into the deep-set room, there was row after row of tall metal shelves. The ceilings were about fifteen feet high. Everything was stored in boxes and tagged and labeled. Some of the boxes had new, printed labels cataloging the contents in detail. Others were faded, handwritten labels, the cursive on the outside almost nonexistent. I cursed low under my breath. Unless I lucked out and found a box labeled *Hatshepsut's personal belongings*, I was in for a long night... or a few of them.

I took a breath, steadied my nerves, and decided to start at the back and see what was there. At the very worst, I'd at least be far back enough that should a guard come by to check on anything, I would have plenty of space and time to hide.

The shuffle of my feet on the concrete floors was barely a whisper. No matter the cost, the darkness had come through on the unseen and unheard front. The storage room was deep, maybe the size of a basketball court, and the shelves were stacked close. A narrow space between each row was enough for one or two people to get through but close enough to touch either side without fully stretching your arms out. The deeper I walked, the more it felt like the room was closing in on me. I wasn't normally claustrophobic, but the looming sense of what I was doing in there gave me tunnel vision either way I looked.

I searched for hours quietly through huge metal drawers filled with artifacts and papers. Not everything was labeled and what was were handwritten labels that were all but crumbling with age. It was a frustrating and slow process that yielded nothing but sweat and dust. I finally gave up around six in the morning. My eyes were crusty with exhaustion, and my back ached from poring over shelves all night. I knew it was time to go, and I'd have to make the trip later to try again.

Tracing my steps back the way I'd come, I leaned against the wall close to the door, waiting for the right time. I'd been inside for so long that the nerves from earlier had all but gone while I was alone in the archives. A flush of heat had them back and spreading all over me while I waited to escape. It took longer than it had to get in. The wait stretched on for almost an hour before someone finally came to the door. It was a little after seven, and the shift change had started. A fresh set of guards began to file in, making their way to the break room to prepare for the day ahead. I decided to wait a little longer, assuming that the shift leaving and heading home for the day would pay less attention as I slipped past them .

Sure enough, a handful of guards, sleep weighing heavily on their faces finally came around the corner. They shuffled their way to the door, the night blanketing over them, focusing purely on getting home. I tread carefully, barely breathing, and slipped through the door, grateful that the first guard had propped it open for the others.

I made it back to the hotel, washed off the grime and layers of dust, and crawled into bed, falling into a deep sleep.

# 31

## *Awry*

When I woke later in the afternoon, I had a renewed sense of hope. I hadn't expected to find the amulet on the first try. I knew that it would take time if it were even in the archives. But the magic had held, and so had my nerve, so I knew I'd find it. I had to. Failure wasn't an option.

I spent the afternoon resting up and eating a good meal ordered from room service before choking down a couple of bitter espresso shots and donning my dusty break-in garb. I could smell the dried sweat on my clothes from the night before and knew I'd have to wash them in the hotel sink in the morning if I had to go back in again. There was no way that more than two days' worth of dust and sweat would evade the guards.

I arrived at the museum a little earlier than the night before, hoping to get some extra time searching. As luck would have it, the same two guards came out for another smoke break, but this time, I was closer, and I slipped in after the shorter of the two came out of the door. The whisper of my long cardigan pulled against the doorway as I hurried past the guard. He paused and looked behind him, and I pressed myself against the wall inside the building, heart pounding, mouth dry with fear. He said something I didn't understand to the other guard, but the meaning was clear. Something had caught his attention.

*You are the darkness. You are the shadows. He can't see you. He can't hear you any more than he can hear the shadows outside. You're safe.* I said to myself in my mind, eyes squeezed shut. The darkness wrapped tighter around me, comforting me and making itself known. The other guard answered, and the door closed against the brick they propped it open with. I let out the tiniest sigh, swallowed down the bile that threatened to come up, and turned toward the corridor. I hurried back to where I'd been the night before, my heart still slamming behind my ribs, the stench of fear strong in my nose.

I took a moment in the archive room. I tucked myself deep into the room in one of the aisles. I slid down the back wall, crumpling to the floor. My breaths were ragged, and I was shaking with adrenaline. I'd come so close to being caught. At least, it felt that way. The night before had been so easy; no one had noticed. But I'd gotten cocky and should have waited a bit longer. I *had* to find the amulet tonight. I didn't think I'd be able to work up the nerve to come in another night.

But I did have to work up the nerve for three more nights. I still had more of the archival room to search, and I'd not found the amulet yet. Exhausted and disappointed, I left each night the same way I had the night before. I repeated my day, sleeping and eating after washing my clothes and hanging them in the bathroom to dry.

For the next two nights, I didn't have any more close calls. My timing had improved, and the guards had changed, though I was lucky they all smoked and took plenty of breaks during their shifts.

When I woke up on the fifth evening, I took one look in the mirror and started. The circles under my eyes were as dark as the shadows I was purposefully becoming, like they were flowing out of my eyes and masking my sallow skin. And there was not a shred of the confidence I'd felt the first night staring back at me. I knew I couldn't keep up my nighttime wanderings much longer. I scrubbed my face with my hands and then splashed cold water on my skin to help wake me up. The failures of the last few nights weighed on me. The last shred of hope I clung to was getting harder and harder to keep hold of. I wasn't sure what to do if I walked away empty-handed tonight.

The night was the same as every other night. Getting into the museum was all but effortless now. The shadows held and clung tight, and after so many nights spent in the darkness, I knew the magic wouldn't drop away unexpectedly. I made it to the far end of the archival room undetected and started my search. I had a small section left to check, and I took a deep breath, steadying myself before I pulled out the first drawer. I rifled through papers, only half reading through them. Most of the notes were in a mix of English and Arabic, the loopy and faded swirls of proper British handwriting the majority of what I shuffled through.

The next shelf held an old cardboard box. Inside were small trinkets wrapped in straw and crumbling paper. A flutter of hope flit through me. If there was a box that held the moonstone, this was it. I pulled everything out, unwrapping each thing, mindful of the fragility and pricelessness of each artifact I held. I found a small carved scarab with a *rehkyt* engraved on the bottom, and I paused and smiled—the sign of the sisterhood. I went to wrap it back in its paper but couldn't bring myself to leave it behind. It wasn't what I was looking for, but it was a piece of the sisterhood. Of Hatshepsut and what she'd stood for and started.

Carefully, I tucked it into the small pocket of my leggings and kept going. I reached the bottom of the box with no other significant findings.

I put everything back inside its box and looked at what I had left. I was on the last shelf of the room. My time was coming to a close, and I hadn't found the moonstone or any hint of its existence. I held on to the metal shelf and hung my head between my arms, bracing myself against the possibility that I was leaving the museum with no moonstone and no idea where to look next. Hot tears of frustration brimmed in my eyes, but I refused to shed them. I couldn't give up yet. I took a breath, swallowed back the tears, and carried on.

I moved to the next large drawer and found more folders and files. I flicked through them and found a heavy envelope in the middle of the drawer that wasn't flush and flat with the rest. There was Arabic scribbled on the front of it, along with some hieroglyphs I had no hope of reading. But something in the envelope made me pause. My hands started to shake, and I wiped them on my leggings. This felt like the last hope. Even though there were a couple of drawers left to search on this shelf...something told me this was it—the last shred of possibility.

I sucked in a breath and carefully, I broke the seal and looked in the envelope. A crumbling sheet of paper was folded over something bulky in the bottom. I reached in, pulled out the small package, and felt a rush of power. The magic inside me stirred, sitting up and paying attention like a student called on unexpectedly in class. My heart was in my throat as I peeled away the paper. It was so old and fragile that it crumbled in my hands, revealing the dark glint of gold and the luminescent moonstone glowing back at me.

It took everything in me not to shout in the silent archival room. Pure elation spread through every inch of me, all but lifting me off the ground in joy. I untangled the thin chain and slipped it over my neck and under my shirt, the moonstone snuggly between my breasts. The magic of the moonstone settled against me, and with it, a sense of right within the world—like things were finally falling into place, and I was going to be able to help Andrew.

Quickly, I packed the envelope back into the drawer and made sure I put everything back the way I'd found it. And, heart singing, I headed to the door, struggling to keep my relief and excitement in check and quiet enough to get out unheard. Someone had left the door propped open wider than expected, and I could slip right out without waiting on a smoke break, sucking my stomach in and making myself as small as possible not to shift the door.

I was met with the middle of the night—when the sky was the darkest before turning towards morning. That time when the night is thick and heavy in the air, the whole world feels silent and slumbering in the dark, and the sunrise feels impossibly far away. I forced myself to stay in control, to stay shadowed as I stole around the side of the building and a few steps closer to freedom. The escape was always stressful, and then the success was heady. The rush of victory tonight was intoxicating, and I was thrumming with excitement.

"Did you find what you were looking for, little witch?"

The deep voice came out of nowhere, and I whipped around, slamming my back against the building and looking everywhere to find its source. My magic reared up, ready to protect me.

"Oh, did you think no one could see you wrapped in the darkness, little witch? Did you think you were the only one with magic here?"

The voice was closer, but I couldn't make out anyone in the dark night. Not even the magic of the shadows gave a hint to the owner of the voice.

"Who are you?" I asked, my voice quivering. The limestone was cool against my clothes, seeping into my hot skin. Every inch of me was lit up with worry, and my eyes darted every way, searching for the voice and an escape. I heard a prolonged intake of breath and then a loud, almost moaning exhale.

"You smell like her," the voice said. "Like magic and fear and defiance and..." He inhaled. "Ahh...and power. Lots of power." The dark voice was resonant and deep but filled with something akin to desire. I shuddered and pushed off the building, squaring my stance to run or fight; I wasn't sure which. The voice laughed, low and easy. "Let's not pretend you can get away so easily, little witch. I want to speak with you."

I swallowed and rolled my shoulders back, remembering my power and strength.

"If you want to speak with me so badly, then show yourself. I'm not going to stand here talking to the night air, waiting to be caught by the museum guards," I said, confidence growing as my magic shifted and fortified inside me. The moonstone grew warm against my skin, pulsing against my chest like a second heartbeat. I knew I was pulling power from it in preparation to defend myself from whoever stood before me.

Another low, rumbling chuckle came.

"As you wish." No sooner had he spoken than the air before me shimmered, and the shadows formed a man. He was a few years older than me and broad-shouldered. He stood only a few inches taller but oozed power despite his shorter stature. And he oozed darkness. He leaned against a towering stone statue set into the ground, one of many that encircled the museum. His arms were crossed against his chest, and he wore a dark suit with a white shirt open at the collar. As soon as he was visible, the darkness pooling around his feet, he stretched out his arms, god-like, palms up, and spoke again.

"Happy now, Julia Wheelright?"

My blood turned to ice when I heard my name cross his lips. The darkness was tugged off of me, like someone pulling on my cardigan, and it fell away, revealing me to the night. I knew I had paled enough in the darkness for him to see it. I had no words—only cold fear in the face of extreme power. I suddenly felt small and very, very alone.

# 32

## The Shadow Man

"Come now," he said, voice deep. "Are you so afraid of the big, bad wolf?" He sounded playful, like he was toying with a child playing hide and seek.

My voice was caught in my throat, fear holding it in place while my magic warred within—wanting to fight back. I was pulled in two different directions. Fight or flight. Fear or power. He pushed off the statue and stalked towards me. I was frozen in place; from his power or my terror, I couldn't tell. I took a breath and readied myself to scream. If nothing else, the guards would hear and come running, hopefully in time. But as I opened my mouth, he raised his hand and made a fist in the air like he was grabbing hold of my voice.

"Ah, I think not," he said. "And besides, it would do you no good. These are my men, and they would only arrest you for stealing, you little thief." He tightened his fist, and my throat squeezed in response. When he released his hand, air came flooding back into my lungs, and I sucked in precious oxygen like I'd been held underwater.

"Who are you?" My voice croaked. I cleared my throat and asked again.

He looked me up and down, measuring and weighing the very sight of me. I was stripped down to my core. Not in a sexual way, but like he was taking stock of my essence. My power—the magic that thrummed through my veins. I wanted to hide it from him. To wrap myself in the darkness and disappear once more.

"I am someone who knows you, Julia. Maybe even better than you know yourself." He answered, still intent on me. Still seeing straight through me. "As soon as you found a way into the museum, I could feel you. And I've been watching you for the last five days. All I want is to know what you've stolen away in your pocket there." He pointed to my hip where the hidden leggings pocket held the scarab I'd secreted away earlier.

"Why?" I asked. "Why do you want to know what I have? Why not just turn me in and have me arrested?" I stood straighter, hoping that feigning confidence would eventually give me the actual thing. He crossed an arm across his chest and brought the other hand to his face. He thoughtfully rubbed his face, five o'clock shadow dark against his golden skin. He came closer, studying me. I pressed myself harder against the building, trying and failing to get away from him.

"I'm sure you'd love me to tell you all of my secrets, little witch." The light-hearted tone was gone from his voice as he loomed in front of me. His eyes were dark pools of midnight, with no light in them whatsoever. "But first, you're going to tell me yours." He was close enough that I could smell his cologne, rich and heavy scents of *oud* and sandalwood. A rush of magic flared between us, and the darkness inside me preened. His responded in kind. His magic smelled hot, like the burning sand under the Egyptian sun and peppers so spicy they burnt the tongue on scent alone.

It stole my breath, his magic. And then it pressed my arms to my sides and tilted my chin towards his face. He hadn't moved a finger. He closed his eyes and inhaled deeply, our faces close but not touching. My magic answered, and, in a rush, the invisible bonds he'd wrapped around me broke, and I pushed past him, freedom at my back.

"You seem to know everything about me already," I said, hands curled in a fist as if sheer force of will would get me out of this.

"Well, I didn't know about *that* little trick." The amusement was back in his voice. "What have you stolen from me? Hand it over, and I might let you go."

I knew he was lying. Anyone could plainly see that. But the one thing I realized was that he hadn't asked about the moonstone—only what I'd slipped in my pocket. The Scarab. I played along.

"I don't believe for one second that you'll let me go if I hand this over. You don't even know what it is." I made my voice sound small and weak. I shrank away from him in fear.

"I know that whatever it is was important enough for you to risk imprisonment. You've spent the last week trespassing and mishandling things worth more than ten of your lives. So, what is it? What could her little lap dogs possibly want from the archives? I've *personally* cataloged everything in that room and taken everything that held even a whisper of her power."

He said *her* with a violent edge to it, and I shuddered, unable to contain it.

"There was nothing of any sort of power in there. Nothing more than trinkets of a bygone era. Things to draw in the masses, nothing else."

I stilled. Then, he'd not felt the power of the amulet. It was safe. I had to think. To keep him talking.

"I don't know what you're talking about," I said. I didn't know how he knew about us, but I knew I had to protect them at all costs. My heart pounded even harder. I tried to tamp it down, but I could taste the coppery and acidic fear in the back of my throat. He laughed again.

"You, my dear, are a terrible liar. So very many tells. You should never play cards." I pursed my lips and did my best to school my face to a semblance of neutrality. "I will only ask one more time before I come and take it from you. Hand over whatever is in your pocket." There was no laughter in his voice. Only power, raw and angry.

As much as I hated to give up any piece of Hatshepsut, the only way I had any hope of escaping this man was to hand it over. I reached into my pocket and pulled the beetle out. I closed my fist around it and squeezed tight, mind racing, plan forming. It was madness. What I was planning was madness. But it was all I had.

"I just wanted a small trinket. That's all. It doesn't mean anything," I said. I bit the inside of my cheek, trying my best not to give anything away. "If I give this to you, you'll let me go?" I asked, gathering the magic inside of me, willing it to spool together and ready itself for a battle. There was no way I wasn't leaving this place. My heart beat faster, pumping and fueling the power in my veins. The moonstone throbbed in time with my heart, and I sent a silent prayer of thanks to Hatshepsut for storing up magic in it before it was lost to time.

"Let's see what you've taken, and then we can talk about your release," he said. He leaned against the building, underestimating me, nonplussed and unworried about what I might do. He knew he had the upper hand. And I knew that I'd played my part well.

"Oh... okay..." I stammered. One last trick before I made my move. I opened my hand to him, let him see the scarab in my palm, and then tossed it high and far into the air. At the same time, I sent a burst of magic toward him. Magic threaded with shadows headed straight for his dark eyes. I saw the moment it hit him, and I spun around, wrapping my cardigan tight against me and feeling the rush of shadow and power cloak itself over me. And then, I ran.

"You'll regret that, little witch!" I heard him shout behind me. "When your false Queen defied me, I squeezed the life out of her from the inside out!" His voice boomed through me, thrown by powerful magic. His words hit me like they were corporeal and reverberated through me, rattling my bones. And still, I ran.

# 33

## The Truth

I ran until my lungs felt like they were going to burst. And then I kept running. One foot in front of the other. I wound my way through the streets, zigzagging until I finally reached the hotel. I knew I had moments, if that, to get to my room and clear it out before the man found me. I only hoped that he hadn't had people waiting here for me.

I fumbled with my key, sliding it into the lock multiple times before it slid home. As luck would have it, no one was waiting. I rushed into the room, barely thinking, shoving things into my bag and making my way through the small room, ensuring I'd not forgotten anything. I hadn't brought much with me, and I got it all shoved into my bag and left the room in less than five minutes. Still cloaked in the shadows, magic pinging through my system, I snuck down the stairs and into the night.

I kept to the shadows, skirting around buildings and into tighter-knit areas of town. There were buildings everywhere, roads littered with cars, stray cats, and dogs. Few people were out at night, but I tried to stay within screaming distance of anyone on the street. I wracked my brain, trying to figure out where to go or how to get back to Luxor. I hadn't purchased return tickets yet. I knew a train went from Cairo to Luxor, but I didn't know anything about the timetables or details. I figured he'd be watching public transport and knew I'd be caught as soon as I tried to get out that way. I hadn't found out who the man was, but he exuded power and influence, and if the guards at the museum were at his beck and call, I knew that many more had to be as well.

I pulled out my phone to check the time, and it hit me— *Dell*. I could call Dell and find out if she and Naomi were in Cairo. They often came to work with the street kids and the foundations that Naomi supported. It took a few rings, but she answered, voice heavy with sleep, at almost five in the morning.

"I'm so sorry to wake you, Dell. I need to know if you and Naomi are in Cairo or Luxor," I said, voice quick but barely above a whisper.

"I'm in Luxor, but Nay is in Cairo. Why?"

"It is a really long story, and I promise I will tell you as soon as I get back. I have to call her now, though. It's urgent."

"Jules, I don't know what's going on with you lately, but you and I are going to sit down, and you've got some explaining to do as soon as you get back. Are you safe, at least?"

I bit my lip and paused. I didn't know how to tell her yes without lying and no without delving into the whole thing. "For now, yes. But it's been one hell of a week," I said honestly. "But now I really have to go. I love you, and I'm sorry." I hung up the phone without waiting for her response and immediately dialed Naomi. She answered on the second ring and was wide awake.

"Who'd you kill now?" she said sardonically.

I rolled my eyes, even though I knew she couldn't see me. "No one, thank you very much," I replied. "Dell said you were in Cairo, and I am too, but I need somewhere safe to go."

"I'm texting you my address. Where are you now?" She asked.

"I don't know," I said. I looked around for anything that could tell me exactly where I was but saw nothing I recognized. My phone vibrated quietly, and I pulled it away from my ear and clicked the link Naomi had sent. Walking directions placed me ten minutes away from her. I sighed in relief. "You're only ten minutes from me. I'll be right there and explain everything when I see you," I said.

She grumbled something in Arabic that I didn't understand and then answered in English.

"Yeah, you will. See you in ten."

I snuck along the streets of Cairo, the city slowly coming to life. The stirring of the people and animals around me brought me some comfort. There was anonymity in a town full of people. I was exposed, alone on the street, even shrouded in shadows. I found Naomi leaning against the outer wall of her flat building. I pulled the darkness back inside me when I was a few feet away from her and took great pleasure in watching the shock on her face as I appeared out of thin air in front of her.

"Well, that's new," she said, shocked. I took a dramatic magician's bow and smiled at her, unable to help but feel a little pride in her surprise. "Why is it that I always have to be the one you call to get you out of some super fucked up mess?" she asked, arms folded across her chest.

"It's not like I try to get into super fucked up messes, okay? Sometimes things just happen." She raised her crazy Egyptian eyebrow at me and narrowed her gaze my way, pointed chin tilted, and her lips pursed. "Can we get inside, please? I'll explain everything." She pushed off the building and turned to go inside.

"These things don't just happen to you. You go looking for trouble."

I knew arguing was futile, and I had just called her for help, so I stayed silent. I followed behind her, checking over my shoulder in case and seeing no one. We went up to the fifth floor of the building, and she let us into her flat. It was dark, save one small table lamp glowing on a side table next to her sofa.

The flat was small but cozy, and it felt intimate to be standing in her space in the middle of the night, like I was privy to this private side of her uninvited. I knew the least about her out of everyone in the group. We didn't fight like we had done in the beginning, but there was no love lost between us, and most of the time, we barely interacted. She had been tender and kind to me when Andrew first fell in the temple, and I held on to that feeling now, remembering her compassion. I was going to need every ounce of it after coming clean with her.

"Okay. Out with it," she said, not beating around the bush. She tossed her keys on a painted wooden table by the door and walked into the open kitchen. I dropped my bag, grateful to have it off my shoulder. "You look like shit. Do you want some water or something?"

I nodded and unwound my damp cardigan from my body. I could smell the sweat, dirt, and fear, and looked at Naomi. "Can I take a quick shower? I smell as awful as I must look."

"Yeah, I didn't want to be rude, but you also smell terrible. Shower's through there. Towels are on the shelf above the toilet; feel free to use any soaps and shampoos. You need clean clothes? Dell has some things stashed here, and you guys are close to the same size."

I unzipped my bag and rummaged through it, coming up with some clean clothes to change into. "I've got some stuff, thanks." I closed the bathroom door behind me. It was modern and well-outfitted, with a huge walk-in shower and a massive rain shower head. I stripped off my sweat-soaked clothes and looked in the mirror. The woman looking back at me looked exhausted and haunted. I wanted nothing more than to crawl into bed, onto Naomi's sofa, or hell, even the bathroom floor, and sleep for days. But I owed her an explanation for coming to my rescue yet again. I toyed with the moonstone hanging between my breasts. I couldn't bring myself to take it off, so I showered with it on, assuming it had lasted so long that a short shower couldn't hurt. At least, I hoped not.

I took a blistering hot shower and scrubbed the dirt and fear off my skin. My mind raced, recalling every detail of the shadow man. Nothing about him was familiar except for his magic. The shadows and the darkness inside of me responded to him with familiarity. How he moved out of the darkness was precisely how my magic worked. Other than that, I had no clue who he was. He had power and influence over the museum. He exuded confidence and power- the kind that spoke to someone in a position of authority and used to being in charge. He wasn't handsome, but he wasn't ugly either. The only feature that stood out to me was his eyes; they were dark and fathomless and would haunt me for ages. I shivered in the hot spray of the water, mind reeling and trying to piece together who he was. There was something niggling at the back of my mind. He'd said something I knew would put it together for me, but it was just out of reach.

Once I'd finished my shower and gotten dressed, moonstone still fully intact, I emerged to find Naomi on her sofa. Her legs were curled underneath her, a pink knit blanket tossed over her lap, a cup of tea steaming in her hand. She was reading a book and waiting for me. I found another cup of tea and a tall glass of water waiting on her coffee table. I sat on the opposite side of the sofa and gulped down the water, my throat working hungrily. When I'd finished, I grabbed the mug and settled into the corner of the couch. I took a sip of the tea, fortifying myself for the telling, and began.

I spent the next hour telling Naomi everything. I told her all about Hatshepsut, our friendship, and the magic and strength in the liminal space. I told her about the amulet and, reluctantly, about the magic that granted me invisibility and everything I could recall about the shadowed man I'd escaped from. Once I started, it all poured out of me like a great purge that had been waiting to happen. I told her what we'd lost sight of, all the things Hatshepsut had told me and shown me. I felt lighter after telling her everything and waited for her to say something. She sat quietly, weighing her response, and I drank down my tea, letting the malty warmth spread through me. My empty stomach roiled a bit when the caffeine hit it, but I swallowed the nausea and sat still.

"For once, I am a bit speechless," she said. "I really don't know where to start with all of that." She looked at me like she was seeing me for the first time. "You are such an enigma, Julia. One moment, I think you're a weak, powerless witch. And the next, you've harnessed this massive power and searched out our Queen for answers when you couldn't find any here. I just... If I'm honest, I don't know whether to be in awe or terrified of you."

Whatever I'd been expecting her to say, it wasn't that. I shrugged my shoulders by way of apology.

"Sorry to... freak you out?" I said. "I don't really know how to feel about it all if it makes you feel better. None of this was planned. I... I did what I had to do. What I thought was right to try and find answers." I could taste the bitterness of my words on my tongue. "Everyone was doing what they could, but it wasn't enough. I took matters into my own hands. And here we are." The words were flat, my voice cold. But it was the truth.

"I actually don't disagree with you," Naomi said quietly. "I told Hanan as much. There was more we could have been doing—things we *should* have been doing for both you and Andrew. Giving you space wasn't the answer, even though that's what it seemed like you wanted at the time. You shouldn't have had to go to these lengths and do all this alone. We're supposed to be a sisterhood. We're supposed to have each other's backs; no one has had yours these last months. Not in the way that you needed us. I'm sorry for that, Julia. I really am."

I knew I'd felt abandoned but didn't realize until that very moment how much I needed that feeling validated. I'd insisted that I needed space, and I had pulled so far away from everyone and had leaned into the abyss of my loneliness and grief. But they hadn't come to pull me out. And there was a bitter disquiet I recognized more clearly now. That bitterness had festered into anger and had pushed me down this path, and I wasn't sure there would be a way back.

# 34

## Unlikely Ally

Naomi and I talked through the early morning, and she was as upset as I was. She'd been asking Hanan for years to do more. To learn more. To be more… she'd felt the calling for something different for a long time, and Hanan had brushed her off.

"I've said for years that we're acting like a magical book club, gathering together to discuss the latest great read each month and then going our separate ways for the rest. Not moving towards anything together." She sounded as exasperated as I'd felt for the last few months. Something silently shifted between us in the soft morning light of her living room, and we became allies.

We both grew quiet then. I knew we were trying to figure out how to tell everyone else what was happening and what it all meant. I watched the dust motes floating in the shafts of light coming in through the tall windows, mind busy but sluggish… like my thoughts were trudging through mud.

"I can't stay upright much longer. I've got to crash," I finally said. Exhaustion was pulling at me, its fingers gripping tight and pulling me under. All the adrenaline from the night was long gone.

"That's fine. It's an eight-hour drive down to Luxor. I normally fly, but I don't think that's a great idea given that we don't know who the man you encountered in the night is," she said, sitting up and stretching, rolling her head side to side to wake up a bit. "Can you sleep in the car?"

I nodded. "I could sleep anywhere right now. It's been a long week." I felt like someone had pulled a plug out of me. It was all I could do to hold my heavy head up.

"Okay. Grab your stuff, and let's go, then. The sooner we get out of Cairo, the better."

I grabbed my bag and went to the bathroom before we left. The circles under my eyes were even darker than before, and I was so pale I was surprised I couldn't see through my skin.

We took the elevator down to the parking garage under Naomi's building. She unlocked a small, pearlescent white SUV with dark-tinted windows. She'd grabbed a pillow and blanket for me and gestured to the backseat, and I almost cried in relief. I shoved my bag onto the floorboard and climbed into the back seat, setting up my makeshift bed.

"Listen, Naomi," I started.

She held up a hand and made eye contact with me in the rearview mirror. "Don't. This is what we should have been doing this whole time, Julia. Get some rest. We'll figure it out in a few hours. Together."

She started the car, and the quiet purr of the engine settled the last of my nerves. I was on my way out of the city and away from the shadow man. But I wasn't leaving empty-handed. Not only did I have the moon-stone, but I had an unexpected ally.

# 35

## The Reckoning

I slept for hours. Now and then, I'd surface to the sound of Naomi on the phone, coordinating movements and things for her non-profit, or her quiet voice singing along to music, surprisingly melodic and soft—the opposite of her persona. But mostly, I slept and slept hard.

We arrived at Hanan's before dinner. Naomi had called Dell sometime in the morning and told her we were coming and to have everyone at Hanan's for dinner that night. Sheepishly, I'd hoped I'd have a little time before confessing to everyone else what had been going on the last few months. I shrugged it off. There was no time or space for regret. Besides, they all had their transgressions to answer for. I needn't waste my worry.

---

When we arrived, everyone was gathered in Hanan's kitchen. I tried to beg off and drop my stuff in the guest house, but one look from Naomi had me following in behind her.

Marwa and Reem were in the kitchen, cooking dinner, and everyone else, save Hanan, was around the kitchen table with glasses or mugs in front of them or cradled in their hands. Hanan was leaning against the counter and snapped to attention when we walked into the room. She'd schooled her face into an unreadable mask, but the energy in the air snapped with irritation. Pale and concerned, Dell jumped up from her seat, the chair scraping against the floor and my nerves. She rushed me and pulled me tight against her. I stood stiffly, arms pinned to my sides while Dell squeezed. Everyone else took turns making worried noises and spouting platitudes too late for comfort.

"*Habibti*, we've been so worried! What happened last night?" Marwa asked, standing beside me, rubbing her hands up and down my back while Dell held on. A bubble of hysterical laughter came out of nowhere, and Dell pulled back and looked at me. I pushed her away and stepped back.

"*Last night?*" I hissed. "Last night? How about *what happened in the last few months*? How about you would all know if you were actually the sisterhood you fucking claim to be?" My fists clenched by my side, and I was shaking. I wasn't surprised by my anger towards everyone in the room. It had been festering for months, an open wound that no amount of pressure could stop oozing. It was fortifying to lean into it... the comforting bite of pain there to give credence to the anger. I should have leashed it, held tight to it, and dealt with it later. I should have. But I didn't. It came boiling to the surface and spewed all over the women gathered together.

"Julia," Naomi hadn't left her sentry behind me, but she stepped close and touched my back. "This isn't going to get us anywhere. I know you're angry. And you've every right to be. We *haven't* been there like we should."

My vision was spotty with anger, but I looked around the room at each face. Reem, Marwa, Marina, Dell, Renee, Salma, Hasina—they took turns looking at me and down at their feet, their faces a mix of sadness and horror. The only face I couldn't look at was Hanan's. But she was looking at mine, not breaking her gaze as it bored into me. She was fuming, and it rolled off of her in waves.

"Let's all just sit and talk it out, okay?" Naomi put hot hand on my back in solidarity or warning, I wasn't sure.

I nodded, and Naomi pulled me into the living room and gently pushed me towards the sofa.

Everyone spread out, each woman taking a seat in the room. Dell took the spot on the other end of the couch and angled toward me, but everyone else gave me some space. Naomi sat beside me in solidarity, perched on the arm of the sofa. I cleared my throat and started.

Everyone gave me the room to tell it all. It was a bit like being called to the Principal's office and being forced to recount something wrong I'd done, especially with Hanan taking a seat directly across from me at her desk, her chair spun to face me. I avoided making eye contact, focusing hard on my hands in my lap as I picked at my cuticles, little pinpricks of pain stinging. It was too hard. No matter how justified I felt, sitting in that room recounting everything I'd been doing without them knowing felt a little sketchy. More than once, Marwa or Renee tried to send out some soothing energy, and I stopped them.

"Leave me be," I said, looking up at Marwa and then at Renee. Renee bit her lip, and her magic receded, but Marwa argued.

"You can stop with the self-harm, *Habibti*. We can calm you and make you feel better." I looked at her with cold eyes, and my eyebrows raised slightly.

"I'm asking you to stop. I am fine," I snapped at her. Deep down, I knew that she meant well. But I needed the sting of hurt to power me through without tears. I refused to cry, cower, or behave like I'd done anything wrong. And I refused to have my feelings manipulated. She finally pulled back, face filled with hurt. I could hear the rustlings of everyone shifting uncomfortably in their seats. I carried on.

When I got to the part about the shadow man, Hanan stood up, chair banging against her desk, startling me from the retelling.

"You compromised our safety!" she exclaimed, her face pinched with fury. I'd never seen her angry before. She'd always been calm and clear-headed in the face of stress. But no longer was she our serene leader. She was a storm of emotions. "You set out on this power trip, going against everything I expressly asked you not to do. And you've compromised the safety of every single one of us in this room. And for what? Because you are a selfish, selfish woman who can't see past her own deluded reasoning that anything or anyone else matters but you."

She was shaking with rage, fists clenched, and body coiled with anger. Every word Hanan bit out slapped me in the face and stung me as much as if she'd physically done the same. She took another pointed look at me and stormed out of the room. The door slammed, making me jump, and Dell reached over and grabbed my hand.

"I'm sorry, everyone, but I've got to go to her." Salma stood up and headed for the door, hot on Hanan's heels. "She'll cool down. She needs some time, I'm sure." She glanced back at me, and I couldn't read the expression on her face.

"Anyone else?" I asked the rest of the room, my voice shaking a bit. My palms were clammy, and adrenaline was zinging through my system, making me hot.

"You can't be upset with us for feeling like you've gone behind our backs to do this, Julia," Marina said, her voice calm and steady. She was never quick to emotion, but I could hear the sense of betrayal in her words.

"Yes, Julia, it sounds like you've lost faith in us completely. Are we not allowed mistakes?" Reem asked.

I looked up at her and saw wet tears track down her cheeks. My stomach hollowed out. The pain in the room was palpable.

"The same could be said of me if that's your argument," I replied, hugging my arms around my waist. I waited, but no one else said anything for a beat.

"I think we're all losing sight of what we need to focus on," Hasina said. "Everyone has made mistakes. Julia." She looked directly at me. "You pulled away. You couldn't do the full moon ceremonies. You didn't come to anyone with your grief. You made choices. And we all did what we thought you wanted. We respected your choices. Respected your unvoiced ask for space. And, obviously, we were all wrong. But the fact of the matter is something bigger than all of our feelings has happened. And we need to find a way forward."

"Yes, let's continue." Marwa finally broke the silence. "After the man asked about what the sisterhood wanted, what happened? How did you get away?"

I closed my eyes and tried to picture what had happened in the night. *Had it only been hours ago?* I took a breath and let it out audibly, shaking off the ominous feeling that the timing felt impossible.

"Um... he said he'd gone over everything in the archives and felt nothing of *her* power. He didn't say who, just *her*. And he thought I'd only taken a scarab. He didn't know I got what I had come for and had the moonstone under my clothes. I don't know how. The scarab was the first thing I'd found and taken." I paused, thinking back, eyes still closed.

"Then he said I was a liar when I told him I didn't know anything about what he was talking about. He'd said that he knew me. Knew all about me..." I trailed off, the night playing out in my mind.

"He got angry and did some sort of magic to take my voice. He squeezed a fist from steps away, not touching me, and closed my throat. Then he came up against me, almost touching me, and froze me into place. His power... his magic... it felt big. He held me in place, my arms pinned to my sides, and my face tilted up, and he sort of... inhaled me in. Whatever he did, whatever he was looking for, my magic answered and bubbled up. But his responded to mine, and I could break out of his ho ld."

My heart was beating fast with the recounting. I couldn't open my eyes for fear of losing the vision of what had happened. It played out like a film behind my eyelids.

"Is that when you got away?" Reem asked. I shook my head.

"No, there was more. He underestimated me. Even though I'd spun out of his hold, he casually stood against the museum, like he knew I couldn't escape. And then I took the scarab out of my pocket and gathered up as much power as possible—the moonstone was throbbing on my chest. I squeezed the scarab so tight it left an indent for a long time. I pretended to be small and scared. And I kept drawing up power. And when I could hold the power in no longer, I threw the scarab past him, sent a huge burst of magic and shadows at his face, and shrouded his eyes in black so he couldn't see me. And I turned and ran. He shouted at me that I would regret it. That my false queen had defied him, and he'd killed her. Or something like that. And then I—"

"Wait, Julia," Naomi interrupted me. "Go back. What did he say?"

"He said I'd regret it. And that he'd choked the life out of my 'false queen'... why?" I asked, confused.

"If he knows about the sisterhood, then he's got to be talking about Hatshepsut?"

I shrugged my shoulders. "There's no way. I don't know. It felt like a threat, not a fact or anything. And I assumed he didn't know who I was and was pissed."

"But why would he use the term *false queen*? Or even lap dogs? Like he knew there was a group of us?" Hasina asked. I could see the wheel spinning in her mind, trying to pinpoint the threat and his identity. "Or even earlier when he said *her*. When he'd searched all the archives for anything that held *her* power. What if he was talking about Hatshepsut's power?"

"I... I don't know. No..." I stammered. "That's impossible."

"As impossible as this?" Naomi waved her hand and lit all the candles Hanan had around the room. "Or anything else any of us can do?" She swiped her hand again and extinguished the lights.

"As impossible as becoming a shadow?" Dell said.

It was the first thing she'd spoken since we'd come to the living room, and her voice was small. I looked over at her, and she was still pale and scared. Dell looked at me, and I saw the fear in her eyes. Not fear of the shadowed man but fear for me. I opened my mouth to answer her, but I closed it again. My mind was reeling. *Could* he have meant Hatshepsut? Stranger things had happened. Dell and Naomi were right. We had magic at our fingertips. Hell, I had visions of a long-dead Pharaoh. How was this possibility any different?

"How are we ever going to find out who he is?" I asked.

"Now, *that* is where I come in," Hasina said, standing up from the armchair she had been sitting in. "I can probably hack the security camera footage from the museum, get a clear picture of his face, and then find him from there. I'll be right back." She left the room, presumably to grab her computer and return. I looked at everyone else. Renee still hadn't said anything since I'd snapped at her and Marwa. Reem had stopped crying, but she still looked pained. Marwa and Dell, however, looked the most upset. They both had broken-hearted and disappointed faces that would have brought me to my knees if I hadn't been sitting down. All the anger had fizzled out of me, and I was left raw and hollow.

"You know you're going to have to fix things with Hanan. I've never known her to be this upset before," Naomi said. "I mean, I've butted heads with her plenty, but this is different."

Everyone made noises of quiet agreement around the room. I hung my head and nodded. We were silent then—words hanging in the air, mingling with emotions, and floating around like dust motes.

"I need to get some air," I finally said, breaking the silence. I didn't wait for anyone to argue. I left and hurried out to the garden. More than air, I needed to escape the room's choking emotion. Reliving the last few months and, especially, last night was a lot on its own, but add to it the high emotions of nine other women, and it was too much. Too thick to try and wade through a moment longer.

# 36

## *Search and Find*

I wanted nothing more than to escape to the guest house and fling myself at Hatshepsut through time and space. But I knew that was impossible with the sisterhood at my back, waiting for Hasina and me to return. It was a reckoning of sorts. I was being called to the carpet to answer for what I'd done. It rankled, but I knew there was no escaping it. Not really.

The last few months had been long. Lonely, save for Hatshepsut. Scary. And exhausting. In a way, I was ready to hand some of the stress over for the others to help me carry. And in another way, I knew I needed to prepare myself for more disappointment. One evening of apologies was no match for the seclusion and hurt. Though everyone had been doing things to help Andrew—making salves for his body, lending their energies to try and heal him—it paled in comparison to what *I* felt we needed to be doing. I'd argued with Hanan over and over again. I'd begged her to do more—to search the scrolls, to do anything but wait. And everyone, in turn, had agreed with her. If they wanted to talk about feeling betrayed, I could match them.

I scrubbed my face with my hands and let out an exasperated groan.

"Fuming and festering will get you nowhere, you know?" Hasina came from around the corner of the house, her laptop bag slung over her shoulder.

"Am I that easy to read?" I asked.

She shrugged and made a face that answered the question. "You forget, my friend. We know each other on a different level. Your pain calls to mine. It is too easy to let your anger and your hurt suppurate. But it will get you nowhere. Come. Let us track down this shadow man." She nodded towards the kitchen door and held open her hand in question. I nodded and came with her, arms folded against my chest. She opened the door for me, and cold air billowed out into the hot night. We could hear the quiet murmuring of the women in the living room as we walked in. At the closing of the door, they quieted.

Hasina and I walked in together. She took the center part of the sofa, pulled her laptop out, and took control of the room. I sank next to her and watched her fingers fly on the keys, too fast for me to make out much. Everyone was quiet, letting her work. Marwa stood up, and she and Reem returned to the kitchen to finish dinner for everyone. My stomach was hollow, but it had been a long time since I'd eaten more than snacks or protein bars, and it grumbled at the thought of an actual meal .

It took surprisingly little time for Hasina to hack into the security footage at the Egyptian Museum.

"I don't know why everyone thinks I'll be challenged by these things," she said smugly. "It was simple. I could have broken into this when I was fourteen." She started searching through the previous night's footage, pulling up all the outdoor cameras on one screen and working her way through them. I watched as she sped through, guards coming and going on their shifts and stepping out for smoke breaks. Not once did I catch sight of myself.

At the 3 a.m. mark, a dark sedan pulled up and parked behind the museum in a space marked with a placard we couldn't make out. A dark shadow of a man unfolded himself from the driver's seat and leaned against his car. He was barely perceptible in the darkness as if the shadows were leaking out and around him, camouflaging him in the night. He waited, still and silent as the night itself. Naomi and Dell perched on the arm of the sofa next to me, and Marina sat on Hasina's other side, all of us watching, holding our breaths.

We watched the minutes tick by on the camera footage, and he barely moved. After ten minutes, he checked his phone, the light from the screen flaring against him and lighting his face as he read for a moment before tucking it back in his jacket pocket. He pushed off his car, and the shadows wrapped around him as he walked towards the statue where he'd surprised me before he winked out of sight completely.

A few more minutes passed, and he came on the screen again, leaning against the statue directly across from where I knew I stood, still sheathed in shadows. Suddenly, we all watched as the shadowed man made a gesture. The darkness fell off of me, and I stood there, visible to the world, against the side of the building. Watching it play out on the screen in front of me was chilling. It was like watching a film in a detached way, but my heart picked up in anticipation, nerves on fire, waiting for my escape.

"Is there audio?" Renee asked Hasina.

"I can try, but most businesses won't spring for the extra cost of having audio. And places like the museum probably wouldn't bother since they get so much traffic it would be impossible to zero in on whatever they needed to." She bit her lip and focused on the computer. "Ah! Got it!" She jerked back and pumped a fist in the air.

"Wait, they have audio?" As the question left my lips, we heard tinny voices from her speakers.

"*Who are you?*" My voice sounded so small.

"*I am someone who knows you, Julia. Maybe even better than you know yourself. As soon as you found a way into the museum, I could feel you. And I 've been watching you for the last five days. All I want is to know what you've stolen away in your pocket there.*"

Hasina looked over at me, and I shrugged. We listened together; everyone hovered over the screen, intent on what was happening. It was bizarre to watch it when I had lived it less than twenty-four hours before.

"*So, what is it? What could her little lap dogs possibly want from the archives? I've personally cataloged everything in that room and taken everything that held even a whisper of her power.*"

"Oh, you're right. He says *her* like he's ready to destroy whoever she is. And he definitely implies a group. Who *is* this man?" Hasina paused the video and looked around at all of us. She fiddled with the controls and zoomed in on his face. It was grainy, and he looked unremarkable and barely recognizable. "I'm going to leave it zoomed like this while we watch, and if I can get a clearer image, I'll be able to screenshot it and use it," she explained as she hit play, and we continued watching.

"*I don't know what you're talking about.*" I heard my panicked voice ask.

"*You, my dear, are a terrible liar. So very many tells. You should never play cards. I will only ask one more time before I come and take it from you. Hand over whatever is in your pocket.*" The tension in the room was thick enough to cut through with a knife. Everyone knew I'd made it away from him, but there was no mistaking the danger in the man's voice.

"*If I give this to you, you'll let me go?*" My voice was small and weak over the video. I braced for what was about to happen and felt my heart pounding like I was back there. We were still zoomed in on the man, so I couldn't see my arm raise or watch myself pitch the scarab behind him, but we could see the moment my magic pummeled him. A black shadow slapped against his skin like a superhero mask framing his eyes. He grabbed at his eyes, squeezing them shut and swiping his face with his hands, face contorted in rage.

"*You'll regret that, little witch!*" He bellowed, and it sent chills down my spine. "*When your false Queen defied me, I squeezed the life out of her from the inside out!*" His voice boomed through the speakers on Hasina's computer. He moved out of the line of the camera as it was zoomed in close, so Hasina corrected it and zoomed out. He shoved his hands into his pockets and pulled out his phone, barking orders into it in angry Arabic within a few seconds. Hasina held up a finger to acknowledge to the non-Arabic speakers in the room that she'd tell us what he was saying in a moment. Dell and I were the only ones who didn't know enough to follow along. Marina was a whiz at languages and frequently switched in and out of English and thickly Italian-accented Arabic. Everyone else who was still in the room was a native speaker.

He hung up the phone call, and Hasina paused the video. "Basically, he orders whoever is on the other end of the call to track you down. To go to the hotel and get ahold of you and bring you to him at his home office. He says at the end, "*Somehow, I know she's behind this. My mother was a calculating bitch. They all are. She knows I'm close to finding them, and she would do anything to stop me and protect her precious priestesses. Not this time. I will find them and root them out. I will not fail again!"*

She hit play on the video again, and we watched him storm off, flashlight beam from his phone sweeping across the grounds until he found the scarab. He paused, his back turned away from the camera, seeming to stare at the small token in his hands before tilting his head back and screaming a furious growl into the early morning sky. After that, he got into his car and sped off. Hasina stopped the video and sat back.

"Well, he seems pleasant," she said.

We all looked at each other, unsure what to say or do. Watching him on the screen, the violence in him. The power... I was overcome with relief that I had managed to get away.

"What do you think he meant by *priestesses*?" Marina asked. "And that bit about his mother? Maybe he was raised by someone who was part of the sisterhood?"

We all shrugged our shoulders, each perplexed.

"First of all, let's go back and see if we can get a clear shot of him," Naomi said distractedly. I could tell she was wracking her brain for the next move.

Hasina nodded and sat back up to her computer. Muting and rewinding the video, she manipulated the controls until she had a solid picture of him. It was grainy but recognizable enough. "We'll give this a shot and see if it turns anything up," she said. "Unless you recognize him just by seeing him again."

She looked at me, hopeful. I shook my head.

"I don't. I've never seen him before." Someone shifted behind me.

"I think I recognize him," Naomi spoke up. "I don't know... he looks familiar, but I can't place where I might know him from." She trailed off, thinking.

"It's fine. Let's see if a quick search will turn anything up." More fast fingers on the keyboard, and Hasina had a web browser pulled up and searched the man's grainy face. We looked through a few rows of images before I stopped her.

"There," I said. "That's him." I pointed at the screen, and she enlarged the photo. I looked at the man looking back at the camera. It was a formal photograph taken with a light background and a symbol in the bottom corner that I didn't recognize. He was smiling, but the smile didn't reach his dark eyes. He had jet black hair and light brown skin with a neatly groomed, few days growth beard that was dark against his skin. He looked to be in his forties, with the barest wrinkles marring the skin around his eyes and forehead.

"Are you sure?" Hasina asked. I nodded. My stomach dropped as I flashed back to another night in front of Hasina's computer, with another cold face staring back at me. I shook the memory from the front of my mind and focused.

"Absolutely. That's him." She clicked on the hyperlink under the photo, and a new window opened to the Egyptian Ministry of Antiquities office. The symbol in the corner of the image was larger on the website— a golden eagle with a shield and the colors of the Egyptian flag on its breast. "Holy shit..." I gasped.

"Well, it looks like our shadow man is the Minister of State for Antiquities Affairs," Naomi said.

My mouth dropped open in shock.

"What the fuck are we going to do?" I stammered, terrified of the ramifications of such a powerful man on the hunt for me.

# 37

## *Revelation*

After the revelation of who the shadowed man was, Hasina shut her computer, and we all headed to the kitchen to eat, needing a moment to process and step away from the seriousness of the news. We ate quickly and quietly, no one knowing what to say. At a certain point, Salma called her mom to let her know that Hanan would stay with her for a few days and to lock the house up if Dell was going to leave to stay with Naomi. We all visibly relaxed—I didn't think anyone was ready to be in a room with the two of us any time soon. I was relieved. I certainly didn't have it in me to face Hanan again.

We all cleaned up after dinner, and Dell and Naomi decided to stay at Hanan's and be close in case anything happened. None of us thought it would just yet, but there was always safety in numbers. There was nothing that could track me to Hanan's or even Luxor. We had a little bit of time. We made plans to make sure we weren't alone out in public until we could get a handle on the threat from the Minister. It took some light arguing, but I assured Dell and Naomi that I would be fine in the guest house and begged off to get some sleep after everyone else had gone home. I wasn't truly alone— they were behind the same outer walls I was. If anything happened, they'd be able to hear me call for them. I grabbed the cat from her spot on the back of the couch and brought her to the guest house.

---

I showered, changed into pajamas, and climbed into bed, grateful for the cool sheets against my skin and the now-familiar pillow behind my head. The one good thing about having had such a transient lifestyle in my adult years was that I was pretty good at making new places home, and it hadn't taken me long to settle into the guest house. Lumee jumped up on the bed and walked up the length of my body, stomping on my chest before leaning over and head-butting me. I scratched under her chin and murmured to her until she'd had enough and slunk down next to me. She kneaded a bed out of the duvet and my arm. The occasional prick of a nail kept me awake, but she finally settled down, and I closed my eyes, absentmindedly stroking her soft fur.

I took a deep breath, focused my worried mind, and searched for Hatshepsut.

I found her in the ritual room. She was seated on a cushion in the middle of the room, candles lit all around her, incense burning, the scent of smoky sage, a thick cloud hanging in the air. Before I was even fully corporeal, her eyes opened, and her hand flew to her chest.

"Julia! *Merit!* Thank the goddess!" Relief washed over her face, and she got up and came to me in a flash. "I have been terrified for you. It has been so long since you've come. I feared you were lost to me forever."

She wrapped her arms around me, my powerful queen tucked away. Shesout, my friend, was shaking in my arms. I pulled her close and breathed her in. The burning sage suffused her hair and mixed with her myrrh and rose scent. I drank her in, taking comfort in her and taking pleasure in being able to comfort her. I whispered platitudes and apologies into her hair, holding tight as she cried in relief.

A few moments later, we pulled apart, and she held tight to my arms while she looked me over.

"Did you succeed? Did you find the moonstone in your time?" she asked breathlessly. Her face was soft with release.

I nodded. "I did. It took me days to search, but I found it, and it's safe with me there," I reassured her. I held her gaze as hers bore into my eyes.

"What else has happened, *Merit*? There is darkness in your eyes where there should be light from the success of your trial. Is it Andrew?"

"No. It isn't Andrew." I quaked. "Something happened, and I got caught. And, the magic held. The shadows cloaked me and didn't fail," I said before she could ask. "But I wasn't alone the last night I broke into the museum. When I left, a man found me. He could see through the magic." The relief that had flooded Hatshepsut's face fell away at once.

"A man was there? Who was he?"

I bit my lip, unsure how to answer her. A minister of antiquities wouldn't be a role in her time.

"He's a powerful man in the government. Not a king but what they call a minister. He's in charge of what we call antiquities now. So all the things discovered from the past, all the pieces of Egyptian history that tell us about your life. He's charged with the protection and collection of those things."

"But he didn't hurt you?" she asked. I shook my head.

"No. Not really. But he had magic of his own. And he threatened me. I think he's searching for me, and he's got a lot of power—magical and otherwise—that will assist him."

"May I see what happened?" she asked, holding her hands up, hovering away from my temples. I nodded my permission. It would be easier for her to watch everything from my memories than to delve into the retelling again. Even in the liminal space, I was weary from it all and felt exhaustion pulling on me. I needed a proper night's sleep in my bed.

Hatshepsut placed her fingers lightly against my skin, and I felt the barest amount of pressure against my temples. She sucked in a breath, and I closed my eyes as if I could hide and spare us both from the vision of what had happened. She had been still for only a few moments when she gasped a shriek that reverberated off the walls of the ritual room, and she pulled away from my face as if my skin had burned her.

"What is it? What happened?" I begged. The shock on her face was nothing I had ever seen before. The color had drained from her skin. Her eyes were wide, petrified from what she'd seen in my mind. She worked her mouth, trying hard to find the words to say. When she finally spoke, her voice quavered, barely above a whisper, but she might as well have shouted in my face for the thunderous statement she made.

"He...he lives still," her voice shook, and she choked on her words, tears pouring down her face. "Thutmose... he found the magic he was looking for. He... lives."

# 38

## *Minister of Secrets*

I didn't stay with Hatshepsut for long after that revelation. The knowledge that the man wasn't only the Minister of Antiquities but also the man responsible for Hatshepsut's death. Also, the leader of every iteration of man who had hunted down and snuffed out as much of the sisterhood as he could wasn't something I could sit on for long. I left Hatshepsut with the express vow that I would return to her as soon as possible. I returned to my body with a gasp that upset the cat where she had curled against me.

"Sorry, Lumee," I mumbled. I scrubbed at my eyes, rubbing the gritty sleep from them and wishing I could close them again and sleep the rest of the night. Instead, I groaned and reluctantly climbed out of bed. I pulled on leggings and a sweatshirt, grabbed my phone, and headed out the door and to the main house. Letting myself in through the kitchen door, I ran up the stairs to find Naomi and Dell.

They were sleeping in the room Dell had claimed as her own; Naomi curled against Dell, their faces soft in sleep. I sighed, not wanting to disturb them. I gently knocked on the door frame. I waited a moment and knocked again. Naomi shifted, and I whispered their names into the dark room. Dell grumbled a response, but Naomi said straight up in bed.

"What is it? What's happened?" she said, coming fully awake as she reached over and turned on the lamp on the bedside table. Warm, low light filled the room, and Dell pulled the blanket over her head and mumbled something under the covers.

"Get her up. I have news." I was wide awake now, my body zinging with a fresh hit of adrenaline.

Naomi pulled the duvet off Dell, who groaned even louder. "Unless someone's bleeding or on fire, can it please wait till morning?" Her voice was heavy and scratchy with sleep, and I felt guilty for waking her in the middle of the night two nights in a row.

"No one is bleeding or on fire yet. But this is big. Scoot," I said as I walked over to their bed. Naomi sat up against the headboard and pulled her feet up. I sat at the foot of the bed, tucking my legs under me. "I didn't go straight to sleep." I began. I raised my hand to stop them chiding me. "I know, I should have. But I didn't. I went to Hatshepsut."

Dell shifted then and pulled herself up to sit against the headboard.

"And you had to wake us up to tell us that?" she asked.

I narrowed my eyes at her. "No. Not to tell you that, but to tell you that the Minister isn't just the Minister of Antiquities. It's Thutmose."

Naomi scoffed, and Dell glared at me.

"Yeah, right," she said. "What is he? Thutmose the seven hundred and eighty-second?"

"No, jackass. Thutmose the Third. Hatshepsut's stepson."

Naomi shook her head. "You're taking the piss, aren't you?" she said.

I threw my hands up. "No. I'm not taking the piss. This isn't a joke; it's Thutmose," I insisted. "Hatshepsut can do this thing with her magic, where she can see inside your mind. Into your memories. I don't know how to describe it other than that. But she can. And she looked to see what happened at the museum, and she wasn't *there,* or whatever, long and pulled away petrified. I finally got her to speak, and she told me it was him. That he must have found the magic he was searching for and was still alive. There was no doubt in her mind. None."

It was Naomi and Dell's turn to pale.

"Yeah. *That's* why I woke you guys up. This isn't some rich and well-connected asshole we're dealing with. It's *Thutmose.*"

It took a long time for either one of them to respond. But Dell finally spoke up.

"I know you don't want this to be the answer, but we need to call Hanan. She needs to be here. They all do. This is huge. You were right. This is can't-wait-till-morning-huge."

Naomi nodded in agreement.

"I'll call Hanan. She's with Salma, so that's two in one. And I'll call Marwa after that. Hanan and Salma can pick her up on the way. Dell, you call Renee, and she can bring Marina with her. Julia, call Hasina and Reem. Have everyone get here within the hour."

She reached for her phone and opened it up. I got up and walked downstairs, pulling my phone out and calling Reem first. She answered on the third ring and sounded surprisingly awake for two in the morning. I didn't tell her about Thutmose, but I told her we had news and she needed to get to Hanan's within the hour. It took me three calls to get through to Hasina. She was *not* as awake as Reem, and it took a little more coaxing to get her to agree to leave her warm bed and come.

"Just tell me now, and I can get some sleep, and we'll deal with it in the morning," she insisted.

I stood my ground. "I'm not telling anyone until we're all together. Hasina, I promise you this is can't-wait-till-morning huge. Just get here."

I walked into the kitchen and started prepping tea and coffee. After the night we'd all had and the very few hours everyone had managed, I knew we needed vats of caffeine to get through the rest of the night and the coming day. I turned on the oven and popped in a batch of muffins. I'd made them the month before and had frozen, grateful that I'd had the foresight to prep a big batch of breakfast for a gathering like this.

Salma, Marwa, and Hanan were the last to arrive. Everyone was waiting in the living room, with various states of exhaustion around the room. Still, everyone was clutching a mug of something caffeinated like it was a lifeline. The smell of coffee, cinnamon, and sugar made the room warm and comforting. It was still the middle of the night, the darkness outside beaten back by the glow of the lamps in the living room. The three latecomers entered the room, Hanan looking like a stranger in her own house, unsure of where to go or what to say. Salma threaded her arm through Hanan's and pulled her into the room. We'd left the sofa to the three of them, and they took their seats. Marwa poured coffee for the three of them and then settled, looking up expectantly. I cleared my throat and stood up from the desk where I'd been sitting. I held tight to my mug from Marina, the heat of the tea inside steadying me.

"I'll cut to it," I said, looking at all their expectant faces. "Long story short, I had a vision of Hatshepsut tonight. She can do amazing magic, and she could see into my memories and watch what happened at the museum. And, um... she knew who the Minister is. I mean, who he really is." I took a breath and braced myself for the coming outbursts. "It's not just the Minister of Antiquities. I mean, it is. He is that, I guess. But he's also, and more importantly, Thutmose the Third."

I paused and gave everyone a minute for the news to sink in. And then the room erupted.

"How?"

"What are you talking about?!"

"Unbelievable!" Everyone shouted at once, surprise waking them up better than the most robust cup of coffee. I gave them a few moments more before continuing.

"Look, I know. It seems impossible. But apparently, that's the kind of magic he was searching for in the scrolls. And he found it. He found a way to stay alive all this time. And he's been behind the brotherhood, or whatever you want to call them."

Everyone in the room looked frantically around at each other for some sort of reassurance. No one had any to give. We were all in shock. Even *I* was still in shock, I'd barely had time to come to terms with it. Hanan, the only one who'd been quiet this whole time, finally spoke.

"How do you expect us to trust what you're telling us?" She bit out. Every word was filled with the same venom as earlier, and each word still carried the same sting of a slap. Her anger was quieter now—the calm yet unrelenting fury of someone betrayed.

I stood my ground, willing to take the hits as they came in the face of my truth.

"You don't have to believe me for it to be true. And if you no longer trust me enough to be a part of the group, then I'll leave. But know this: I'm not lying. And I'm not wrong. The Minister is Thutmose the Third. Some way, somehow, he found and harnessed enough magic to live this long, and we heard him say on the security footage that he was close to finding us. He called his mother a bitch. There's enough evidence to at least warrant looking at him closer and being on our guard," I implored. If Hanan wouldn't listen, maybe everyone else would. She crossed her arms over her chest and sat back on the sofa, quiet defiance written across her face. I turned to leave the room, and Marwa spoke up.

"No. Julia, *Habibti*, we've had enough secrecy these last months. Enough time apart. We are stronger together. We will get through this together. We will fight this man. But we will only do it together." She put her hand on Hanan's leg and pleaded with me with her eyes. I nodded once, and Hanan responded in kind.

"You and I aren't finished," she said directly to me. Months of hurt mixed with fear hung on her words. A ripple of my own defiance wanted to flex back at her, but I swallowed it down. I took a seat at the desk and waited.

Everyone spoke in turns, their voices still threaded with incredulity. Still, the reality remained that we were a coven of women with magical powers passed down from the great Pharaoh Hatshepsut... anything was possible.

We talked through the night. The muffins were long gone, and I'd lost track of how much coffee and tea we'd made, everyone taking a turn to go to the kitchen and bring something back to eat or drink every now and then. By the time the sun was high overhead, we were all exhausted but restless. Those with jobs and children to look after had begged off for the day, passing responsibilities so we could all stay together. No one would say it, but the thought of leaving each other was simply not a possibility.

Hanan and I avoided each other to the best of our abilities. Bless her, Marwa flitted between us, doing her level best to temper each of us. But after a few hours, her exhaustion darkened her eyes and made her tremble. Finally, Renee called for a break and ordered everyone to rest on a bed or sofa. No one argued.

I went back to the guest house, and Marwa came with me. I closed the door behind us, and she turned towards me, slipping her shoes off as she braced against the counter. In her tiredness, she looked every day her age. Usually vibrant and bright-eyed, she was pale and wrinkled with exhaustion and worry.

"*Habibti*, I know you're hurting. I feel as if I've done nothing more than add to your hurt when—"

I cut her off.

"Marwa. I know. It's fine," I said, too tired to try and patch things up with her at that moment.

"It is not fine, my dear one. But, if you are willing, it will be." She held her hand, and I took it, her skin warm against mine. She squeezed, hopeful. I squeezed back in return and nodded.

"Let's try and get some rest. I can barely stand upright." I shucked off my sweatshirt and crawled under the covers, my body physically aching with tiredness. I groaned, low and long, as I stretched my body under the blankets. Marwa chuckled, too tired to do much more than a quiet laugh.

"*Habibti*, I feel the very same way. Though my bones are much older than yours, they will groan and creak on their own alongside me."

I gave a half laugh in response, and my eyelids closed, too heavy to hold them open any longer. Marwa got into bed, and then I was out.

# 39

## *Secrets No More*

When I woke again, it was the middle of the afternoon. The blackout curtains in the guest house were doing an excellent job of keeping the room curtained in darkness, but the edges shone bright with the sun. Marwa snored softly next to me, and I quietly shifted, grabbing my phone from the bedside table to see if anyone else had woken up. The only text was from an unknown number. I opened it.

*"Well, well, little witch. I would have never guessed you had it in you. As I said, you will pay. Now that I've got your attention let me be clear about what I want from you. I want something you and your sisterhood have. I am willing to forgive your transgressions from this week in exchange for what I am seeking. My only ask is that you keep this between us. If you bring anyone else into this, I will hurt your husband, and the pain will be so great he will have no choice but to wake."*

The last dregs of sleep were whisked away instantly. My mouth went dry, and my hand trembled, the phone screen wavering in front of me. I locked the screen and pressed the phone to my chest, pressing it hard against me and biting back a sob so I wouldn't disturb Marwa. How did he connect me to Andrew? We didn't check him in under his real name, and the staff was paid for their discretion. I had nothing in my name here in Egypt. I was even using a contract-less SIM card for my phone.

Silent tears leaked out of my eyes. I was so exhausted. At what point in my life could I be free of power-hungry mad men who threatened me and the people I loved? I was haunted by the ghost of Gordon Mitchell and his father, along with Thutmose. How similar these men were. They thrived off threats and power, and I was expected to fall in line, behave myself, and cater to their every whim.

I lifted my phone off my chest and opened it back up.

*"What could you possibly want that I would have any power to give you? And how could I ever trust that you wouldn't take what you wanted and kill us anyway?"* I hit send before I could lose the tiny smidgen of bravado that had bubbled up. I waited. It didn't take long before the little dots showed up… Thutmose was typing a response.

*"I think you know exactly what I want. And you'll find a way to get me the scrolls, or I will pick off each member of the sisterhood, one by one, like gazelles in a weak herd."*

"Julia, what is it? What's going on?" Marwa's voice was quiet with sleep.

"He's sent me a message. He tracked my phone number down and messaged me. He's threatening us. And Andrew. If I don't get him the scrolls." I heard her sharp intake of breath. "I don't know what to do. He's warned me against telling anyone, but I can't keep any more secrets. They're too heavy to hold on my own." Marwa reached out over the blanket and grabbed my hand in hers.

"Secrets are a heavy burden, dear one. But there's no reason you have to hold this one alone. We'll figure this out together. Let us get the others." She was exhausted but resolute. And I couldn't help but feel a little hope that we could shore up our defenses and come together to fight this off like we were supposed to.

When we made our way to the main house, most everyone was up and milling around. Reem was cooking and baking up a storm in the kitchen, giving directions to Renee and Marina, who wore flour-covered aprons. Marina shoved her short, bobbed hair out of her face with the back of her hand, smearing flour on her forehead. She grabbed another handful of flour and tossed it on the dough in front of her with practiced ease.

"Good afternoon, ladies. Reem has us cooking to bring everyone some love and comfort. I am making my family's pasta recipe. It's good for hard times." She kneaded the dough in front of her with enough force that her forearm muscles rippled with the effort.

Renee turned towards us. "There's a fresh carafe of coffee on the side table there. Did you sleep?"

Marwa and I both nodded and made our way to the side table. Despite my preference for tea, I didn't want to add one more cook to the kitchen to get to the kettle. I poured myself a cup of coffee, doctored it with enough milk and sugar to make it palatable, and took a sip. It was bitter and hot but strong enough to promise a jolt.

Marwa and I took a seat at the kitchen table, both of us looking at each other, wondering when to break the news of Thutmose's contact.

"I'm not going to wait for everyone," I said. "I'll tell it again if need be."

"I agree," Marwa said. "Get it out. It feels too big to keep in any longer."

"What was that, mama?" Salma asked as she came into the room.

"I woke up to a text message from an unknown number, and it was Thutmose. Threatening me. Us. He wants the scrolls and doesn't want me to involve anyone else. He's threatened to—" I opened my phone and read directly from the message to avoid missing anything. "*Pick each of the sisterhood off like gazelles in a weak herd.*" I put my phone down and looked up. Everyone was frozen in place, mouths agape.

"How could he have gotten your number?" Reem asked.

"I don't know. It's not even a SIM card that needs a contract. I top up every month. There's no paper trail." I worried over my phone, turning it over like it might have the answer.

"Here, lovey, have something to eat." Reem came over and set a plate of fresh fruit down and another plate of warm cookies. Chocolate, sugar, and all the magical goodness I was sure Reem had poured into them lifted my spirits a little bit. "I spelled them with peace and grace." She looked at me, and I knew I'd been forgiven.

I smiled softly up at her. "Thanks, Reem." She reached down, squeezed my hand, and turned back to the kitchen.

"Simon has the kids for the next few days. I told him to lay low and that I was needed here. They'll be fine without me while we figure this out," she called over her shoulder as she returned to the stove and stirred a huge pot of something. Steam billowed out in a cloud as soon as she lifted the lid.

"Yeah, Omar is good with ours, and I've shifted the one tour group I had coming in tomorrow to someone else. Hanan is working on moving her schedule around as well. Still, I think everyone else got things sorted enough that we can be together for the next few days and figure out our next steps." She was standing next to the table, her mother's arms wrapped around her hips, Marwa's head resting on her side. Their connection was so effortless, so easy. I smiled, and I didn't feel a pang of envy or hurt for the first time. It was... sweet.

Within an hour, everyone was seated around the table, eating and drinking and speculating on Thutmose and his power. Everyone had varying opinions, and while there wasn't the sort of angry arguing that would lead to door-slamming and tears, there were definitely a lot of disagreements around the table.

Hanan, who barely looked at me and didn't speak directly to me once I'd relayed my text from Thutmose, was of the mind to lay low and keep living our lives. She wanted to focus on shoring up the defensive spells on our homes and ensuring we didn't call unwanted attention to ourselves. Marwa, Salma, and Renee were of the same mindset.

Marina and Reem wanted a slightly more defensive approach and wanted to scout him out and figure out what Thutmose was up to in his day-to-day life. Their thought was if we could figure out who he was pretending to be and what he was doing each day, we could figure out what he wanted from us and the scrolls.

Hasina and Dell wanted to hit him where it hurt... his finances. Once Hasina suggested digging into his money, and where it was going and freezing some accounts, Dell was all over that in response to his tracking me down— to prove we could do the same, and he didn't have the upper hand.

Naomi and I were the only ones who wanted to go after him. As in, come up with a plan and confront him in person, prepared to fight. I had a weird sense of confidence after escaping him once. Naomi was always spoiling for a fight and firmly believed that attacking things head-on was the best way to see them finished. It went against my every normal response of shutting down and running away, but something in me had snapped. I was tired of being ordered around and forced into doing something I didn't want to do. I was ready to fight.

Where Naomi and I differed, however, was how to go about fighting him. I wanted to get the scrolls and find a surefire way of defeating him. We had no idea the sort of power he'd amassed from those very same scrolls or what he'd come across in the thousands of years since he'd used them.

Everyone vehemently disagreed with me. And Hanan finally had no choice but to talk to me.

"Absolutely not. I told you before, and I will continue to tell you no. The scrolls are to be protected at all costs. We don't understand their power. We don't understand the gravity of what that kind of magic would ask, and I won't put us any more at risk than you already have." Her cheeks were flushed with anger, and her voice wavered with it. "We don't even know what sort of risk you've put on yourself by accepting this darker magic into you. I will not have a repeat of what happened when my grandmother was Steward."

I sucked in a breath and pinched the bridge of my nose, trying to steady myself against saying something I knew I'd regret.

"Nothing in life is without risk," I said, voice preternaturally calm. It was the exact opposite to what was happening inside my body. I was a storm of emotions that couldn't be reigned in. "How we choose to face the risk and the ramifications are what matters. I know something awful happened before, and Hanan, we're all sorry for what it did to your mother, but we can't sit behind these walls hiding and waiting for something to happen. We have to be proactive. He wants the scrolls. Why? What's in there that he doesn't know already?"

Hanan's jaw clenched.

"It doesn't matter. The answer is no. *I* am the Steward of the scrolls. I have vowed to protect them with my life and my magic, and I will do just that. That protection extends even to you, Julia. To all of you." She looked around the room at everyone, but no one argued with her.

"This is ridiculous. The answers could be right there, and you wouldn't know because you refuse to even try, like finding something to help Andrew. You're too scared of power to even look. Why should the rest of us suffer?"

"*Enough*!" Hanan's yell was so out of character that Marwa jumped, and Dell's face blanched.

Everyone looked down or at each other, trying their hardest to shrink away into nothing. Everyone except me. For the first time, I stood my ground.

"No," I answered. Adrenaline was pinging through my central nervous system like a pinball in an arcade, but I kept going. "You can't stand there and shut down every mention of the scrolls and more magic than your parlor tricks. Have *you* been meeting with Hatshepsut? Has she been telling *you* what she truly wanted for the sisterhood? What was her vision? And how far we've fallen from that vision? You are weak. And blinded by your weakness. We could be so much more. But you refuse even to entertain the possibility of more. You're content to sit here and play at magic. To light candles with thought and send out good intentions into the world. It's not enough. Not now. Not ever. It won't be enough when Thutmose comes calling. And what will you do then?"

Everyone was staring at me, eyes wide. I was usually content to fade into the background and let other people lead and argue. But this... I *knew* the scrolls had the answers we needed. I would fight and argue and make everyone uncomfortable if it made them see reason.

"I think that's enough, Julia," Salma spoke up and made her way over to Hanan to stand by her in solidarity. "Let's not forget that we're all on the same team. We're losing sight of what really matters, and this is no longer a productive conversation." She put her arm around Hanan, who was glaring daggers at me, hands fisted at her sides. I waited for her to turn on her heel and storm out again. But she stayed. Everyone else may have been content to forgive my secrecy from the last few months, but the reckoning I was getting from Hanan made up for their grace.

"Salma is right. This is getting us nowhere. We need to strike a balance between offensive and defensive, and we'll get it figured out," Hasina piped up. "First things first, let me do some digging on him. He's high up in the government, so he'll have an easy enough surface footprint to follow, and I can dig in deep from there."

Everyone fought against the tension in the room and busied themselves with tasks. Salma, Hanan, Naomi, and Marina left to go to the temple to ensure the wards there were strong. Renee and Reem left to get groceries for the next couple of days, and Dell cozied up with Hasina to help her search. Which left Marwa and me, which I knew she'd done on purpose.

"*Habibti*, you need to take it easy on Hanan. She feels like she's failed you, and now she's failing the others."

"Maybe she is failing," I said quietly. "I know no one wants to think the worst of her, and I don't either. But the fact is, we *have* to do something other than sitting around repeating the same mistakes over and over again."

Marwa narrowed her eyes at me. "I don't think you're being fair. The mantle of leader is a heavy burden to carry."

I made a noise in the back of my throat and fought back the urge to roll my eyes like a petulant teenager.

"Be that as it may, we must change how we're doing things if we have any hope of protecting ourselves against whatever threat Thutmose is going to be."

"She won't change how things are being done, *habibti*. She knows the dangers of the scrolls all too well."

"Yeah, I've heard about Ilse and all that she did. But it doesn't have to be like that!"

Marwa put a hand on my arm and steadied herself.

"Not just Ilse, dear." She took a breath and I knew I wouldn't like what was coming. "When her grandmother returned from abroad, they found a spell for forgetting. Hanan only meant to take away the guilt she felt over her daughter's death. Instead, it wiped her memories of ever even having a child. It—"

"You have got to be kidding me?" I hissed through clenched teeth, not letting her finish. "So the scrolls can be used when it's convenient for whoever is in charge? But no one else can have access when they need them?" I squeezed my hands open and shut next to my sides—they were vibrating with anger.

"It isn't like that, Julia," Hasina argued, turning away from her computer to face us. "The ramifications of that spell were great. Her grandmother doesn't even remember Hanan's her granddaughter. Everything about her mom, and Hanan herself have been wiped from her memory. The good and the bad. The risk far outweighed the reward."

"But that shouldn't be for her to decide for everyone else," I countered. My voice cracked with emotion and the sadness threatened to overtake the anger. I didn't want to let it. I had been sad for far too long. Too worried. Too upset. I wanted to burn with anger a little while longer.

No one had any arguments after that, and I stormed outside, needing something other than more bickering or sympathetic looks.

How dare Hanan. To have used the scrolls for her own personal reasons and then to decide no one else could use them because things didn't work out for her grandmother? What kind of leader was that? And *I* was the selfish one? A part of me was grateful (and another part was disappointed) that she wasn't home. I wanted nothing more than to scratch her eyes out and steal the scrolls out from under her.

# 40

*Dreams*

It had been over a week since I'd seen Andrew, and I needed to be sure he was safe. As soon as Reem and Renee returned with groceries, I left to go to the clinic, bringing Reem along to appease everyone's nerves. The desire to be alone was great, but the fear of facing Thutmose again was even greater.

Reem was quiet the whole journey. The car was filled with unsaid words, rubbing against us and taking up space, but we ignored them and pressed on. I didn't say anything about Hanan using the scrolls. I figured everyone knew or they didn't, but all the fight had fizzled out of me in that moment. She entered the clinic but waited outside the room while I slipped in and checked on my sleeping husband.

Time was not being kind to him. Though they were moving and exercising his body to prevent bed sores and the deterioration of his muscles, he was wasting away before my eyes. He was sunken in on himself, eyes shadowed, and cheeks gaunt, but he at least looked peaceful in sleep. I felt like I could reach over and shake him awake at any moment. But no touch brought more than the tiniest tremors from him.

"Drew..." I whispered his name in prayer and wish and mantra. Hope, the precarious thing it is, was slipping further and further out of my grasp. I shook my head, trying my best to clear the doubt. "I'll find a way, my love. I *will*." I'd made the same promise and spoken the same vow for months, and it was growing weaker and weaker. I hoped, wherever he was, Andrew was holding on to hope for both of us, ever the optimist he was.

I didn't stay with him for long. I couldn't bear it. Reem looked at me and put her arm around me to walk us out. I was hollow. Numb. All the anger from earlier in the day fizzled out.

When we reached Hanan's, I retreated to the guest house, crawled into bed, fully clothed, and sought out Hatshepsut.

She was in her bedchamber and turned, facing the window, face tilted up to the sky, lost in thought. I walked over to her, my steps whispering on the floor. I stood behind her, our bodies barely touching, and looked out at the sky. The moon was split almost perfectly in half, and the dark night sky was alive with the twinkling of thousands of stars and no modern-day light pollution. The sky was a riot of light and shadow, and it stole my breath. It was amazing.

"We are both so troubled, *Merit*. Let us hold our worries together, for I am sure they are one and the same."

I rested my head against her shoulder and nodded, not having the words but not needing them with her. We stood like that for a long time. She put her arm around me, tucked me in close, and I did the same. To be held by someone who truly understands you and what you're facing is a gift that knows no price.

We didn't speak that night. We didn't need to. We held each other and our burdens, there in her room, together with the stars. And when I kissed her shoulder gently and slipped out of the liminal space, I felt better for having been there.

I slowly came to and found Marwa next to me, sleeping peacefully. I quietly got up and padded to the bathroom, sliding the door shut behind me. Even though I'd 'slept' the afternoon away, I was bone tired. I couldn't even muster the energy to scrounge around the kitchenette for a snack, so I crawled right back into bed and fell asleep.

But I did not sleep the quiet, restful sleep my body craved.

"You are more powerful than I anticipated." Thutmose's voice rang out in the dark recesses of my mind. I was asleep but somehow cognizant of that, and the chill from the sound of his voice seeped into me. "I haven't felt a taste of her power in centuries. And now, little witch, I can feel her all over you. How is that?"

I wasn't anywhere in particular in the dreamscape he found me in. I was surrounded by darkness lit only by tiny pinpricks of stars that surrounded me entirely. I was barefoot, and the ground beneath me sparkled with stars and a puddle of ice-cold water no deeper than the tops of my feet. I shivered in my dream and hugged my arms tight to my chest.

"How are you doing this?" I asked.

"How do you think, little witch?" he said lazily. "Magic." His voice was coming from everywhere and nowhere. I shivered more. "You can ignore me in the normal world. You can delete my messages and ignore my phone calls. You can strengthen your wards. But you cannot hide from me here. Your dreams are as open to me as if you've hand-written me an invitation." His voice trailed away, and I was left in throbbing silence.

The rest of my dreams were quiet, but my sleep still felt disturbed, and I woke the next day feeling more hollow than before.

# 41

## *Time*

*Andrew*

"Time passes among your people." Khonsu's deep voice rang out behind Andrew, pulling him from a deep meditation. He squeezed his eyes shut and scrubbed at his face, still disconcerted over the fact that no matter how many months he'd been here—for he knew it had now been months—his beard never grew. Everything was on pause in this place, this... stasis. His fingernails didn't grow, his stomach never rumbled, and he never even had to relieve his bladder. It had taken a long time to ignore the mind's need for order and familiarity that went against the body's current needs or lack thereof.

"I know it does. I know that a great deal of time has passed with them," Andrew said, his voice carefully measured. He might not need to inhale and exhale on the plane where he existed in this form, but it certainly didn't stop his emotions. He stayed where he was, lying on cushions, propped up in the supportive supine position he'd perfected in his time alone.

"It is but a tiny drop of water in an endless ocean of time, child."

Andrew rolled his eyes, and Khonsu answered with a deep chuckle even though he couldn't see him. "I know you find offense in my calling you a child, but to me, you are an infant. I mean no harm, Andrew."

Andrew sat up, crossing one leg underneath himself. At least in this place, he was more flexible than in everyday life, and half lotus was effortless. As he constantly did, Andrew wished that Jules could see him here. He filled his days with meditation and yoga. Movement and breath and stillness. All the things she'd tried to impart that never took before. It seemed like they took when all he had was time and no distractions.

"You speak of time, Khonsu," Andrew mused. "About drops in an ocean. But your ocean is much larger than that of a human. These drops in *my* ocean are beginning to spill over. It has been too long. Too much." He took a deep breath and tightened the hold on his emotions. It would do no good to reason with the god using emotions. He didn't understand desperation or urgency.

"I do understand your urgency, child. Even if you weren't screaming it in your mind. I would understand. It is written on your soul. And it is written on your path."

Andrew straightened up. Maybe this was it. It was time for him to go back.

Khonsu shook his head. "Not yet, Andrew. But, soon."

"It's not soon enough," Andrew bit out. His hands were clenched at his sides. He released his fists, trying to calm himself by smoothing out the soft fabric of his trousers.

"It will have to be, I'm afraid." As usual, the god gave nothing away. He should have been used to it. But something was tugging at Andrew. An urgency that was not his own. Though it seemed to match his. "She is close," Khonsu said, and Andrew froze.

"She? Julia?" Andrew demanded. "What is she close to? What's happening?" He was frantic with worry. He knew that she was not okay. More than once, her grief had found its way through his unconsciousness. It was heavy and raw and too great a burden for any one person to bear after all she'd been through.

"Do you want the great burden of knowing? When there is nothing yet you can do?"

Khonsu was earnest and calm, whereas Andrew was anxious and beside himself. He worried over his words, knowing there was always more to what the God of the Moon said.

"My wife carries burdens far too heavy. I can carry the burden of knowing. Because when I return, the knowledge will help her."

Khonsu studied him closely, a faint twitch in his right eye, his only tell that he was holding back the whole truth.

"You only wish the knowing will help her. But you do not know. There are many truths, Andrew. Many things you need to know. But none of the knowing will be easy."

Andrew nodded, knowing he had no other choice. He could sit idly by no longer. No amount of meditation or raging at the empty sky would get answers further than his own self. This was the time for truth.

# 42

## Plans

I slept in fits and starts over the next two days. Any time I lapsed into a deep sleep, Thutmose was waiting. Sometimes, he spoke. Other times, it was his presence lurking in the darkness. But it was enough to haunt me and keep me from allowing myself to go to sleep for any length of time. Suddenly, all the time I'd been spending in a sleep-like state to visit Hatshepsut was gone. I was left with hours upon hours of wakefulness that was burdensome, stressful, and without escape.

On top of not sleeping or visiting Hatshepsut, I was forced to spend more time with the Sisterhood than I had in a long time. Everyone was still scared, anxious that there would be an attack from Thutmose at any moment, and they were hunkered down together at Hanan's. They were all in planning mode—trying to figure out a way to stop him.

"What if we found a way to bind his power during the next full moon ceremony?" Naomi asked one afternoon. Everyone was spread out throughout the house—some on computers or phones, others nose-deep in books. I was in the kitchen, absentmindedly stirring a big pot of soup for dinner, and Marina was kneading bread for dinner rolls behind me. Naomi was perched at the counter, a strong cup of coffee half drained in front of her while she worked frantically at her computer.

"What are you thinking?" Hanan asked, coming in from the living room. She leaned against the door jamb, relaxed but curious. We still weren't speaking and avoided each other as best we could, but we'd figured out how to at least coexist in a houseful of people. I had tried to argue about her having used the scrolls on her grandmother, but she refused to talk about it past reiterating what Hasina had said—the risk outweighed the rewards, and what had happened to her grandmother had been nothing short of a nightmare. I finally gave up.

"Well, I wonder if we can come up with, or find, a spell that would bind his powers. Even a bit. If we can keep him from doing his dream thing to Julia or any one of us, then we'd have an advantage there."

"Hmm, that is true. I'm not sure if I know of anything like that," Hanan said. She crossed her arms over her chest and thought for a moment.

"Yeah, but we could figure something out, surely," Salma stood in the doorway next to Hanan.

"I can't imagine it would be terribly difficult," Hanan said, still thinking. "Besides an incantation, I think we'd need to do something to physically represent a binding. That way, we could pour the magic into something tactile to hold the spell."

"Okay, so something that binds. Like... a book bound together? Glue? Staples?" Salma trailed off, still thinking.

"What about a wrapping of some sort?" I asked, back to them, still stirring the soup. It was the first time I'd really added anything to the conversation since relaying everything that had taken place in my dreams. Everyone knew my stance on using the scrolls. I hadn't felt like there was much to add past that since no one agreed with me.

"A wrapping could easily come undone," Hanan said stiffly. I deflated a bit. At least, I'd tried.

"What about knots?" Dell piped up. "I read a book once about a witch who wrote spells and bound them with knots. And that's an old, old pagan thing anyway, so there's got to be some truth to it working."

"That's a good idea," Salma said. "Worth giving it a try, anyway."

Hanan agreed with her and they bounced ideas off each other, tossing them around like balls in the air, some landing, some rolling away, discarded and forgotten. I stood by the stove, the space between us gaping wider and wider.

# 43

## *Gat a'la elgarh*

I went to sit with Andrew the next day. I was bone tired. My limbs were heavy, and my mind groggy with lack of sleep, but I needed some escape from everyone else. What had once been so amazing and inclusive had become suffocating and lonelier than when they gave me the space they thought I needed. I had begged off the afternoon, tired of twiddling my thumbs with everyone else. Instead of taking a bath in the guest house as I'd said, I'd wrapped myself in the shadows and slipped away. I needed the quiet. To hear Andrew's breathing and be reassured that he was still here and there was something more significant than Thutmose that I needed to focus on.

I hadn't been in his room long enough to put my bag down or spell the door with privacy when the doctor overseeing Andrew's care came in. He was an older man, his hair long gone gray, but still thick and wavy on top and cropped at the sides. He had a kind face and had been so encouraging when we first sought treatment for Andrew. He'd been willing to think outside the box and try different therapies I'd researched online and did his own research. I'd not seen much of him lately. Though, truthfully, I hadn't been to see Andrew as often as I had been, occupied as I was with the search for a more magical cure.

"I know that when your husband came into my care, we were hopeful about his prognosis," he started. His voice was heavy, and his eyes sad. I nodded. He moved his pristine lab coat out of the way, shoved his hands in his pockets, and rocked back on his heels. "Well, there's no way to sugarcoat this, and it kills me to say it, but... I'm sorry, I think we need to face the reality that your husband isn't likely to wake up."

The bottom of the floor dropped out from under me. I opened my mouth to say something... anything. But the words wouldn't come.

"I'm so sorry, Julia. I truly am." I couldn't look up. Couldn't look in the face of this man I had trusted to do something to help. Over and over again, people failed me. Failed to help. "It doesn't make sense. It truly doesn't. He's healthy. He should be..."

He spoke a few minutes more, but his voice sounded like it was underwater. My heartbeat throbbed in my ears, and I nodded and stuttered words to get him to leave. Finally, he bowed his head and stepped away. I closed the door and leaned against it, my fist in my mouth to hold back the threatening sob. I couldn't fall apart. This couldn't be it. I couldn't lose Andrew after all this time. I couldn't.

He was still and quiet, a peaceful effigy lying there alive, though just. But I could still feel him tethered to me. And I knew, deep down, that this couldn't be it. Not yet.

I walked over to him, swallowing down painful lumps of grief with every step. I looked down at him, this shell of the man I loved. That I *needed* with every fiber of my being. When I crawled next to him and lay against his chest, I couldn't help but succumb to sleep, lulled by the sound of his steady heartbeat.

"I can think of nothing else, beloved. Truly." I'd fallen to my knees in front of Hatshepsut as soon as I'd found her in the temple. "You have the amulet. It should be enough power."

"But it's not!" I cried. "Nothing I have done is working! I've not had it long enough to do a full moon ceremony with it, and I drained it of its stores when I escaped Thutmose. There are still days until the full moon. And even then, I fear Hanan won't let me use it. She's terrified of the power. Of what it could do." The simmering anger bubbled to the service, crazed now that my desperation to help Andrew was at a fever pitch.

"My dear one, I am so sorry. I—" She cut herself off before she could finish, and I watched her skin go pale. "What is that?" she asked, looking above me. I spun around and saw nothing out of the ordinary.

"What?" I asked, confused.

"There is something there—"

Without warning, I felt the twist and tug on my belly. Hatshepsut's voice faded away as I was yanked violently out of the temple. I called her name, terrified, as I slammed to a stop in the dark, watery dreamscape that Thutmose favored.

"Ah, there you are," he said, pleased with himself. "And ripe with her once more." I shivered as he looked me up and down, piercing through my skin with his gaze. "You really are much more powerful than I ever expected. Do they know? The other priestesses? Do they let you lead them? For surely you hold the most power?"

"What do you want?" I bit out, still disoriented from being pulled away so abruptly.

"The same thing I've wanted for centuries, my dear." His footsteps echoed behind me and came closer to me. I spun around and faced him. Usually, his dream visits were filled with only his voice. Now, he appeared in front of me, barefoot, soft linen pants rolled past his ankles to keep from getting them wet. His button-up shirt was rolled at the sleeves, casual. Like we were friends meeting for a walk on the beach.

"I don't give a fuck what you want," I said, too tired to entertain a fight with him. Worry pulled on me and loosened my tongue. He clicked his own at me.

"Ah, Mrs. Wheelright, what a mouth you have on you," he snarked. "What if, should you decide to *give a fuck*, as you so eloquently put it, I said I could help you?"

I crossed my arms in front of my body, hugging tight to myself and trying to shrink away from his penetrating gaze. My skin crawled with discomfort, but try as I might, there was no escaping his hold on my dreams. I bit down hard on my tongue and tasted blood, the coppery pain anchoring me and keeping me from spiraling out of control as I tried and failed to escape him. I swallowed down blood and bile.

"Such hatred for me," he crooned. "I can taste it. You are radiant with it." He closed his eyes and inhaled deeply like he was testing the bouquet of a glass of wine. "But we are the same, you and I. The darkness fuels you, you know. The fear and grief and hate. The loneliness. The scared little girl you keep ignoring. The feeling unheard. Misunderstood. Unseen. Ahh..." He exhaled and continued. "It's all there, feeding you. Feeding your power. You only need to harness it. I can show you how."

I swallowed again, uncomfortable with how clearly he saw me. The darkest parts of me I tried to keep hidden away.

"*Gat a'la elgarh,* little witch."

Something in me shifted when he spoke those same sacred words Hasina had spoken the year before. *Gat a'la elgarh... that came on my wound.* I looked at him then, really looked. And I saw it. The same hurt. The same grief and fear. And yes, the same hate and loneliness.

My stomach clenched, and I hated myself for feeling even an inkling of sympathy for the monster standing in front of me. He *killed* Hatshepsut. He lied and stole and did things, unspeakable things, to gain immortality, and he had the audacity to say we were the same. That *darkness* was what fueled me. It was love. Love and desperation for my best friend. The love of my life. That's what fueled me. Not darkness. That was nothing. That was a blip. A power I needed to get what I wanted. Not what *fueled* me. I shook my head, teeth gritted, the hate rolling off me in waves. If he wished for the stench of it, I'd give him enough to bottle and sell.

"We are nothing alike." I bit out each word, feral with rage. He merely shrugged his shoulders and maintained his calm facade.

"Well, should you change your mind, you know where to find me. All you need to wake that husband of yours is inside you." He nodded and then released his hold on my dream.

I came to next to Andrew, sweating and shaking with anger and fear, the stink of it acrid and more pungent than the chemical hospital smell of the room.

# 44

## With Sympathy

I didn't even pretend I hadn't left Hanan's in secret. I walked through the gate and the front door, desperate for someone to give me hope again.

"Julia!" Hasina, on her way to the kitchen, stopped. "We've been so worried about you."

I stared blankly, not knowing what to say or how even to start. She put her arms around me and pulled me tight against her, so out of character for the stoic woman she always was.

"Karim called. Dr. Hamada contacted him to let him know what was happening. I'm...I'm so sorry, Julia."

I tucked my face into her scarf, breathing in her clean cotton scent. The tears were painful behind my eyes. I heard the soft footsteps of the other women as they filled the entryway of the house.

They passed me around like a newborn baby, hugging me tight to each one of them and whispering sympathies and condolences like Andrew was gone already. Even Hanan, who'd been so cold and angry since my return from Cairo, folded me into her arms and spoke her quiet consolations. That was what it took for me to snap out of the numbness and talk to them.

"He's not gone yet." My voice was choked, but I pushed on. "There has to be something else we can do. I'm not giving up. I can't. Not yet." I looked around the room at each of them, imploring them to agree. To jump up and say, *let's do this!* But they all had the same sympathetic look on their faces. The same tear tracks ran down their cheeks. The same defeated air about them.

At that moment, I hated them more than I hated Thutmose. I hated them more than I hated myself.

I shook my head, mouth dropping open, ready to spew the anger at them. But it wouldn't come. I was incredulous. Shocked at their weakness. At their defeat. And I knew then that I was alone in my last little dregs of hope. I clutched my hand to my chest, trying to find that hope to hold on to physically. They mistook it for grief.

More tears flowed. And yet more anger simmered.

I played the role of a pre-death widow the way they wanted me to. I swallowed the anger and was left with a numbness that I welcomed, for it was a respite from the madness threatening to spill over.

I had spent months fighting. Searching. Begging and pleading with anyone who would listen to find a way to bring Andrew back. The thought that these women, my *sisters*, would give up and encourage me to do the same felt like the most profound betrayal.

"I called Edie," Dell said, "She said you haven't been responding to her calls or texts. The girls miss you, Jules. Edie misses you. Maybe you should go back and visit after..." She trailed off without saying the words that were hanging on her lips.

"Dell, I—"

She interrupted me before I could argue. "I'm not telling you to make any plans or big decisions right now, Jules. Just letting you know... you have people who need you. Who miss you. And they're not the only ones."

I nodded, biting my tongue and continuing to play pretend until I could get away.

After forcing myself to eat something to appease the masses, I left them to go to the guest house. I couldn't stand their nervous hovering a moment longer. Every one of them with their sad eyes and resigned condolences. I couldn't take it. Every step I took was a mix between hurried and weighed down. I was desperate to get away, to wash away the stink of fear and the dried tears on my cheeks. And I was desperate for some space to think.

I turned the water on as hot as I could stand it and stood under the hot spray of the shower, eyes closed and skin stinging as the day washed down the drain. Moments of the day, snippets of conversations with the doctor, Andrew's still form, Hatshepsut, Thutmose. They all played out in my mind on a loop. I growled into the steam, a frustrated howl rising from the depths of my very soul. I dropped to my knees. My body was wracked with sobs that clawed up my throat and forced their way out violently.

# 45

## *Infiltration*

When I had howled into the steam long enough to release at least a little of the pressure that had built up, I crawled into bed. Marwa had asked before I left Hanan's if I needed company tonight. I'd assured her that, more than anything, I needed some space for tonight. I couldn't imagine facing anyone now.

Days of not sleeping and the stress of being in close quarters with everyone, compounded with the news of Andrew, had drained me of what little energy I had. I crashed, face-down, on the bed. I was asleep within moments. And, of course, Thutmose was waiting.

"Ahh, little witch, we meet again," he purred. "You've been avoiding me."

I huffed out a groan and walked away from him. The ankle-deep water was cold against my feet. I was exhausted and not in the mood to deal with a centuries-old asshole. No matter where I turned or how far I walked, there was nothing in the dreamscape except the pinprick of stars at my feet, and the enveloping darkness.

"You are troubled, little witch," Thutmose said. His voice was gentle and that, more than anything, startled me. I turned to face him and found him close behind me. I hadn't heard his footsteps.

"That's an understatement? Of course, I'm troubled. How can I not be?" I turned back around and kept walking. For all I knew I was walking around in circles in this place that Thutmose kept me, but I didn't care. I needed to move.

"What is it that has you so angry today? Surely it isn't only me?" He stood in front of me, blocking my way.

"Contrary to popular belief, the world doesn't actually revolve around you, Thutmose," I quipped. He raised an eyebrow at me, curious.

"I haven't been called by that name in a very long time, little witch." I couldn't tell if he was annoyed or amused.

"I'm sure you've been called a lot of things in the last few thousand years," I said, and he laughed. He might have been amused, but I was annoyed. "Besides the scrolls, can you just tell me what you want and leave me alone? I have no idea where they are, so I literally can't help you."

He quirked his head to the side, studying me. I fought every instinct to look away and met his eye contact. A ripple of unease spread through me.

"For the first time in a long time, little witch, the scrolls aren't entirely what I am after," he finally said.

I was deeply uncomfortable. Somehow, he was seeing every part of me and there was no escape from the intrusion. Finally, the spell broke and I turned away, pacing some more. This time, he let me be. I ended up circling back and found him on a low wooden bench, waiting, still studying me.

"What?" I asked. "Why do you keep staring at me like that?"

He motioned for me to sit. I stood, arms crossed over my chest.

"We don't have to be enemies, you know," he started. He opened his hands, palms facing up as if to show he wasn't hiding anything.

"The minute you killed my queen, you became my enemy," I said.

He hung his head, and I glared. I wouldn't let him trick me into thinking it had been some sort of accident.

"I wish you could see the truth of everything I've done. In the beginning, my intentions were pure," he said quietly. "There are many things in my long life that I regret, little witch. But everything I have done, I have done with a reason and a purpose. Reasons you couldn't begin to fathom." He was quiet for a long time, then, and the words hung in the air between us. I shifted uncomfortably, and he looked up at me. "Sit down. I promise I won't bite." Reluctantly, I sat.

"So you're telling me that you're just some poor, misunderstood man?" I said, breaking the silence.

"Aren't we all poor, misunderstood people?" He quipped back, looking up at me, his eyebrow quirked again, questioning. "You're misunderstood by the very people who are supposed to stand by you and support you, yes?" I refused to meet his eyes. I crossed and uncrossed my legs, nervous energy needing somewhere to go. It was all the confirmation he needed.

"Your sisterhood vilifies you. They make you question your sanity and your ethos. But, are you wrong, little witch? Are you evil for wanting more? Or for having more power than the rest of them?" He paused, letting the words ring out in the dreamscape. "I don't think so. I think they *fear* you. They fear power and strength. And they want to hobble you. Control you. I was hobbled once, too."

I snapped my head up and met his gaze. Another quirk of his eyebrow and I clenched my jaw against the argument I wished I could spew at him. But there was no argument. He wasn't wrong.

He sort of bowed to me, one arm outstretched, and then he and the starlit dreamscape were gone.

I slept peacefully, and uninterrupted, the rest of the night.

# 46

## *Gifts*

The gift of a few nights of uninterrupted sleep had me slightly warming to Thutmose. It was amazing how human one could feel without their dreams infiltrated by their sworn enemy. He had also sown the tiniest seed of doubt in my mind. I wondered if maybe we all misunderstood him. If even Hatshepsut had misunderstood what he had been searching for all those years ago. The seed of doubt still didn't excuse the murder of my friend, but it was enough to leave me with questions.

The next time he came to me was different. The water pooled at my feet in his starry-floored dreamscape was warm against my skin instead of cold. The air was humid and tropical in the way the temple was—I found it oddly comforting.

"You look well rested, little witch," he said. He was seated on the wooden bench, the only thing in his dreamscape besides the wet, starry floor.

"Thank you," I answered him. "You've given me peace these last few days, and I needed it." He looked surprised at my gratitude. "I'm not some evil bitch, you know. I recognize a lifeline when it's thrown to me."

He chuckled. "How about another one?"

I looked at him, confused. "Another what?"

"Lifeline, as you said," he answered. "I'd like to prove to you that I'm not some evil monster out to get you."

My stomach flopped over and I swallowed thickly. It was getting easier to drop my guard around him and the thought alone was enough to unsettle me. I didn't know if I could keep the fire of mistrust kindled if he threw me anything else in the way of goodwill.

"I know what you're trying to do," I countered. "You're trying to get me to lower my guard, and then you'll swoop in and do something awful."

He hung his head in his hands and let out a shuddering breath.

"All this power, and I will forever pay for the transgressions of my youth." His voice was heavy, and my heart gave a little lurch. "Are you so pure of heart, little witch, that you've never made a mistake?" He asked the question with his head still hanging, not making eye contact with me. The dubious hold I had on my feelings for him continued to waver. "Let me give you this one thing, little witch. Come, take my hand."

Without thinking, I reached for his outstretched hand. It was warm against my own, the skin soft and well cared for. He took a deep breath and looked into my eyes. I wanted to tear my gaze away from him, but I was frozen in place. My hand began to warm in his, and I could see a soft glow in my peripherals emanating from our clasped hands. Thutmose closed the space between us, pulling me closer to him. Still, I was transfixed by his eyes.

He reached up and gently caressed my face. His eyes softened, and I could see... longing... cross his face for a moment, and then it was gone.

He held his hand against my temple, his touch featherlight and warmth spread out of his fingers, the same soft glow spreading across my face. After a few breaths, it became so bright that I shut my eyes against the light, finally breaking our gaze. My body jerked forward, and the dreamscape tilted and spun like a carnival ride. I slammed to a stop, my stomach protesting at the movements. I opened my eyes, and the dream had changed.

I was in a temple. It was familiar but also not. It couldn't have been any we'd seen on our tour of Egypt- it was intact and pristine. The walls were a riot of colors from the painted stories and recorded histories. I looked up in awe at the painted ceiling above me.

"Wow," I breathed.

"Jules?"

I spun towards the voice I hadn't heard in months, and there he was. Andrew.

We stood across from each other in shock. Here he was. Standing. Skin flush with health, eyes bright with life.

"You're welcome," I heard the voice in my mind, a whisper of Thutmose and a reminder of his power, I knew. But at that moment, I didn't care. Finally, Andrew was before me. Even if he was just a dream, he was here. I took a step gingerly, afraid he'd vanish if I blinked or moved suddenly. Andrew mirrored my movements. Doubt and joy spread across his face in equal measure. When we were close enough to touch, he finally sp oke.

"I am terrified to touch you, my love," he whispered. "I don't want you to disappear."

"I'll hold on as long as I can, Drew," I promised. My voice croaked, the shock of seeing him giving way to a tidal wave of emotions streaming down my face. He carefully reached up and wiped the tears from my face. His fingers barely skimmed my skin, echoing Thutmose's moments ago.

He brought his knuckle to his lips and kissed away my tears like he'd done a thousand times before.

I couldn't take it anymore. In the back of my mind, I knew I could be ripped away from this dreamscape and plunged back into the darkness with Thutmose. I stood on my tiptoes, wrapped one arm around Drew to pull him close, and brought the other to his face. I crushed my lips against his and did my best to drink him in. For months, I'd chastely kissed his lips, and finally, he kissed me back. He threaded his hands through my hair and pulled me closer, tight against him. He tasted like honey, the damp clean after a rain, and salt from both our tears. Emotion bubbled up, and I laughed and sobbed against his lips.

"I love you," I said. There were a thousand words to say, but I could bring none to mind except the most important ones. He kissed me again, words lost between us as our bodies took over.

We were delirious. Time, stress, space, fear, and longing made for a frenetic reunion. I pulled his shirt over his head, breaking our kiss momentarily so I could feel his skin against mine. He answered in kind and pulled mine over my head. He crushed me against him, our bodies flush, mouths working together. Every nerve ending was on fire as his hands roamed up and down my back, and our bodies met again.

His skin was supple under my fingertips, muscles working and hard, unlike the yielding flesh of his sleeping body. Feeling him so alive and healthy filled me with something more precious than joy.

He broke away from my lips and kissed my cheeks. His lips grazed my jawline, and I tilted my head towards the painted night sky of the temple. He licked and kissed his way down my neck, burying his face and breathing deeply. He reached his hands up and cupped my breasts, lifting them. He squeezed them and bent his head, kissing and licking the whole way. My eyes fluttered closed. He wandered back up my neck and found my mouth again, our lips and tongues, trying to make up for lost time.

We lost ourselves in each other, and time fell away like autumn leaves. Frantic. Chaotic. And then slow and sensual. We came together, bodies moving so perfectly in sync as if no time had passed. In those moments, there was no hurt. No wounds that needed mending. No cross words that needed to be forgiven. There was only us. Our skin. Our love. And the promise of hope.

Afterward, we lay together, bodies still touching as much as possible. I tucked my face in the crook of his neck and breathed him in. He smelled like mountains—crisp and clean, verdant and alive. His hands tangled in my hair, and he murmured promises and declarations into my curls. I felt it before I saw it. A shimmering that rippled through me. I opened my eyes to see his form wavering in front of my eyes.

"Drew," I started. "I'm losing my hold. I love you so much, please, please come back to me."

He answered, but I couldn't make out what he said. The edges of my vision darkened, and the nauseating journey that had transplanted me into the dream swept me up once more.

When I opened my eyes, I was alone in my room. I curled up into the fetal position and cried myself to sleep, knowing there would be no more dreams of Drew.

# 47
## Choices

Many times, I had tried and failed to have a vision of Andrew. I had hoped I could somehow visit him the way I did Hatshepsut, but I'd never managed. I assumed it was because she was long dead and Andrew was still alive, however tenuous his hold on life may be. I hadn't even dreamed of him since he'd slipped into his coma. So the dream Thutmose had gifted me—those precious moments with Andrew had done nothing but fuel my need for answers.

I thought about going to Hatshepsut. But Thutmose and his promise kept playing out in my mind. He was here. In my time. What if we'd been wrong about him? He'd been *kind* the last few days, only showing up briefly before letting me sleep uninterrupted. And then, the dream...

"No," I said to the empty room. "He killed Hatshepsut. He's not the hero of this story." I paced the room, unable to sit still. My nerves pinged with frustration, anxiety, and anger, bouncing back and forth between them all, making me dizzy and unsettled.

I fretted and paced most of the night, stuck in a sort of manic loop of thinking out loud and growling in frustration. I don't know how often I sat on the bed, smoothed the covers over me, and laid there, eyes forced shut, willing sleep to come. But it wouldn't. By four in the morning, I'd talked myself out of going to the clinic and dragging Andrew to the temple again, calling Thutmose, and giving up and running away, leaving everyone behind. The last one was the least likely scenario, even though I was desperate to be feel anything other than this howling desolation and helplessness.

I slept then, worn out from my frantic pacing and worrying. I moved on autopilot for the next few days, just getting through. If anyone said anything to me, I barely noticed it. I was stuck in a battle of wills between my heart and mind.

Finally, after a few restless days, I gave up and made a decision that there would be no coming back from. I picked up my phone and called the number Thutmose had texted me from.

He answered on the second ring. I swallowed my pride and morals in one gulp.

"Well, isn't this a surprise, little witch?" I could hear the amusement in his voice and could picture it on his smug face.

"I am not going to beg. Or barter. Or steal. I am just going to ask. How can I heal my husband?" I gritted my teeth hard enough that I was worried they'd crack under the pressure. I couldn't believe what I'd done. But I thought of Andrew lying in the hospital bed, everyone else around him having given up. I wouldn't. I couldn't do that to him.

"Why are you asking me? Have you finally realized I am not your enemy?" Thutmose sounded genuinely curious, not snarky or petulant like I'd expected.

"Because there is no one else. The doctors have said there's nothing more they can do. The sis... my fri—" I cut my words short, not knowing what to call them. The women who were supposed to be standing beside me and helping me face whatever came our way.

"Ah, they won't do any more to help, will they?" He at least had the decency not to sound happy.

I let out a sigh. "No. But I am not ready to give up. So, do you know how to heal him?" Thutmose was quiet on the other end of the line. I shifted from foot to foot, anxious for him to answer. Terrified for him to answer.

"Yes," he finally said. "I know how to heal him. But it would be easier to teach you in person. Where are you? I can come to you."

I wasn't *that* desperate yet.

"No. I can't tell you that, and I can't leave where I am. Tell me over the phone. Or do your dream walk thing and tell me there."

"Dream walk?" He chuckled. "You make it sound like a dance move. But, yes, that could work. Shall we meet now?"

"I haven't been able to sleep all night, but I can try."

"Need I remind you that you have magic, little witch?" He sounded amused, and I stopped picking at my nails and internally groaned.

"I've never done any sort of magic like that on myself. I don't even know where to start," I said honestly.

"Well, I'm not sure what all you know, but a sleeping spell is quite simple. And can be very useful in times of trouble." He took a moment and explained what to do, and I felt like an idiot. It was simple. I'd even tucked aside the right words to use should I have needed them on the guards in the museum. I don't know why it never occurred to me to use magic like that on myself. I thanked him, the friendliness of our conversation feeling foreign on my tongue, and ended the call.

I looked down at my phone, surprised at what had happened. Had I really done that? Had I really called Thutmose and asked for help? How desperate must I be to stoop that low? I thought about the shadows that were living inside of me... the darkness that I'd invited in, and thought about the risk and trepidation from everyone else around me and how it had been the best decision I could have made. How no other magic I performed felt as easy or fated. Maybe this would prove to be the same.

I sighed, knowing there was really no turning back now. I'd invited him into my life and my dreams. The best I could do was show up and be on my guard but get the answers I needed. Hopefully, whatever he asked for in return wouldn't come at too great a cost.

I spoke the spell into the darkness of my room, and my eyes fluttered closed, immediately dropping me into a deep sleep.

Thutmose was waiting for me. We were in a botanical garden, empty of other patrons but beautiful and lush; plants from all over the world were planted together and thriving. The air was verdant and intoxicating, and I stood in the warm light of dawn and felt it warm my face. I took in the clean, green air. It was steadying and wonderful and... peaceful.

"You like it here," he said. I nodded.

"I do. It is peaceful, and I haven't felt peace like this in a long time." I looked at him and found him peaceful as well. He was barefoot, his toes digging into the grass, grounding down into the earth. He was in linen trousers and a loose T-shirt, comfortable and effortless. I was in leggings and Andrew's ratty band T-shirt that I loved so much.

"I love a good garden," he said simply. "They are brimming with so much life and possibility. And when cared for, they can go on forever."

"Gardens like this always feel magical to me. Like there are fairies around every corner or doorways to another land just beyond a low-hanging branch," I sighed wistfully. It gave me a pause, the ease with which I spoke to him. We were supposed to be enemies, but here, in this peaceful place, we were two people admiring the beauty of the world.

"Shall we begin?" Thutmose held out his hand for me. I knew that I was standing on a precipice. I looked from his outstretched hand to his face. His eyes were dark, shadowed, but not unkind. At that moment, I made my choice.

And there was no coming back from it.

# 48

## Trial and Error

I couldn't look anyone in the face the next day for fear that they would see my betrayal written plain as day across my own. I'd spent hours with Thutmose in the early morning light in the garden of our dreams. He had taught me about his magic and taught me a spell to heal Andrew. It was simple, really, and it bothered me that none of us had thought to try it.

We'd been trying to heal the injuries he'd sustained at the hands of a madman. The cuts and bruises, the breaks and scrapes. But what none of us had realized, and what Thutmose suggested, was that his soul required healing. When he'd undergone the healing ritual, the fear he'd felt going in had finished fracturing him into pieces, too much for a soul that was hurting and hanging on by a thread.

My goal was to reach deep and try and speak to whatever it was that was tethering him to life. To hold on to it and to help heal the soul. I had no idea if he was full of shit or being honest, but I had nothing more to lose.

I tried to sneak away to the clinic, but Dell caught me and insisted I not go alone. It wasn't hard to look the part of the pre-death widow. The bags under my eyes were etched deep, and I was exhausted beyond words from my frantic night. My skin was pale and sickly-looking, and my clothes hung loosely on my frame. I was wasting away almost as much as Andrew. Would we even recognize each other when he woke? I shuddered at the thought of him not recognizing me, and Dell reached across the car and held my hand, thinking I was shaking with grief.

I talked her into staying in the car and letting me see Andrew alone when we arrived. I walked in, and the nurse at the desk was somber when she saw me. I nodded at her and kept walking down the corridor and towards a miracle.

I closed the door behind me, spelled it for privacy, and turned to Andrew.

"So, I did a thing," I said, trying to make light of my choices. I stopped and made a face. "Sorry, I'm trying to ignore that I probably fucked up and invited the big baddie into our lives. But I'm desperate, and I really, really need this to work, Drew. I need this to have been worth it. For it not to have been a giant mistake. So please, if you can, hear me. If there's any part of you listening right now. I need you to pull it together and come back to me. Please," I pleaded and begged quiet tears falling on my cheeks as I held his hand in my mind.

It was warm but not with life. I brought it to my chest and cradled it against my breast. "Please," I begged one more time before I began.

I took a breath and settled myself, digging deep for the calm I had spent so many months mastering. It fell upon me like a cloak, my shoulders dropping and jaw unclenching. The darkness stirred, but I held it at bay with an imperceptible shake of my head. This was not the place for shadows. I needed to bring him back into the light.

I reached out, imagining tendrils of awareness like smoke searching out the brokenness in my husband. The bruises were gone. The breaks were mended. The blood in his veins whooshed quietly through with each thump of his heart. His breath was slow and even. Steady. Quiet. I sent the tendrils of magic deeper.

Suddenly, my awareness snagged on something sharp and dark. I focused on it and pulled it towards me. Light filtered through the edges of the darkness like the shadows snuffed out the light in this one sharp spot.

Andrew moaned, and his body jerked in response. I paused, my own heart thumping hard in my chest. I started again, and his body convulsed, his hand jerking out of my grasp. I opened my eyes, and his face was broken out in a sweat, a pained look on his features as he twitched.

Terrified, I pulled back, leaving the sharpness and pulling my magic out of him. Instantly, he settled. I bit my lip. Thutmose didn't say anything about it hurting him. But he was obviously in distress. Something wasn't right. I got up and crossed the room, wetting a washcloth with cool water and returning to Andrew to clean his face. He relaxed under my touch, features softening once more. It was the most animation I'd seen from him since we came to the clinic. I held his hand to my chest again and cried hard then.

I tried two more times, each time bringing on more and more distress in him and draining me more and more. When I gave up, I was wringing with sweat, and Andrew was red in the face. I knew I had to stop and figure out something else. I blotted at his face with the cold washcloth, soothing the pain and washing away the beads of sweat and my own tears as they dropped on his cheeks and rolled down. It was as if we were crying together.

"I'm so sorry, Andrew," I whispered, my voice choked with tears. I laid my head on his chest and peppered him with apologies and tears.

I washed my face in cold water, trying to hide the redness of sobs shed, and headed back out to the car. I avoided Dell's questions and her worried glance the whole way home. My mind reeled.

# 49

# *A Whispering of Shadows*

I sat at the kitchen table shortly after Dell and I returned, surrounded by the chatter of everyone still gathered at Hanan's. They were on edge, the threat from Thutmose seemingly imminent. But the secrets I was keeping from them kept mounting, and I left them to worry.

My mood was dark, and something inside me preened with it. It whispered terrible things through my veins, maddening things. Terrifying things. It lurked in the corners of my mind and smoothed away the wrinkles of hope in my thoughts and worries over Andrew. At that moment, the darkness and shadow felt intrusive instead of welcome. For the first time, my stomach soured as I wondered if I'd been wrong in doing the spell. After all, it had gotten me the amulet, but it hadn't brought Andrew back.

I wrapped my hands around my glass of water, the condensation on the outside wetting my fingers. It was cool against my skin, and I shivered ever so slightly with a cold chill. Brought on by the water or my thoughts, I wasn't sure. The prickle of someone staring at me made me look up, and I saw Hanan from across the room studying me. We made eye contact, but she didn't look away or acknowledge that she was staring. I shifted my gaze back to my hands and the water dripping down my glass and onto my fingers, but I could still feel her watching me.

It made me want to crawl out of my skin. Or melt into the floor. Anything to get away from her gaze.

I tried to focus on what everyone was talking about. Their findings on Thutmose, their fears over his plans, and what they wanted to do to remain out of his clutches and somehow defeat him. The darkness inside of me bubbled up to the surface of my mind, chiding them for thinking they could outwit or out-magic an ancient immortal sorcerer who had actually seen and *used* the scrolls they were so scared of. My frustration with them simmered. There were answers in the scrolls. I knew it. And I knew we could be so much more than we were if they would just wake up. Naomi was right. We were nothing more than a witchy book club, playing at parlor tricks and good vibes.

"Julia, you've been quiet all evening. What are you thinking?"

Hanan's voice shook me out of my own thoughts. I met her eyes again, and her gaze was far more intense than it had been, like she was seeing through me and reading my dark thoughts about them. Or maybe they were written across my face or in the clench of my hands on the glass. I wiped my hands on my jeans, the water leaving marks behind, and straightened up. I tried to make my face as neutral as possible but couldn't muster a fake smile. No matter, no one else was smiling around the table.

"Nothing, really," I shrugged my shoulders gently. "I'm feeling a bit overwhelmed, is all." I lied through my teeth, and the darkness inside purred like a cat. She looked at me over her nose, head tilted slightly, still studying, the corners of her eyes narrowing slightly. The tension between us pinged like a tightly stretched rubber band. One more inch and one of us would snap.

When did that happen? When did we go from sisters to enemies?

*When she refused to lend her aid. When she continued to choose weak-ness over strength, and you finally saw through her facade of 'leadership.'* The shadows inside of me answered a whisper of voices low and silky through my mind. I shuddered and tried to hide my discomfort. Dell reached over and placed her hand on my back, quietly lending comfort, though I'm sure she thought it was for Andrew's plight. Not the plight of my sanity.

I sat quietly after that, letting everyone's voices wash over me, not really listening to anything but the shadows in my mind. They were much harder to tune out than the women before me.

# 50

## Demands

"The spell you taught me didn't work," I hissed into the phone, clutching it so tightly my knuckles were white.

"The spell I taught you works fine, little witch," Thutmose purred into the other end of the phone. "Maybe you did it wrong." He didn't pose a question so much as to offer a statement about my incompetence.

"I literally did it exactly as you said," I ground out through gritted teeth. "And instead of healing him, all it did was bring him more pain. So, again, the spell you taught me didn't work. Teach me something else." I squeezed my eyes shut and rolled my neck along my shoulders, doing what I could to try and release some tension. My body was keyed up, shaking with anger and adrenaline.

*He knows exactly what to do.* The shadows purred. The sound was like velvet rubbing against my skin. I squeezed my eyes tighter, trying to block out the voices. I didn't have the time or the energy to deal with them.

"Explain to me exactly what happened, little witch," Thutmose said, a demand instead of a request. I hated him at that moment. I hated that he held so much power and had the knowledge I needed. I hated that I had to choose between him and my integrity.

*Fuck integrity.* The shadows whispered. *You want something. You get it by whatever means necessary.* I gritted my teeth and told him everything.

"I tried again and again. But it was clear that he was in extreme distress. In a lot of pain."

"What did his pain look like?" he asked.

"What do you mean?" I countered. "It looked like pain. Like he'd be crying out if he were awake." I pinched the bridge of my nose, frustrated that this was getting me nowhere.

"No, I understand that. But what was his bodily response? Did he make any noise? Did he move? Sweat? Cry?" His voice was calm, and I hated him even more for that even tone. He spoke of Andrew like he was nothing. Like he didn't matter. I shook my head, trying to clear it. Trying to force my way past the darkness to get answers and more help.

"He groaned. Didn't cry out. But his body jerked, lifting off the bed. He broke into a sweat; it was pouring off his face by the third try. He sort of... convulsed on that third try, too. That's why I stopped. I was afraid of doing more harm than good," I trailed off, back in the room with Andrew, reliving my worst nightmare of hurting him. The memory of sweat on my skin and the scent of fear in the air was strong. My face was hot with shame, and sweat dripped down my spine. Thutmose was quiet. I was about to ask if I'd lost him when I heard him let out a long exhale.

"I was afraid of this," he said quietly. And for the first time, I heard the emotion in his voice.

"Afraid of what?" I asked.

Another deep sigh.

"Afraid that you didn't possess enough healing power on your own to infuse the spell with calm and peace." He paused. "This is difficult magic. It inherently causes fear and pain. It is the nature of what you're trying to do. What you need is the ability to calm and soothe the spirit. Like a balm on burnt skin. You bring relief. And then you bring the pain."

I let out a frustrated breath and shook loose the truth.

"I've never been able to do that," I said, almost a whine. "I'm not *good* at magic. The only magic that has ever come easily is the shadow magic I used at the museum the night we met." I had no idea why the words quickly tumbled across my lips. Why was I being so honest with him? I should have been hiding my inability and my weaknesses from him. I knew, without a doubt, that he would eventually find a way to exploit them.

*We will exploit him first.* The darkness hummed. *He enjoys weak women. He mistakes your honesty for weakness, and he will help us. He will think that he's not. But he will.*

I tried to ignore the shadows— the murmuring sweetness that the darkness wove through me. It both terrified and soothed me. And I didn't know what to do with either feeling. There was nowhere I could run. No one I could turn to. It was inside of me. And yet... that meant that I wasn't alone.

"I, too, have never been very good at soothing or calming magic," Thutmose finally answered. "It is not in our nature to be nurturers, it seems. We have that much in common, at least." I wanted nothing in common with Thutmose, but at that moment, I didn't care as long as he could help. "If you have someone you can trust to go with you and us e *their* magic on your husband, that would work."

"There is no one. No one here will help me. They've written him off already," my voice was cold as it forced its way out of my emotion-clogged throat. No matter my feelings, it was the truth of the matter. No one who could help me would.

"There is another way," he offered. "But I know you won't like it."

I swallowed down my emotions.

"I don't care what it is. I'll do whatever it takes," I answered. And I knew then and there that that statement was the most genuine thing to come out of my mouth in a long time. I was done failing. Done feeling weak or scared. Done with not being able to do anything I needed to do on my own. The shadows stretched inside of me, velvet rubbing up against the walls of my skin, sending another shudder through me. Still, this time, it was pleasure instead of discomfort.

"Are you sure, little witch?" Thutmose asked. "It requires a great sacrifice."

I nodded to my empty bedroom.

"It can't be any more than I've already sacrificed." He laughed a hearty laugh on the other end of the line.

"You'd be surprised, little witch." He was no longer laughing.

My blood ran cold as he described what it would take to do the spell on my own. Apparently, I *could* be surprised and could be asked for more sacrifice than I'd already offered the universe. Thutmose described, in great detail, what I had to do. He promised that, without a doubt, it would work and I would be successful. To get the magic I needed, I would have to steal it... from someone who carried their strength in healing. It would be the ultimate betrayal. To someone I once loved and to myself.

I warred with myself all night. The shadows whispering promises and growing louder and louder, drowning out the lighter parts of myself that I tried to grasp hold of. But it was no use. The shadows had their grip on me. And it hadn't been the violent, piercing grasp one would expect but the menacing caress of quiet betrayal. All this time, I'd thought I'd mastered the darkness. Felt that it was magic meant for me. Little did I know that it was the darkness that had mastered me.

---

I knew that my time was limited. The doctors hadn't said exactly what they planned to do with Andrew. I knew they wouldn't haul him out onto the street, but I feared they'd release him to my care at home or force us to find somewhere else for him on short notice to make room for someone else.

I went to him again the next day, in the early morning hours, before the night nurses' shift ended. There, in the quiet of the darkness, I poured out my fears to him. I held his hand and cried, my tears hot on my cheeks. I thought once I felt him squeeze my hand, but it was nothing more than my imagination and the last little bits of hope floating around in the darkness.

Andrew was gaunt. A shell of his former self—skin sallow and pale, longing to be kissed by the sun. I missed the rosiness in his cheeks and the warm brown that brightened his face in the summer months. His lips were dry and pale, and I smeared ointment on them, hoping to give him some relief if he could feel it.

What I missed most were his eyes. They were the eyes that saw the deepest, darkest parts of me and loved me anyway. Eyes that could see through little white lies that I was okay. Eyes that could make my heart pound and my skin flush with desire in only a moment. And eyes that sought mine out in a crowded room that could speak a thousand things without saying a word.

He never really liked his eyes. He always said they were muddy brown. But to me, they looked like home. Like the solid earth of the mountains he climbed, flecked with the gold of a thousand years of crystals hidden in those same mountains. They were warm. Comforting. And I was beyond tired of not seeing them behind his purpled eyelids.

My tears slowed, and I held his hand in my own, turning it over in my palm. His skin was paper thin, the muscles worn away with time and illness, and I wished, more than anything, that I could go back in time and keep everything from happening. Maybe even keep our Egypt holiday from ever happening. It led us down this path, and now I was faced with a point of no return. And for what? Childish dreams that irrevocably changed the course of our lives.

The shadows were quiet then. The innate darkness I'd battled my entire life drowned out the soft intrusion of magic. My heart felt heavy in my chest like I could reach in and pluck it out and rid myself of pain. Of suffering. To be lighter again.

"I refuse to let us be some tragic love story, Drew," I whispered. "I've lost too much. I can't lose you too." I stood up and smoothed my hair out of my face, unruly, sweaty curls pinging back behind my ears. I'd made up my mind. I'd do what Thutmose suggested. The shadows rose to meet my darkness and crashed together in a burning wave of pleasure and pain. I gasped aloud, the breath sucked out of my lungs.

I turned from the room and walked out, mind made up and fate sealed.

# 51

## *Fever Dreams*

I didn't do it immediately. I couldn't. I had to work myself up to sell my soul and forgo my integrity. Well, that wasn't really true. Ultimately, Marwa held my movement off. She'd gone home for a few days, taking care of things she'd left in the wake of our emergency meetings to figure out Thutmose. I was alone in the guest house for the first time in days, and surprisingly, I didn't relish it. I longed for the distraction of her soft snores or even my annoyance at feeling babysat. Anything but the waiting.

The first night, I slept and slept hard. And while I slept, I dreamt.

I walked an overgrown path lined with the biggest tangle of honeysuckle bushes I'd ever seen. Their scent was sticky and heady in the air, almost choking in its floral sweetness. My mouth watered, the memory of nectar on my tongue so visceral I had to swallow multiple times. The air stirred and crackled with magic and birdsong, the buzzing of greedy bees as loud as my thundering heart.

I turned a corner and was met with another overgrown path, darker, more verdant, and grown. The smell of petrichor was thick in the air after only a few steps, and I knew I was somewhere else from the first path. I carried on. One foot in front of the other, each twist and turn opening to a new path, new scents, new sounds. The only static thing was the snap and twang of magic in the air. I didn't know whether it came from me or someone else. Still, I carried on.

One last turn, I found myself on a shorter path, the overgrowth lighter here, the sunlight peeking through openings in the foliage and lighting the way. There was light at the trail's end, a bright meadow glowing with the warmth of sunrise. I hurried my steps, the meadow and the light beckoning. The air grew heavy with morning dew, a crisp bite in the air that spurred me on. It reminded me of home. Of Saturday mornings with my grandparents and their comfort and peace. I could almost smell Gram's perfume and Gramps' pipe tobacco. My heart felt like it would burst when I stepped out of the tunneled path and into the clearing.

I looked around expectantly, knowing I'd find them, the pit of my stomach dropping when I didn't. I was alone in the meadow. Save the birds and buzzing insects. I stood there, the sun rising with the day, the heat rising with it, prickling at the goosebumps along my skin.

Before long, the meadow was rippling with shimmering heat. I was sticky with sweat, the tiny curls along my hairline coiled tight. The air was thick, like the summer heat I'd grown up with. The south's reason for iced tea and window air conditioners that whirr louder than the bird-sized mosquitos that get more prolific each year.

I slowly wandered around the meadow, keeping the edge of the forest to my left. The heat grew with each step I took until it was oppressive and left me panting. Someone was there with me, and I was convinced it was Gram or Gramps. Or maybe I longed for them.

A branch snapped behind me, and I whirled around, a hopeful smile on my face. Nothing. The air was still and sweltering, and no one was there. My shoulders dropped, and disappointment swept through me. Maybe if I kept walking, I'd find them.

Hours passed, and the sun was high in the sky, heat burning down on me. My skin was blistering, hot burns opening all across my face, arms, and legs. I was dressed in my sleep shorts and tank top, something I was deeply regretting. Every time I tried to walk in the shade, the trees swayed and moved to shade the forest, not the meadow— no matter where I walked or stood.

Finally, something shifted in the air. I looked across the meadow that had started so small and inviting but had morphed into a stretching expanse of open land. Shimmering in the distance, like a mirage, was a figure. It was small at first. Blurry in the heat and distance. I walked towards it, and it came towards me. Slowly, the form took more shape, and I recognized his gait. Then his shirt became clear— the soft band T-shirt we fought over, and my heart leaped up into my throat. His face was still a blur, features muddied like I was looking through water. But it was Andrew, no doubt.

I opened my mouth to shout, but my tongue was sandpaper, and nothing came out. I clawed at my throat, desperate to speak. He stopped and cocked his head to one side, curious. I fell to my knees, unable to take another step but so close to him. Slowly, his shadow inched nearer to me. Finally, he was close enough to shroud me in shadow, and I heard the whisper of his voice.

"Jules..."

When I looked up, he blocked the bright sun behind him, and his shadow grew and grew, swallowing up the sun and casting us into complete darkness. The shock of the dark and the cold from the missing sun startled me, and I reached out for Andrew. My fingertips met nothing but air.

I came to, burning with fever, soaked to the bone in sweat, my teeth chattering with heat boiling me from the inside and the frigid air outside my body.

The fever held me tight for days. I came in and out of consciousness and fever dreams— each more confusing and disturbing than the last. I was wracked with pain, tortured with some unknown illness. In my lucid moments—of which there were very few—I knew that this was somehow my soul's reckoning. It felt like a purging of the darkness that wouldn't loosen its grip.

I saw my grandparents in my dreams; they were quiet and cold, disappointed in me like my parents had been. That was more gut-wrenching than the terrible visions of Thutmose and I hovered over old papyrus, calling forth monsters and demons from the depths of Duat and every other hell we could grab attention from.

I had visions of shadows swallowing me whole. Andrew was the only thing I didn't see, though I searched for him in fevered panic. I heard his voice calling out to me every now and then. He sounded strong again. He sounds like himself again. From before... he sounded like... home.

# 52

## A Healing

When my fever finally broke, I was tucked into my bed, sheets and blankets freshly laundered. Dell was sitting in a chair I'd pilfered from Hanan's sitting room months before. Her laptop was perched on her lap, keys clacking away while she worked.

My mouth felt disgusting, all cotton and thick, and my head throbbed in painful relief that the fever had finally loosed its grip. I shifted in the bed, and Dell looked up from her computer.

"Oh, hey," she said quietly. "You're awake. Need anything?"

I shook my head and opened my mouth to speak but could only croak a half-garbled noise. I gestured to drink, and Dell hopped up and grabbed a glass, filling it from the tap. I drank greedily, the water cool and crisp in my mouth. I cleared my throat and spoke, barely a whisper.

"What happened?" Dell sat on the edge of the bed with me.

"We're not really sure. You were in here alone, Marwa had gone home for a few days, and everything was fine when you went to bed. By the next afternoon, we hadn't heard anything from you, so I came to check on you, and you were running a crazy high fever." I could hear the worry in her voice. The fever dreams still seemed surreal, but I knew it had been bad.

"How long was I out?"

"Almost five days." She looked down at her lap. Despite her work as a corpsman in the Navy, she had a hard time when someone she cared about was sick or hurt. It always took its toll. "We called in Karim, and he drew some blood. Do you remember that?"

I nodded. "Vaguely. But not really. I was in and out of it, so much everything seemed like one big blurry mess." My throat was sore and dry, so I drank more water. The last five days were a discombobulated mix of dreams, fever, and the rare flash of muddy cognizance.

"Yeah, it was pretty scary. You were raving, talking gibberish in your sleep, and thrashing around. And nothing we did could get you cooled off. Your fever stayed between 104 and 105 the whole time. But all the tests came back normal. No raised white or red blood cells. No sign of infection. Everything functioning as normal. It was weird." Dell reached over and rubbed my leg on top of the covers, the movement absentminded and for her own comfort as much as mine.

"That's so weird," I said. "Did Karim have any guess as to what it was?"

"No," she said, shrugging her shoulders. "No clue. He said they have to run their course sometimes, and fevers can be hard to diagnose. Renee says you were fighting off something more internal than bloodwork can trace. But that seemed a little wooey— even for me."

I smiled, and my lip cracked a bit. I winced and licked at it, tasting blood. I sucked on it, the pain from the pressure, good and bad, in the way those little wounds always were.

"Have you been here this whole time?"

"We took turns," she answered. "Everyone sat with you and lent some energy, trying to at least give your body some relief from the fever. It was bad, Jules. It felt like when…" She trailed off, but I knew what she was saying without the words.

"Andrew," I finished for her, and she nodded, tears in her eyes. We sat quietly together after that, no more words needing to be said. After a few minutes, she got up and sat back down with her computer, knocking out some more work after ensuring I had everything I needed. Despite having slept for most of five days, exhaustion tugged at me, and I fell back asleep quickly.

This time, instead of a fever dream, I was thrown into a vision with Hatshepsut. It was the first time in a long time I'd not gone searching for her, and my subconscious, or hers, had sent me.

"*Merit*!" she exclaimed. "Where have you been? I've been so worried for you. I thought something had happened!" She rushed at me as soon as I entered her room.

"I'm sorry, Shesout. I've been sick. I've only just come out of a fever," I explained as I wrapped my arms around her. She enveloped me, soft curves and strong arms pulling me tight, surrounding me with her myrrh and rose scent.

"Fever?" she asked.

I explained the science as best I could. The Ancient Egyptians knew about fevers and that infections caused them. But they also believed that an evil spirit could be to blame.

"I'm fine now, I think," I assured her. "The doctor didn't know what caused it, but it seems to have run its course. I'm exhausted. I can feel how tired even from here." The fatigue weighed me down like a stone. I wanted to lie down and sleep for three more days. My limbs felt weak and my mind fuzzy. Typically, in my visions, there was clarity and strength.

Separate from whatever my earthly body might be going through. This was not the norm.

"If there is no sickness on the inside. It must be deeper than your blood, *Merit*." She raised her hand against the argument on the tip of my tongue. "No, no. If you *insist* it isn't an evil spirit, then you must be having a healing," she said matter-of-factly. I looked at her, confused.

"A healing?" She nodded.

"Yes, a healing. There is something inside of you that needs to be repaired. Something deeper than your body. Deeper even than a spirit from the outside. Your *Ka*."

"My *ka*?" I asked, not familiar with the word.

She clucked her tongue at me, chiding me lightly. "Surely you know of *ka*. It is your life force. Your essence. It is the part of you no one can see or touch but can feel." I nodded, understanding.

"Oh. We call that the soul now," I said. "But it's the same thing."

"If there is nothing in the body that needs to be healed, then it must be the soul that needs a healing. Something needs attention on the soul level, and the mind and body work together to try and fix it."

It was similar to what Renee was suggesting. Again, I was struck by the weird similarities that seemed to exist beyond time and space. I didn't say anything, but my mind immediately went to what Thutmose had told me to do to save Andrew. I didn't want to tell Hatshepsut because I knew she would disagree. And I couldn't imagine disappointing her or having to tell her the truth... that I was in league with the man who betrayed her and killed her.

"I don't have to ask, Julia, for I see it written on your face," she said. "There is something in your soul that needs attention. Is it the darkness? Have you let it run wild inside of you? Or do you still feel you have control?" She looked me up and down as if looking hard enough would uncover the truths I was doing my best to hide. I bit the inside of my cheek, willing myself not to tell her everything.

"No," I finally said. "I don't think it's the shadows. That all seems fine." I lied. "Really, it's fine. I'm sure it's nothing, and I'll feel better soon."

Hatshepsut clucked her tongue, such an ordinary, mundane response, and I couldn't help but smile at her. This epic Pharaoh clucking around me like a mother hen, trying to find out what was wrong. But before I could insist that I was fine, I felt the pull from the other side. I knew my time was limited.

"I have to go," I said quickly, holding her hand and squeezing gently. "I'm being pulled back. But I'll come back soon. I promise." With a tug to my solar plexus, I left Hatshepsut, her fingertips still like ghosts in my palm when I came to in my bed.

The room was dark, and I could hear Dell sleeping beside me. I rolled over, facing away from her, and quietly cried myself back to sleep, the heaviness in my heart at my betrayal too heavy to hold in a moment longer.

# 53

# The Unthinkable

I knew there was no turning back. No second guessing. No more waffling back and forth. I had to do it. I had to steal Marwa's calming magic. Maybe I should have stolen Renee's. Made her pay for using her magic on me without permission. Her healing magic had always felt intrusive and uninvited. But I knew there was no way I could get to her and get it done. It had to be Marwa.

When Thutmose had suggested that was the answer, I had balked. Surely, there had to be another way. But I had tried and failed too many times, leaving Andrew for too long. Death was circling like a buzzard, and I wouldn't let him have him yet. Maybe this was the final piece of the puzzle I had been searching for.

In the end, taking Marwa's magic wasn't the violent, severing theft I'd thought it would be. It was quiet. Peaceful. As if her magic gladly left her and came to me happily. A dark thought rushed through me... would she have freely given it had I asked? Would she have lent her help so I didn't even have to ask her to hand over an intrinsic part of her soul?

I shut down the thought as quickly as it had come on. The sisterhood had given up on Andrew. They were all content to let him go quietly to his death. I was the only one still kicking and screaming, or, in this case, stealing and scheming, to save him.

Once my fever had passed and showed no signs of returning, Marwa gave Dell a reprieve from her sentry duties. Everyone was terrified that the fever would come back unexpectedly and refused to let me be left alone. Dell had asked if I would move into her room in Hanan's with her, but the space between Hanan and me was still a gaping maw of distrust and unsaid words. The less time I was in her space, the better.

Hanan had a late tour group, and Marwa brought food to feed Dell, me, and Naomi, who was staying over. We'd eaten and talked all through dinner like everything was normal. I'd finally gotten really good at pretending everything was okay, like I didn't feel a deep sense of betrayal from everyone around the table.

The conversation was light. No one mentioned Andrew, or Hanan, or the upcoming ceremony where we'd try to bind Thutmose's power, though it loomed over us. We spoke of films and travels and easy things with no drama attached to them. Dell regaled everyone with tales from our time in California, when we'd been young and wild and free. Well... as wild as a girl from an extremely strict upbringing could be.

After a particularly hilarious story involving Dell, Edie, and me getting locked out of a parking garage at midnight and walking home in the days before Uber when our husbands were out to sea, I laughed so hard I cried. As I remembered it, the story was fairly stressful, and the most random things happened to us that night. It wasn't until a few days later that we could all have a laugh about it. But the way Dell told it was something straight out of a movie, and it stripped away all the worry and stress from the night. I laughed until my sides hurt, and tears leaked from my eyes.

As our laughter died down and we moved on to another story, I realized that I couldn't remember the last time I'd laughed that hard. Or even truly laughed at all. The past year had been fraught with grief and trauma and more grief. With fear and sadness, that left little room for belly laughs. The sweet release of laughter that deep felt foreign... and wrong. A wave of guilt washed over me, sending my thoughts spiraling inward. While I was joking and laughing, Andrew was lying in a hospital bed, the world having given up on him.

Thinking of Andrew and the guilt that followed was enough to sober me the rest of the evening. I grew quiet, and everyone noticed, but I didn't care. I was angry with myself for losing sight of what needed to be done. Rationally, I knew that Andrew would want me to live my life, be happy, and find those moments of joy, but it didn't feel right knowing there was a clock ticking even louder now.

When we finally retired, I didn't make small talk with Marwa. We got ready for bed quietly, and I came so close to forcing her to leave to keep myself from doing what I had to do. But, at the end of the day, I made my choice, and she stayed. I lay there in the dark, listening for her breath to slow as she fell asleep.

"Is everything okay, *Habibti*?" Marwa whispered sleepily. "You're all but vibrating the bed with your thoughts."

I stilled, heart pounding so loud I was sure she could hear it.

"I'm fine, having trouble getting to sleep."

"It's alright, *Habibti*. Close your eyes and let your breath take you." The sheets rustled as she shifted in bed. I willed myself to calm down and stop projecting such loud nerves. There was no way I could take her magic if she were awake. I needed her asleep and pliant in her unconsciousness.

I took long, slow breaths in and out and steadied myself. While waiting for Marwa to fall asleep, I repeatedly replayed my conversation with Thutmose in as much detail as I could remember. He had been clear in his directions and a patient teacher, which surprised me. I expected him to be a monster. To be this horrible, cruel thing. But he was... dare I say, understanding? He absolutely had his moments of assholery, but once I'd stopped fighting him and we came to a mutual understanding, he dropped the nasty streak and started to grow on me.

I tried to reason with him and help him understand why the sisterhood was taking such a staunch stance on him getting access to the scrolls. For generations, the responsibility of keeping the magic safe and out of his hands (though no one had known it was Thutmose himself who still sought them) had been paramount. To wash away those years of purpose and identity wasn't going to happen overnight.

It had taken time, but he finally understood and was happy to let me try and win them over. I still hadn't figured out exactly how I was going to do that, but I hoped his understanding and almost friendly nature would hold out a little longer. There was something about him. Something that felt like a kindred spirit. And though it terrified me, that feeling humanized him ever so slightly.

"Little witch," he'd said when he finally gave me the last part of the spell I needed to pilfer Marwa's magic for my own. He said the words differently than how he'd first spat them out as an insult. They'd become almost a nickname. Not quite a term of endearment, but they weren't dripping with disdain. "Don't make me regret this. It has been a long time since I trusted someone and didn't just take what I wanted." He'd narrowed his eyes at me in the dreamscape we walked. Where he'd taught me the dark magic I was about to perform.

The darkness was purring away inside of me, happy as a cat in the sunshine to be in his presence. I know it could feel the darkness and shadows within him... like calling to like. I felt it. The enigmatic pull of our magics wanting to be free and out into the world together, a raging storm of power. It scared me sometimes how dark and powerful I was with him. It wasn't how I felt with Hatshepsut. Or any of the sisterhood. It was intoxicating as much as it was terrifying. I hadn't decided which way to lean into yet.

I'd promised him the world. The scrolls. The power of the sisterhood. Whatever I could give him to get the answers I needed. It had taken a few nights of dream walking and secret texts throughout the day to convince him, even if I hadn't convinced myself how I would make good on everything I'd promised him. But surely, once Andrew was awake, and Marwa's magic was restored—because I would give it back as soon as I was done with it— they'd have to see that he wasn't some evil monster. That he had helped and had goodness in him. And if they didn't? Andrew and I would figure it out together. Because there was no way this wasn't working. I was convinced.

Finally, after what seemed like an eternity, Marwa's breathing slowed, and she drifted off to sleep. I made sure to wait a little longer before I began.

When her soft snores filled the room, I took a breath and reached over, fingertips brushing Marwa's shoulder, making the lightest contact I could.

Slipping into her dreams was as easy as slipping into the shadows. It was almost effortless. It took a little focus, and a few carefully chosen words murmured, and I was there. Her dreamscape was so unlike my own. I walked on a quiet beach— the bright white sand warm between my toes, the ocean lapping softly at my feet. The water was warm, and the air wasn't too hot or sunny. It was perfect and peaceful. I swallowed a thick bubble of guilt in my throat and carried on.

She lounged in a hammock between two substantial palm trees, shaded from the sun, and resting quietly. I stayed far enough away that she didn't engage, thankfully. I don't think I could have faced her in her dreams.

I dug my feet into the sand, reaching a cooler layer, and grounded myself. I took a deep breath and focused all my energy on finding Marwa's own energy. Her magic. It rose up and answered, curiosity piqued. I sifted through, searching for the thread I needed- the calming essence she was so proficient with. It resisted when I tugged gently on it, the feeling of the magic slippery in my hands. But I stayed calm, not wanting to scare it or alert Marwa. I coaxed it with every ounce of calm I had. It yielded slowly, long breath after long breath, a little pop of release as I pulled it free of its host. I reeled it in, almost like a line on a fishing pole. It settled inside me as I slowly backed away from Marwa's private dream oasis, Marwa never even having stirred.

I quietly slipped out of her mind and opened my eyes to the darkness of my room and her still soft snores filling the space. She seemed peaceful. Quiet. But then the light caught on a single tear tracing down her cheek. I turned away and forced myself to ignore it.

Her magic swirled inside of me. It was discomforting and unsettling as it tried to make space amongst my own magic. The shadows swirled around it, displeased at something else taking up space. I internally whispered platitudes and promises, willing the magics to make peace and get along for this one night.

I slipped out of bed, pulled on my cardigan, and tiptoed out of the house, magic silencing my steps and the closing of the door.

I stopped in the moonlit garden and looked at the sky above me. Its vast darkness twinkled with stars and the heavy, almost full moon hanging there, full of magic. Full of hope.

Magic coursed through my veins, still unsettling but now making itself at home. I was like a ripe peach, full to bursting, and I decided to go to Andrew immediately instead of waiting till morning. Maybe I could do the spell, wake him up, and get back before Marwa even woke up. I could call Thutmose on the way and ask him how to return her magic, and maybe no one would have to know what I'd done.

For the second time in a few short weeks, my heart was full to bursting with newfound hope.

# 54

## *Another Kind of Betrayal*

"I did it. I took the magic I needed—the calming, peaceful magic I lacked before," I said excitedly into the phone. I had grabbed Marwa's keys and taken her car instead of trying to find a taxi this late. I'd called Thutmose as soon as I'd gotten behind the wheel.

"I wasn't sure you had it in you, little witch," he purred.

"I had no choice. Nothing else was working, and you know it," I argued. Guilt sat, hard as a rock, in my stomach.

"Have you kissed your sleeping beauty and woken him yet?"

Joy bubbled up in my chest, and I grinned ear to ear.

"I am on my way right now. I couldn't wait till morning," I answered. "I'm hoping I can get in there, heal him, and get home to give Marwa her magic back before anyone wakes up and knows what I did. That's why I'm calling you. What do I need to do to give her magic back?"

"What do you mean?" Thutmose asked, confused.

"The spell won't take long. Even when it failed, it didn't take long to perform it. So I'm going there now, healing him, and returning home. The doctors and nurses will get called in and spend all night running tests and checking him out. I'll have plenty of time to get back and restore Marwa's magic before they all start their days, and no one will ever have to know what I did."

I flicked the headlights on high, bathing the empty road before me in bright light. Something skittered away on the side of the road, and I wondered what nocturnal creature I'd disturbed by the high beams.

"My dear," he said darkly, jerking my attention away from the road. "Did I not explain things clearly enough?" His voice was smooth and rich, its timbre almost a purr. "Once you've divested someone of their magic, there is no returning it."

My pulse throbbed in my ears, drowning out the noise of the car engine.

"No. No— you never told me that! There has to be a way!" I argued. "I would have never done it if I'd known! I'm not some monster!" The heavy ball of guilt that had sat, leaden, in my stomach all evening roiled. I veered off the road and slammed to a stop. I wrenched the door open and fell out of the car and onto my knees. I wretched and heaved my guts up until there was nothing left but the acrid stench of vomit in the air.

I sat back on my heels and swiped my mouth with the back of my hand. The taste of bile was sour in my mouth, but the taste of betrayal was even stronger. A muffled voice sounded from the phone I'd dropped in my scramble to get out of the car. I turned and reached for it, hands shaking. I put it up to my ear and heard the quiet laughter of a madman. Of the joy he found in my undoing.

"You knew, and you said nothing?" I demanded.

"Of course, I knew, little witch. And I assumed you did as well. What spell on earth would grant its user such epic power and also the ability to give it back? Magic isn't a trading card you can swap with friends for something better. You either have power or you don't. Simple as that," he continued to talk, but the words got further and further away, tunneling from my mind as the reality of what I'd done sank into my bones.

I dropped my hand into my lap, and the phone slipped out and landed in the dirt next to me. I could hear the quiet, muffled noise from the earpiece and then silence.

I sat on the side of the road, folded over on myself, for a long time. My knees were burning, and my stomach was cramping, but I couldn't force myself to move.

Marwa. The woman who had taken one look at me and known what I needed. She had stepped in and been the mom I'd always needed. Always wanted. We'd had some missteps along the way, but a part of me had always known that she'd taken me on as hers, and that was that. And I'd taken from her something that was an intrinsic part of who she is. Who she was meant to be.

I had stolen that from her when I'd only meant to borrow it. And there was no way she would ever forgive me now.

No one would.

# 55

## *Pathfinder*

*A*ndrew

"It's time, child. Time for you to return to the land of the living." Khonsu's voice was heavy with sadness, and his eyes were bright and shining with tears. "It is selfish of me to keep you here any longer," his voice broke slightly. "Though I have enjoyed this time with a human companion." Andrew put his hand to his chest, flattening his palm against his heart, and nodded at him, reverent and thankfully.

"Thank you, Khonsu. I don't know what to say." Andrew's time with him had been like nothing he'd ever experienced. He was leaving a changed man, a better man, but he was desperate to get to Julia. To hold her. To touch her. To reassure her. To love her. The dream he'd had of her, of them together, had done nothing but make him more restless in this place.

"It is clear without words, child."

After months of ease, there was a heaviness in Andrew's limbs that was startling. Grief or the pull from his earthly body, he wasn't sure. Khonsu reached over and placed his large hand on the top of Andrew's head, resting it gently on the mass of curls.

"Your return will be anything but easy, Andrew. I cannot ease the pain of life. But I can show you the way to the truth. I am the Pathfinder. I will guide your path and the path of Isis' priestesses. You will encounter darkness. But you are the light. You, my child, will carry heavy burdens along the way... will help carry the burdens of others. But you are strong enough. Trust in your light. In your strength. In all that you have learned here."

He bowed his head to Andrew and spoke in a language he didn't understand. He began to glow, slowly at first, and then shimmering and bright. The brightest light of a fire a halo around his body... in his eyes.

And then the light winked out, and Andrew was thrown into the darkness with a force that ripped the god's hand away from him and sent him spiraling downwards.

There was nothing.

And then there was pain.

Every nerve ending was set alight. Bright red, angry light behind his eyelids. Pain erupted from everywhere as he continued to fall. It was so great Andrew could do nothing but relinquish himself to it. His body wasn't his own. The pain *was* his body.

It was a rebirth. Not the peace of life-giving water but a baptism of fire. Time stretched before him like a never-ending pathway. There was only the fire of his injuries reawakened and the biting cold of falling. Every nerve ending in his body electric with feeling after so long in the peaceful stasis with Khonsu. His brain and body warred against each other, trying to make sense of the assault on his senses.

The stretched-out path of time snapped back— a wave rushing him, and Andrew slammed into his earthly body with such force. It shoved every ounce of air out of his lungs, and he abruptly came to. Awareness violently pinged through his entire system and had him gasping for air and clutching his chest. A fish out of water. A dead man brought back to life.

# 56

## All for Nothing

The clinic building, so unassuming and familiar after all this time, loomed above me. I took a steadying breath and pulled my light cardigan around me tighter, hugging it to me for comfort—without even realizing it, I'd grabbed Gram's old peach-colored one. I was terrified of hurting Andrew again. Of doing more damage. My stomach fluttered with nerves and discomfort—the power I'd siphoned from Marwa still chafing from its newness. Like it knew it didn't belong to me and wasn't freely given. I took another breath and gripped the door handle. The brass warmed from the sun that was beginning to set.

"Miss! Miss!" The nurse at the front desk hung up the phone in her hand and called for me as I hurried in. I absently waved at her, determined to get to Andrew without small talk. I was frantic about the need to use Marwa's magic and try to wake him again before I lost my nerve.

"Hi, Leena. I won't be long. I—" she interrupted me, her excited voice high-pitched and fast.

"We've been calling you! Trying to reach you all evening." The urgency in her voice froze my body in place. She came out from behind the desk and stood in front of me. My heart dropped, and I knew.

I was too late.

My knees began to buckle, and I felt the sob crawling up my throat, the stinging fingers of trapped grief scrambling to find a way out. "No! No— you misunderstand. He's awake." The sob escaped, and the ground pulled me down, the nurse coming down with me, catching me by the arm. She wrapped an arm around me, rubbing my arm, trying to comfort me.

But I could find no comfort.

Andrew was awake... but I hadn't been the one to save him.

The last torturous hours flashed through my mind.

The lengths I'd gone to.

The choices I'd made... Marwa...

The betrayal.

It had all been for nothing.

No, I would find no comfort in my failures.

# 57

## *A Cold and Broken Hallelujah*

*Andrew*

It had been almost six months since Jules had seen Andrew's eyes. Their shape and the depth of the brown that was so much richer than the word alone could convey had haunted her. She had spent days begging him to open his eyes when he'd first gone into his coma. She'd wanted him to open them and look back at her. To meet her blue-green eyes constantly blurred with tears to the point that salt water seemed the only way to describe her own color.

The eyes that looked back at her were wide with fear and excitement, but they weren't her husband's eyes. Gone were the dark eyes with flecks of bright amber. Staring back at her were a stranger's eyes... a brilliant and startling blue with a starburst of gold in the center. Eyes that looked otherworldly and did not belong to the person who knew her inside and out.

"Ju—" He cleared his croaking voice, rusty from misuse. "Jules."

Andrew's voice was no more than a scratchy whisper, but it was all the invitation Jules needed. She threw herself onto Andrew, burying her face in his neck and crying.

"I...how...I..." She choked out half words and sobbing sounds, tasting salt in the corners of her mouth.

"That's a really long story," he said. Andrew raised a hand to rub her back, his fingers tangling in her curls, his own eyes prickling with hot tears at the feel of her against him once more. They held each other for minutes or hours, both afraid to move lest they wake up from a dream. Though his journey back to his body had been excruciating, he was no longer in pain. He marveled at that almost as much as he marveled at the woman draped over him, sobbing into his neck.

Finally, Jules sat up and looked at Andrew, taking him in. Her face was red and swollen with tears, but she'd never looked more beautiful. Or haunted. Deep shadows were carved beneath her eyes, and he felt his belly clench at the remembered words of Khonsu. He cracked a lopsided smile at her, trying to look careless and easy though she could see the worry written on his face.

"What happened to your eyes?"

Confusion knit his brows together as she pulled away from him ever so slightly.

"What do you mean?"

Jules shook her head, petrified. Incredulous.

"It's... they've... they've changed. They're not yours. They're...strange."

The eyes in question widened, and he looked around the room for a mirror. Jules reached for her bag and pulled her phone out. She opened the camera, switched it to selfie mode, and handed it over, her hands shaking.

"What?" He croaked, voice still quiet and raspy. Andrew stared back at the face on the camera, eyes wide and mouth dropped open ever so slightly.

He stared back into Khonsu's eyes.

# 58

## *Consequences*

"Well, well, well," a cold voice said from the doorway. I turned, and even knowing who was standing there, it still shook me to my core to see Thutmose leaning against the doorframe. He'd broken through every ward I'd put on the doors. Every ward we had all put around the entire building. Somehow, he'd gotten past and was standing here, more powerful than I could have imagined. "What a beautiful reunion. Andrew, I presume?"

"What do you want?" I asked. I stood up and made to shield Andrew.

"Who are you?" Andrew asked, confused.

"Oh, I'm a friend of your lovely wife's," he said. His voice was flat and devoid of emotion. I should have known that he'd not leave me in peace.

"You are no friend to me," I argued. "You need to leave." I heard Andrew shift behind me, and I turned to see him getting out of bed. "Andrew, stop. I'll handle this."

Thutmose was a hair's breadth away when I turned back, looming over me. I sucked in a shaky breath, petrified. Angry. He was close enough that we were breathing the same air, but we weren't touching, and I'd not even heard him move.

"Perhaps it is you that needs to leave, little witch," he said. His voice was still flat, but he was close enough for the deep timbre to rumble in my chest. "We had an agreement. And it is past time for me to collect."

His dark eyes flicked behind me, and I heard a strangled noise come from Andrew. I spun back, body bumping into Thutmose's. Andrew was frozen in place, his eyes wide with terror as he tried to fight against the magic that held him.

"Let him go!" I shouted, pushing away from Thutmose. He didn't budge. He looked down at me and smiled a nasty smile. His teeth were straight and perfectly white, and his breath smelled clean. Everything about him oozed money and power. Magic rolled off him in thick waves.

"I will let him go when I feel like it," he said. "You seem to have forgotten who is in charge here, little witch. I've been patient long enough. I want the scrolls, and I want them now."

He didn't move so much as a muscle in his face, but I felt the magic squeeze against me, holding me in place. The power he'd wielded over me at the Egyptian Museum was only a tiny taste of what he was capable of. We had grossly underestimated Thutmose.

"You see, Andrew, your wife here may not think we're friends, but we are. Friends help each other out, right, little witch?" He grabbed my bicep and pulled me closer to him so we were pressed against each other. He was only a few inches taller than me, so we were chest-to-chest. I turned my head away from him, trying to see Andrew. I opened my mouth to speak but could only make a strangled garble. Thutmose had a hold of my voice again.

"Ah ah ah," he tutted. "I'll be doing the speaking for now." He turned us towards Andrew, whose eyes were wide and almost glowing with an eerie and unfamiliar light. "I'm going to take your wife with me for a little while. It won't be long because she will take me straight to the scrolls and hand them over. As soon as she does that, I'll release her back to your open arms." He spoke kindly, but the words were anything but friendly.

I closed my eyes and tried to will my heart to slow down. I grappled for control over my nerves and dug deep for the magic I knew was struggling to get past Thutmose's hold. It gathered inside me, the shadows like smoke curling around and gathering strength. Instead of shoving everything I had at Thutmose, I focused my energy on my voice, wrestling it away from him. Power bubbled up from deep within me, effervescent. It popped like soda bubbles in my throat and mouth, and the squeeze on my throat fell away.

"Fuck you!" I ground out. "I'm not going anywhere with you." I looked to Andrew, trying to find the words to explain how desperate I had been to make a deal with a madman, but the madman in question only gripped my arm harder, leaving a bruise.

"Such a defiant little witch, aren't we?" he said. "I am torn between amusement and annoyance. Amused at the fact that you think you can best me. And annoyance that we're not moving. Let's go." He wheeled me around towards the door, and I threw another glance back at Andrew, pleading with him to understand.

"I'm so sorry, Drew. I'm so, so sorry," I cried. "I did what I had to do... I love you so much."

Thutmose opened the door and shoved me through, waving his hand to close the door behind us. Tears were pouring down my face as he dragged me through the empty halls of the clinic. When we reached the front desk, I saw Leena slumped down in her chair, her head tilted back and her mouth open slightly. I couldn't tell if she was breathing.

"Did you kill her?" I asked, tugging on my arm and stopping Thutmose.

He looked down at me and then at the nurse he'd attacked.

"I didn't kill her, no. There wasn't any point. Someone has to spread the word that I was here." He smiled a cold and calculating smile. "I'm through hiding in plain sight. I want the world to know my power and that I will use it to get what I want, no matter the cost." He pulled me along with him, the whoosh of the automatic doors the only thing I could hear over the blood rushing to my head. Pinpricks of light danced across my vision—the only thing keeping me upright was Thutmose. The ramifications of his power and existence getting out were dire.

Because I did not doubt that as soon as the world knew about him, he would point the world in our direction, and the witch-hunt would begin.

# Acknowledgements

No book is ever a one person feat. Yes, the ideas and words are mine but it takes a village to raise a book baby and get it out into the world.

Pathfinder wouldn't be here without a few very important people.

Lindsey Clarke—I am so grateful that you took a chance on me with this series and that you champion it (and me) as much as you do! Your careful consideration and eye for detail have really helped not only hone my skills but have made my stories so much better than I could ever hope to do alone! Thank you so much!

To my alpha readers—Christoph, Mom, Charlotte, and Denise—you guys are absolute rockstars and I owe you so many thanks for reading my words when they were at their worst and most raw.

To my beta readers—Lizz and Jill—your insight and ideas truly made this story better. It's not easy to hand over a piece of my heart and actively ask for criticism and help, but both of you were incredible, so helpful, and handled the tender parts of me with such care. And Lizz—I hope you like Andrew just a weeeeee bit better than you did before—I did my best with him!

To the Tuesday Night Writer's Club—Jill (our fearless leader and the brains behind the formation of our group), Cara, Connie, Dian, Jennifer, Leslie, and Michelle—thank you guys for your honest feedback, excitement, joy, and most of all, your friendship. I walked into the group not knowing what to expect (and so nervous about joining) and it has been one of the best things to ever happen to me! Tuesdays have quickly become one of my favorite days of the week— I love hearing what each and every one of you are writing and working on and cant wait to see what you create!

To every reader who has taken a chance on a very unknown indie author, thank you from the bottom of my heart. This has been a dream since I was tiny and to have it coming true has been incredible! Every purchase and every review mean more than you'll ever know!

To Stella—not only did you absolutely nail that plot point I was stuck on, you are one of the best cheerleaders for this whole author thing! From telling strangers that your mama is an author to supporting long writing and editing sprints, to pulling out my copies just enough so they stick out at Barnes and Noble, I couldn't do this without you! I know I'm biased but you are one of my favorite humans ever—you are resilient, brave, smart, beautiful, hilarious, and watching you grow is one of my greatest joys. I hope you never forget what an incredible person you are, and that you stand strong in a deep knowing of who you are.

Christoph—I don't think there are enough words to convey what you mean to me. Just know that you are in every word I'll ever write.

# About the author

JW Kingsley has been a voracious reader since the age of four. As soon as she could hold a pencil she was scribbling stories, bad poetry (and some decent poetry), and dreaming about writing her own books.

She is currently making a new home in a small town in North Carolina after spending the last twenty years traipsing around the world with her partner, their daughter, half-feral cat, and their sweet new puppy (because they decided life wasn't hectic enough). If she's not writing she's home-educating, gardening, cooking, or traveling—all while drinking ridiculous amounts of tea and reading a mix of smut, fantasy, and time-travel novels.

*I*

www.ingramcontent.com/pod-product-compliance
Lightning Source LLC
LaVergne TN
LVHW011332030125
800296LV00014B/363